BETTER OFF DEAD

Published March 2025
by Indies United Publishing House, LLC

FIRST EDITION

Cover Art by Richard Burns, Bullet Liongson

ISBN: 978-1-64456-795-1 [Paperback]
ISBN: 978-1-64456-796-8 [Kindle]
ISBN: 978-1-64456-797-5 [ePub]
ISBN: 978-1-64456-798-2 [Audiobook]

Library of Congress Control Number: 2025902816

INDIES UNITED PUBLISHING HOUSE, LLC
P.O. BOX 3071
QUINCY, IL 62305-3071
www.indiesunited.net

To Kit and Geneva

Praise for the Trisha Carson Mystery Series

Dead Code

"An immensely likable sleuth headlines this lively crime tale." – *Kirkus Review*

"Glenda Carroll creates a powerful portrait of not just another murder mystery, but an investigator still recovering from the last one." – *Midwest Book Review, D. Donovan, Senior Reviewer*

"*Dead Code* is an exciting, fast-paced mystery with vivid scenery and very likable characters that readers will cheer for from start to finish." - *San Francisco Book Review*

Drop Dead Red

"A smart, steadfast gumshoe who, in her second book, continues to flourish...Carroll's writing bounces off the page." *Kirkus Reviews*

"Looking for a cool read after a hot weekend? *Drop Dead Red* is great fun, and intriguing - the theme is swimming, the murders are a mystery. Way to go, Glenda!" -- *Lynn Sherr, New York Times Best Selling Author, " Sally Ride: America's First Woman in Space," "Swim" and former ABC correspondent for 20/20.*

"I loved your new book, *Drop Dead Red.* I've always enjoyed murder mysteries and yours was so well written. I kept thinking I knew who the culprit was but loved the surprise ending. I think that open water swimmers, triathletes, murder mystery fans...will enjoy your book." -- *Lynne Cox, New York Times Best Selling Author, "Swimming to Antarctica."*

Dead in the Water

Dead in the Water is....so well written you just can't put it down...If you're like me, you'll be trying to figure out who committed the murder while you're working out." -- *Lynne Cox, New York Times Bestselling author, "Swimming to Antarctica," "Open Water Swimming Manual."*

"Carroll combines a skill for mystery writing...with her sports journalism and Masters swimming background by nailing the details of what it's like to race in open water...I liked Carroll's characters immensely, but it was the story that kept me up late reading." -- *Swimmer Magazine*

"(This) is a swim-centric mystery that will keep you turning pages while you think about your strokes. It's the first open-water-detective-novel that I know of, and it's great fun to read." -- *Lynn Sherr, author of "Swim: Why We Love the Water." Sherr is a broadcast journalist and writer and was an award-winning correspondent for ABC News.*

"It is a great first novel for the author and the main character has secrets to be explored in future books. It is a fast read and will appeal to open water swimmers, athletes and mystery lovers." -- *US Open Water Swimming Connection*

ACKNOWLEDGMENTS

"Though this be madness, yet there is method in't."
Hamlet, William Shakespeare

During the time I struggled to find a plot for book four of the Trisha Carson mysteries, I tutored a high schooler reading Shakespeare's *Hamlet.* I explained how Shakespeare's plays stood the test of time and could easily be modernized. As we discussed what *Hamlet* would sound like today, the proverbial light bulb went off in my head. Later that evening, I started to write *Better Off Dead,* a mystery based loosely on *Hamlet.* Yes, that Hamlet who is consumed with grief and revenge and is driven crazy as the play goes on. So, Will S., many thanks for the idea.

I had a number of modern-day professionals helping me: Lourdes Venard, Kelley Scriven, Lisa Towles. Once again, the cover is the creation of Richard Burns, an excellent graphic artist and a masters swimming teammate and Bullet Liongson.

A special thank you to the women swimmers of Tamalpais Aquatic Masters who kept asking me in the locker room 'how's the book coming along?"

A Trisha Carson Mystery

BETTER OFF DEAD

Glenda Carroll

INDIES UNITED PUBLISHING HOUSE, LLC

Chapter 1

"I really shouldn't be here," I complained to Lena as we drove up the long, pebbled driveway leading to an elegant home in an elegant community in Marin County. I never went to funerals. They made me itchy. That's right, itchy. Within one block of the memorial, I broke out with a bumpy red rash that would probably last the whole day.

"You were specifically invited. You have to be here," said Lena.

My eyes were on the parking valet who motioned for me to stop. "I never met the man who died. Andy Barlow? Who is … was … he?"

"I didn't know him either. C'mon, his son asked us to be here. We are paying our respects."

The last time I saw Harrison Barlow, the dead man's son, dated back almost twelve years. Then, he was a geeky kid, eight years old, hardly talked. His clothes hung on him like wet rags and his hair stuck out of his scalp like porcupine quills. Lena, along with teaching kids to swim at the community pool, often gave private lessons to the affluent children in Marin County. Harrison was one of those.

Now a college junior, he had been summoned back to Marin from his university in London, England, when his father died.

"Didn't you say Andy Barlow died in a boating accident?" I asked, scratching my neck.

Lena shuddered. "The worst kind. A powerboat ran over him … His body was chewed up by the boat's propeller."

My mouth flew open. "That's terrible."

"That's every open water swimmer's nightmare," Lena said, nodding.

We walked up the front steps to a strikingly modern home spread out over one level, all glass and brick and angles. Guarding the immense doorway was a five-foot easel and a large photo of Andrew Barlow, with the words "Celebration of Life" at the top. The photo emitted confidence and contentment. He looked happy and very much alive.

"Bet he didn't look like that when they picked pieces of him out of the water," I said.

"Trisha, that's disgusting," my sister hissed under her breath. "This is a celebration of Andy's life, so keep the snarkiness to yourself. I read in his obit that he was cremated, and his ashes were spread off the San Francisco waterfront in the Bay."

"His teeth are … were … really white," I said, squinting as I leaned forward to examine the photo. "Bet he had some work done on his face."

"And how would you know that?" Lena asked skeptically.

"Just a guess. Lee, look at the area around his ears and near his eyes. The skin looks stretched. Doesn't it?"

Lena sighed.

"How old was he?" I asked.

"Fifties, I think."

"He looks like a guy trying hard to stay young," I said as we walked through the empty entry hall.

For reasons I never understood, Lena received a last-minute invitation to this memorial. Why did Harrison want his former swim teacher to be here? And stranger still, why was I specifically asked to attend? I planned on going in, offering my condolences, then escaping to the car. I'd listen to the San Francisco Giants podcast until Lena came out.

But my sister wouldn't hear of it.

A butler-type person popped out of a doorway. "This way please." He handed us both a program, led us through the highly polished house, and pointed to the beveled glass doors leading out to the side lawn. "Please go through those doors and find a seat. They should be starting momentarily."

"Lena, my neck is one big itch. I won't be able to sit through this. I need to leave."

"Suck it up," Lena whispered. She looked over at me and her eyes grew to the size of dollar pancakes. "How did your neck get so red, so fast?"

"I told you." I desperately tried not to scratch.

We passed a table with a guest book, a bucket of ice, an elaborate silver water pitcher, sparkling crystal glasses, and white linen napkins. I grabbed a handful of ice and wrapped it in a napkin, resting it on my neck and sighing in relief.

The side yard resembled the setup for a garden wedding: rows of white chairs, a podium at the front with another large photo of the deceased. Off to the left, behind a tall iron fence, was the pool. It was a no-nonsense 3-lane, 25-yard competition pool complete with backstroke flags and a 36-inch timing clock on the pool deck. On the right side of the chairs were the rolling golden hills of northern California.

"Was Andy a serious swimmer?" I asked.

Lena shrugged. "Must have been with that kind of a setup." She walked toward two seats in the second row, but I grabbed her arm and pulled her into the last row.

"Here. I want to sit here so I can make a quick getaway."

Rock music from the sixties and seventies played quietly in the background.

"I wish they'd turn the music up," said Lena, absentmindedly pushing her ginger curls off her face.

"Do you think the DJ takes requests?" I asked, hiding a smile.

"Trisha, knock it off. It isn't a club."

As the ice cubes dripped down my neck, I gazed around the room. Some of Marin's finest were here. The mayors of San Rafael, Tiburon and San Anselmo, Larkspur, Ross, Corte Madera, and Sausalito sat together off to the right. Police chiefs in crisp uniforms sat behind them. And then came the local celebrities: musicians, artists, high-flying charity workers, movers and shakers in the LGBTQ+ community, and aging rock stars.

"Isn't that …?"

I pulled her hand down. "Don't point, Lee." But I leaned forward and tried to see who she was looking at.

The music faded away and Justine Barlow, the dead man's wife, walked to the podium in stilettos and an expensive designer black dress that hugged her curves. Her stylish hair, prematurely white, was pulled back in a simple bun.

She blotted away a few tears. "I welcome you all here today to celebrate the life of my wonderful husband and my best friend, Andrew. Andy was the loving father of our son Harrison, a caring and encouraging older brother to Martin, a wonderful uncle to Marty's twins Dawson and Daria, and a devoted friend to all of you."

"Sounds like she's reading from a dictionary," I whispered to my sister. "I didn't know the guy, but I could say something more original if the love of my life just died. Boring."

"Be quiet."

"Maybe he wasn't the love of her life," I said, elbowing Lena. "Bet she's had work done too. What is it with this family?"

Lena glared at me.

Justine talked on and on. I looked around to try to keep myself awake. Off to the side beyond the pool, the two car valets were leaning against a Porsche, appreciating the smoothness of its lines.

Justine stopped her talk with a tearful hiccup. She stretched her hand out to the front row. "Harrison, please come up and say a few words."

Almost imperceptibly, Harrison shook his head 'no.'

"Please. Your dad would have wanted it."

Harrison stayed glued to the chair, his back stiff. He glared at his mother, not moving. A man sitting next to him, I guessed his Uncle Martin, leaned over to whisper something in his ear. Daria leaned in her father's direction to hear what he was saying. Dawson looked down at his sneakers. Harrison jerked as if he'd been pricked by a sharp knife. Red blotches flooded his ashen skin. He stood up rigidly and rushed in the opposite direction of the podium, past his uncle, his cousins, the guests, and the row in which Lena and I were seated.

A melancholy gloom followed the young man like a dark cloud. Wearing a severe black shirt, vest, and pants didn't help his image. I couldn't decide if Harrison was a goth English major or a wannabe malnourished eighteenth century undertaker.

Uncle Martin stood up and walked to the podium to comfort the crying mother. He put his arm around her shoulder and drew her close.

"He's overcome with grief," Martin told the assembled guests. "I'd like to say a few words about my brother, and then there'll be time for all of you to talk about your remembrances of Andy, who died too young."

I whispered to Lena. "I don't need to be part of this."

Before Lena could grab my arm, I slipped out of my chair and moved toward the house. There is something to be said for making an escape in a solemn moment when talking is taboo.

I shooed away the car valets and found my ratty vintage Honda stuffed between a white Mercedes convertible and a slick black Maserati. I planned on sitting here until Lena came out. Trying not to think about my itchy skin, I reached for the radio. The baseball podcast lacked pizazz. Instead, I switched to an easy listening station, closed my eyes, and hummed along with Otis Redding's "Sittin' on the Dock of the Bay."

Almost two hours later, a few people trickled out. In the doorway stood Justine and Martin. But no Harrison. They nodded solemnly at each mourner as they passed by. I strained to see Lena, but she didn't emerge, at least not from the front door. The stream of mourners diminished to a trickle. Valets delivered extravagant cars to the guests, who slowly drove from the parking area into the street. Within fifteen minutes, everyone was gone.

Still no Lena. I slid out of the front seat, moved to the front of the car, and leaned against the hood. From the corner of my eye, I caught a movement back by the pool. Turning to get a better look, I saw Lena and Harrison heads close together, talking intently. Finally, Lena pulled back, cupped Harrison's face in her hands, and kissed him on the cheek. She patted his arm one more time and turned to walk toward the one car left.

"Lena," I called out and her head jerked up. She nodded, took a look back at Harrison now standing near the side door of the house, waved gently, and headed for the car.

"How's your rash?" she asked, slipping into the front seat.

"Much better. Funerals do that to me. Remember at Aunt Anna's wake?" I checked the car mirror and was relieved to see the redness fading away.

"You were a mess."

"So, what were you and Harrison talking about?"

"You won't believe what he just told me," said Lena.

"Try me."

"He's sure that his Uncle Martin killed his father."

"Seriously? He thinks his uncle murdered his dad??"

Lena nodded.

"And that his uncle was having a long-time affair with his mother."

"See. I told you. He wasn't the love of her life. That's ugly. Did the dad know?"

"I don't know. Now Harrison wants you to check it all out."

"Why me?"

"Because you solve crimes."

"Have him call the police."

"He did. But his dad's death was ruled an accident, and they aren't interested in looking into it any further."

"Do you think the uncle killed his brother? For what reason? To be the main man in the mother's life?"

"I don't know. Harrison wants you to investigate."

"I could talk to him, but I don't think it will go anywhere."

"Please, I promised him you would," said Lena.

"Why'd you do that?"

"Tomorrow. He wants to see you tomorrow. Around ten. At the Two Seagulls café down by the waterfront in Sausalito," she continued, ignoring my question.

"I don't want to. Since you set this up, you tell him 'no.'"

"You tell him," said Lena. "Look, it's only a conversation. His father just died and he's upset. He needs to talk. All you have to do is listen to him and smile reassuringly. I know you can do that."

"Yeah, I can. But I don't want to."

I don't know why Lena involved me in this mess. I glanced at her. She had dressed appropriately for the celebration of life ceremony. Trim black slacks, a white silk blouse. Her bouncy reddish curls were pulled sedately back behind her ears. I personally didn't think the black stilettos fit in, but it had been agreed on by everyone in my extended family that I know little to nothing about fashion. I wore wear a dark green, long sleeve dress, totally inappropriate for early fall in the San Francisco Bay area. The afternoon temperature had reached eighty-five degrees, and sweat dripped down the back of my neck.

"Can you tell me anything about Harrison or his family? There were some pretty impressive people at the ceremony today."

Lena pecked away at her phone, but then looked up.

"I know about as much as you do. I haven't seen him since before he went to college abroad. I think his father and uncle were partners. They had something to do with money. If I remember correctly, so did his mother. If she still works."

"Like banking?" I asked.

"Investment stuff, I think."

"Based on who attended today, he was an A-lister in Marin." I paused for a minute and squeezed my eyes shut. "Okay. What we know for sure is that the father had an accident in the Bay and is dead. What we've been told by Harrison is that he thinks his father was killed, and that his father's brother was having an affair with the mother. We think, but aren't sure, that the father and brother were partners in a financial-type firm. Did I leave anything out?"

I opened one eye and looked at her. Lena shook her head.

"That sounds positively Shakespearean," I said.

"How would you know anything about Shakespeare?" Lena asked.

"Just because I didn't complete a four-year college doesn't mean I didn't take any classes."

"And you chose Shakespeare?"

"Well, it fit my schedule."

Chapter 2

The next day, I found Harrison prowling along the Sausalito waterfront. He paused at Schoonmaker Beach, a comfortable sandy beach sandwiched between two marinas with protected waters that paddleboarders and open water swimmers enjoyed. An overcast and windy day was the perfect backdrop for the tall, lanky young man draped in a black cape blowing in the breeze. He could be an extra for an eighteenth-century British movie standing on the dreary moors of the English coast instead of a California local. To me, he looked a little silly but I've seen weirder clothes in Marin.

The desolate beach stretched down to the brownish-green water.

"Harrison?" I called from the edge of the parking lot that straddled the beach. He didn't turn around. I called again. Louder. "Harrison." This time he looked in my direction, nodded, but made no move toward me.

I held my zip up camouflage hoodie tight around my head as I trudged over. The wind picked up sharp grains of sand and sent them flying in my direction.

"How about we find a place inside?" I asked as I approached him from behind. He didn't comment. I pulled the hoodie tighter and shielded my face from the sand with my hand.

"Harrison, can we…"

"I like the brisk air. It reminds me of England," he said, staring out at the Richardson Bay channel.

"Yeah, Lena told me that's where you go to school." The wind whipped his cape across my face and I pulled it down.

"Please," I said, tugging at it again after another gust sent the cape airborne. "We won't be able to talk like this. Or at least I won't."

He finally looked over at me and sighed. "Okay. There's a café at the end of that dock," he said with a slight British accent.

I walked next to him in silence. He never looked my way or even acknowledged that I was there. When we reached the café, he pulled open the door and walked in ahead of me. I scrambled after him right before the door shut in my face. I tugged on his arm and pointed him to a table overlooking the marina.

He remained quiet. His coffee came. He ducked his head and took a sip. I squirmed around in the chair, not sure what to do or what to say.

Finally, I blurted out awkwardly, "I'm so sorry about your father. It must have been quite a shock."

No answer. The clumsy silence grew.

"What are you studying at university?"

"Theater," Harrison said. "I'm at King's College in London studying Shakespeare. And performing. I auditioned for a part in Hamlet, and then I was called home."

"That's too bad," I said. "So sorry about all of this. A terrible reason to come back to California."

Harrison looked out the large glass window at the boats bobbing around in the marina. He remained silent.

I cleared my throat and began. "Why did you want to see me? I don't know you. Haven't seen you since Lena was teaching you how to swim. I don't know your family or anything about your father."

Harrison leaned back on his chair until he was balancing on the back two legs. The dark clothes and cape hid the young man underneath and contrasted sharply with his pale skin and blond hair pulled back in a ponytail. Yet there was something about his broad face and shoulders that belonged on a poster advertising the beach lifestyle. Change the cape out for a wetsuit and a surfboard, and he morphed into a classic local surfer. I had trouble seeing him as a great Shakespearean actor.

"Quick question. Do you surf? I know there's surfing in England."

"Used to" was all he said. "Off the northern California coast and sometimes in Hawaii. But that was a long time ago." He paused, eased the chair down on all four legs, and leaned forward. "Here's the deal. My father is dead, and I think that he was murdered."

"Why do you think that?"

"He told me."

"What? Your father? I thought he was dead."

"Before he died. We were talking when I was at school and he mentioned that Uncle Marty wanted to take complete control of the business. He wanted my father out, and my dad said he seemed willing to do anything to make that happen."

"Even murder?"

"I think so. Yes." As he spoke, his intense dark brown eyes glistened.

"Isn't that a big jump? From wanting to buy out his partner—I'm assuming that's what he had in mind—to killing him?"

"I thought I knew my uncle. But I don't. He's a twit."

"Excuse me?"

"English expression for scumbag."

"What did your father and uncle do?" I asked. Based on the house I saw at the memorial service, whatever they did brought in the bucks.

"They were financiers. They managed money. Banks from all over the world, hedge funds, charities, universities, and people, famous people, like actors, sports stars."

I sat there with my mouth open. These two brothers and their families must be worth billions of dollars.

"And these investments were successful," boasted Harrison. "Everyone earned money. People were very happy with them. But I think my uncle got greedy. He didn't want to share the profits with my father anymore."

"Harrison, do you have any evidence that your father was killed? Did he often swim in San Francisco Bay? It's a pretty cold place to swim, from what Lena has told me."

"He'd been thinking of doing a swim across Lake Tahoe, and he wanted to get in as many long swims as he could before the water really cooled down and he had to put on a wetsuit."

"How long is the Tahoe swim?"

"If he swam the width, it would be twelve miles."

"That's a long way to go," I said.

"But that was only part of his goal. He was determined to swim the length, which is twenty-one miles and change."

"Seriously?"

"For the last couple of years, he's been talking—dreaming, actually—of taking on the California Triple Crown of Marathon Swimming: the Catalina Channel, Santa Barbara Channel, and the length of Lake Tahoe. He wanted to do the width of Tahoe next summer."

"Sounds like he's been swimming in open water for quite some time."

"He started swimming in the Bay last year."

"Just last year?" I asked. Was his father as out of touch with reality as his son? From what I knew, no one would tackle a swim across Lake Tahoe with so little practice time in the water.

"He was a very ambitious man," Harrison said with a sad smile. "Look where it got him. I think that's why he's dead."

"Because he wanted to swim? I don't understand."

"According to what Dad told me, Uncle Marty wasn't happy about all the time he spent in the Bay. But Dad said he had found his passion. He felt he didn't need to work as much anymore. He had all the money he and Mom and I needed. But Uncle Marty was greedy. He wanted more."

"Let me backtrack for a minute. The swim where he died was a training swim? He was in the water before whatever happened, happened? He didn't have a heart attack and fall overboard?" Something didn't make sense. Didn't Lena tell me he had a heart attack? Maybe it happened in the water? Or could he have lost consciousness while swimming?

"Heart attack? Where'd you hear that? No. Normally, my uncle was on the Nereus and followed Dad while he swam around the Bay."

"The what?" I asked.

"The boat's name is the Nereus. She's named after the Greek sea god known for his wisdom."

"And you think on this particular swim, your uncle ran over him?"

"One hundred percent sure. Nobody was there but the two of them. Dad in the water, somewhere off Angel Island, and Uncle Marty on the boat. Two went out alive; one came back dead. In pieces. What would you think?"

Harrison's eyes darkened and took on a deep glow. He leaned across the table until his nose almost touched mine. I jerked backwards, ramming the chair behind me. My heart thrashed inside my chest and I gripped the tabletop, turning my knuckles white.

"Sounds so gruesome. Your uncle must have panicked," I said softly, trying to calm him and me down. "Do you know how the accident happened? Did he accidently put the boat in reverse and back over him?" I picked up a glass of water, took a small sip and stared at him over the rim.

"How would I know? I wasn't there," Harrison snorted. He leaned back and I exhaled silently.

"What about the Coast Guard? Did he call them? There's a station right under the north tower of the Golden Gate Bridge, not far from where this happened."

"I don't know."

"Did the boat have a radio?"

"Of course it did."

"Harrison, are you sure that it was just the two of them? That your uncle was the person driving the boat?"

Harrison wouldn't look at me. Then his gaze found mine. "Absolutely. He was the one on the boat. Who else could it be?"

"You mean, you don't know for sure it was your uncle's fault? Why would you want to blame him for this when you don't even know if he was on the boat?"

He pitched forward toward me again, his face inches away from mine. His voice intensified. "Why? He's been fucking my mother. That's why. He wanted my dad out of the picture so he could have my mother and their business all to himself."

An older couple sitting at the table next to us stiffened.

"Harrison," I whispered, "keep your voice down."

He sat back and crossed his arms.

"I know you're upset about your father. But this sounds—and I hate to say it—like you need to find someone to blame. What you're saying is…."

"That's what Dad told me the last time I talked to him. And I believed him."

A red flush crept up Harrison's neck and bloomed across his face. He shoved back his chair and leapt to his feet. I compelled my hand not to recoil, reached across the table and casually rested my palm on his arm.

"Hold on," I said. "You asked me to meet you today. Why?"

"Isn't it clear?" he asked, sitting back down. His voice dropped to a whisper. "I want you to prove my uncle killed my father. The police aren't interested. I've talked to some people and they said you can do this. Can you?"

"That's hard to say, but I appreciate the offer."

"I have a lot of money. I can pay you."

My Achilles heel. Money. I never had enough. Right now, I was barely working. My car needed repairs and my bank account was as empty as a desert well in a drought.

"Let me think about it, okay?"

Harrison nodded.

"But I need to tell you, if I decide to investigate your dad's death, I have to search out everything. If I find that someone else is responsible, or that maybe no one was responsible, that it was an accident, that's what I'll report."

He reluctantly agreed and then stood up. "I know that my uncle is the one. This is the truth, whether you believe it or not," he said and headed for the door, his dark cape streaming behind him.

When I slid back into my old Honda in the parking lot, I sat there for a few minutes watching my hands tremble. As my heart rate tumbled toward normal, I reran the conversation in my head. Harrison seemed so sure of what happened to his dad. To me, it sounded like bad blood between the families, or at least between the adult brothers. I'd like to know more about that conversation between Harrison and his father. Since Harrison tilted toward the dramatic, did he misinterpret what his father said?

Then there was the bit about his uncle having an affair with his mother. Not that it couldn't be true but come on … really? Harrison and his theatrics. I pulled out my tablet and opened a new file, which I named "Andy Barlow Propeller Death." I put down what I knew about the boating accident. Then I started an ecard for those connected: Harrison, Andy Barlow, Marty Barlow, and Justine Barlow. What information I knew about each one, I put on the card and then looked it over.

"This tells me nothing," I thought, shaking my head.

I had to admit the murder angle was unique. A man chewed up by a boat propeller in San Francisco Bay. You don't hear that every day. And potentially mangled by his brother? It intrigued me. In fact, the whole family intrigued me.

I jotted down my next steps.

A trip to the marina.

Check with the Coast Guard to see if they could—maybe would

was the better word—tell me about the accident.

Talk to both families.

My phone pinged. It was Lena.

Lena: *Well?*

Me: *Well, what?*

Lena: *Harrison? Did u meet?*

Me: *Yeah. Weird guy. Too intense for me. And a little scary. But I feel sorry for him.*

I watched as a couple walked to a nearby pier, pulling a wagon full of boating gear. They unlocked the gate to the ramp and proceeded down to the end of the dock. My only experience on a boat was when I helped Jon, my sweetheart, move a sailboat from Marin County to the Berkeley Marina. It had been a spectacular evening, and that's when Jon became boyfriend material.

Sausalito gleamed in the morning sun. The wind blew itself out and the high fog retreated behind the Marin headlands. Fall was San Francisco Bay's summer, complete with warm weather, dazzling Pacific Ocean sunsets, and cloudless nights. Further out, two swimmers with bright orange safety floats streaming behind them swam for the entrance that led into the bay. Although I had swum in lakes and rivers, I stayed away from bay swimming unless forced to. Even sixty-five degrees seemed too cold for me. I read that half the people who died from drowning really died from hypothermia. Once they hit cold water, their bodies turned into life-sized popsicles as their extremities began to shut down. Inadvertently, I shivered, then switched on the ignition and turned the car heater up to toast.

Chapter 3

Before I headed home, I drove over to the small marina under the north tower of the Golden Gate Bridge and parked. It was positioned in the quiet, protected waters of Horseshoe Cove, right around the point from the Pacific Ocean. I couldn't imagine the Barlows keeping their large, expensive yacht here at Travis Small Boat Marina. The original locals, the Coast Miwok tribes, paddled their tule reed canoes in these waters. Centuries later, it morphed into a no-frills harbor where anglers and recreational boaters docked, not at all like the luxury marinas found in nearby Sausalito.

I took the last exit in Marin before the freeway headed for the Golden Gate Bridge to San Francisco and drove down the twisting road to the marina's parking lot. On the side nearest the bridge, the small Coast Guard station that recovered Andy Barlow's body sat buttoned up against the breeze flowing in from the Pacific. Training must be done for the day since their large motorboats rested secured to the docks. These rescue boats head out to the Pacific Ocean in storms and high seas to aid boats of all sizes. And they also have the grim task of picking up bodies, whether it be forlorn people who jump off the Golden Gate Bridge or sailors who fall overboard. A small white house behind a picket fence harbored their offices. Inside the yard, a young ensign tossed a stuffed rabbit to an obsessed black lab who sprinted in all directions.

"Excuse me," I said with my sweetest smile.

"Ma'am," he answered with a salute.

"Can I ask you a question?"

He walked over to the fence, followed by the happy dog.

"I'm pretty sure a large powerboat was towed in here after an accident. Not too long ago. Evidently, a guy was swimming in the Bay and somehow got chewed up by the boat's propellers. Were you around when that happened?"

The ensign tossed the rabbit one more time and paused. "I heard about that. I wasn't on duty that day. From what I understand, it was grisly. Nasty. The thing is, rescue vessels weren't that far away. They were coming back from a training exercise off of Ocean Beach. But they weren't in time to help the poor guy."

"Is this kind of thing typical?"

"Well, we're trained for water rescue. We're the busiest search and rescue station on the Pacific Coast. It's not unusual to pick up a dead body, but one that's been mutilated … not so common."

"Did anyone mention who was on board?"

He shook his head. The dog, now back at the fence, stood up and tried to give me his rabbit.

"Did you know the guy?" the ensign asked.

"Not really. His son asked me to look into it."

"Are you a cop or a private investigator?"

"No. Only a friend of the family."

"The police and the Coast Guard declared it an accident."

"So I heard. Hey, look." I pointed to the marina entrance.

Swimming into the small harbor was a man wearing a lime green swim cap and pulling a bright orange buoy behind him, heading straight toward the beach. An eighteen-foot inflatable powerboat followed him from a safe distance. The two people on the boat waved to him and motioned that they were going to dock.

"Do you often get swimmers off this beach?" I asked.

"This is the last hurrah. The Bay will start to get colder by the end of the month. Open water swimmers like to get their last licks in."

I waved to the ensign and moved quickly down to the beach, where a small group huddled together. A woman wrapped a towel around the swimmer, and a short dark-haired man threw a swimmer's parka over his shoulders.

"Hi," I called out, but they were engrossed in warming the shivering man up.

"Let's get you out of your suit," said his friend.

I backed up a fair distance to give them some privacy. The two people on the inflatable walked down the sandy beach in my direction. They nodded.

"How long were you out?" I asked them.

"Four hours."

"Seriously? No wonder he's cold."

The swimmer had donned gray sweats, a black knit cap, gloves, and boots. He held a warm drink in his hands. He looked over at me and said, "I'm warming myself up from the inside out."

His helpers on the beach and the boaters that followed him started chatting about best ways to handle the currents in the Bay and keep their swimmer moving forward.

"Are you interested in open water swimming?" he asked.

"Not four hours' worth." I paused. "Do you know other swimmers that use this beach?"

"A few," he said. Water dripped from his hair down across his face. He pulled a towel snug around his neck and patted his bright red cheeks.

"A man, Andy Barlow, was training for a Lake Tahoe swim a month or so ago and he had a terrible accident in the Bay. The boat following ran him over."

"Yeah, I heard about that." The swimmer hunched his shoulders up to his ears and shivered. "Very disturbing."

"Did you know him?"

"Slightly. He was very ambitious. I felt he was in over his head.

All hat, no cattle."

"Excuse me?"

"He talked a good game. Knew all the terminology. Liked to swim, I'll give him that. But he was looking for shortcuts to get himself ready. And there aren't any shortcuts. You have to put in the work. Train. Swim for hours at a time."

"That's what you're doing?"

"I'm trying," he said, "but I know my limitations, I don't think Barlow knew his."

The swimmer in front of me started to shiver again.

"Well, thanks for talking to me."

"Gotta go get warm," he said to his crew. They quickly led him up the beach toward the parking lot.

"Yeah. Go get warm," I repeated quietly. I didn't get a chance to say goodbye. Once he was in a van, I walked past the Coast Guard boat docks on my way to the other side of the harbor. There, a curvy narrow road reached over a hill for a great view of Angel Island, Alcatraz Island, and the piers and skyscrapers about two and half miles across the bay in San Francisco. A few shapeless fishermen sat on the retaining wall, crouched over, lost in thought.

That swimmer did not think too much of Andy Barlow. Not sure that has anything to do with his death, but if both Barlow brothers were neophytes when it came to water and water sports, an accident wasn't out of the question.

Off to my right stood the massive burnt-orange base of the Golden Gate Bridge. I studied the mile and a half long span with its two sky-high towers. From this angle, they resembled the tallest goalposts I'd ever seen. I tried to imagine a placekicker booting a football from the San Francisco Bay over the Bridge to the Pacific Ocean. That silly image replaced the one I had of Barlow's arms, legs, fingers, and toes floating with the current.

As I walked back to my car, I noticed two men at the far end of Travis Small Boat Marina. Trekking down the pier, their arms were filled with boat gear, the dock swaying and splashing beneath their feet. As they opened the locked gate and moved up the wooden plank to the parking lot, I stopped.

"Excuse me," I said. Lost in conversation, they didn't hear me. "Excuse me," I called out again. They both looked my way. "I'm trying to find a boat."

The taller sailor in a dark blue knit cap laughed. "Any particular one? There's plenty here."

"Do you want to buy one?" said the shorter man wearing a faded red waterproof jacket.

"You can have mine," said the other man. "I'll sell it to you. Cheap."

Both men laughed.

"I don't have the money for a boat," I said.

"Nor do I," said the cap-wearing mariner and shook his head. Kindly brown eyes looked at me.

"Come on guys," I said to myself. I needed to help them stick to the point.

"This is a boat owned by Andrew Barlow. I think he and his brother, Marty, often take it out."

"Barlow? I don't know the name. Are they fishermen?"

"No. One is … was … a bay swimmer. There was an accident."

The sailor in the faded red jacket snapped his fingers as he remembered the incident.

"Oh yeah. About a month ago. The Coast Guard towed in a boat and a body. Was that this Barlow guy?"

"Might be," I said.

"I was repairing the engine on a friend's powerboat when the Coasties showed up. Big commotion. There was an ambulance waiting at the Coast Guard dock. The EMTs went up with a stretcher and carried someone in what looked like a body bag out to the ambulance," said the same man.

"Was there anyone else on the boat?"

"I couldn't tell," said the taller sailor. "Lots of people moving around. Whole thing was tragic. On our way to the parking lot, we stopped by the pier and asked what happened. One of the Coasties said it was a terrible accident. The body was ground up like horse meat. The conversation was cut short when their superior officer walked over. That's all I know."

"Did that boat have a slip in this marina?" I asked.

"I don't think so. But I'm pretty sure it used to stop here on occasion and pick people up. I remember seeing it. Sometimes they had teenagers aboard. No adults as far as I could tell. They'd pick up other kids. I got kinda worried about their boat skills, but the boy at the helm, just a teenager, knew what he was doing. It's a real nice boat. Fancy. Expensive," said the taller man. "Sorry, but I gotta go. Need to pick up some parts at Pacific Boat Works."

"Thanks," I said. I sat down on a wooden bench and watched as the men walked over to a black truck. The choppy water in San Francisco Bay swirled around the base of the north tower as the wind picked up. I pulled my hoodie closer and crossed my arms for warmth. The clanking of the rigging against the masts beat out a military tattoo complete with sounds of a fife and drum.

So, was there anyone on the boat besides Andy? He couldn't set a course into the Nereus, put it on automatic pilot, jump in the water, and swim beside the boat, could he? Maybe he was tethered to the boat? That might be an explanation for how the boat backed over him. The boater mentioned teenagers. Harrison's cousins were high schoolers, but were they sailors? Why would one or both of them purposely run over their uncle? According to Harrison, he knew—just knew—that his Uncle Marty went out with his dad and then killed him while he was swimming. I wondered if Marty was that good of a boater that he could make murder look like an accident.

I felt that Andy's connection with reality had begun to slip. Swimming and not bringing in new clients were one thing. But attempting a marathon swim like the length or width of Lake Tahoe with little open water experience was nuts … so said the swimmer I talked to. While Marty attempted to keep their business moving forward, Andy swam and swam and swam. If I was Marty, I'd want control of their financial planning organization too. But would I kill for it?

A fishing boat slowed down as it entered the marina and cruised to its slip. Outside in the central bay, the wind continued building and pushed the small waves into white caps. A gloomy gray fog sunk over the boat harbor. Waves slapped against the retaining wall, flinging cold spray into the air soaking the fishermen. I shivered. Who in their right mind would go out swimming on a day like today?

Chapter 4

We were sitting at Lena's kitchen table. I propped my feet up on my sister's lap and she promptly pushed them to the floor. Across from me sat Dr. T or Terrell Robinson, MD. an emergency room doctor in San Francisco, who was regaling us with strange cases that came into the ER in autumn. Lena and Dr. T's son, Timothy or Little T, sat securely on his dad's knee chewing on a set of multi-colored plastic keys

"You know that fall is the best weather in the Bay Area. The sun is warm, and that means people are outside more than ever. And they overdo. There are so many sports injuries—cyclists, runners, you name it," said T.

"The Bay is the warmest right now," said Lena. "I should get you out for a swim."

"What does 'warmest' mean to you?" I asked her.

"Well, it can get up to sixty-five, sixty-six degrees. Warmer still in some places on a low tide."

"No thank you."

"You're such a wimp," she said.

I ignored my sister and watched a mobile that was shifting around in the afternoon breeze outside the kitchen window. Transparent glass letters of the alphabet reflected in the sunshine in every font and color imaginable. My sister was a graphic artist in addition to being well known in the national swimming community. Her forte was creating websites for the aquatic world.

I couldn't take my eyes off the slow moving, revolving letters. My mind slid back to the conversation with Harrison.

"You know what Harrison said?"

Lena and Dr. T stopped talking to each other and looked at me.

"What?" they said in unison.

"That he really wasn't positive that his uncle was driving the boat that killed his father."

"When did he change his mind?" asked Lena.

"Based on things he brought up, it was always an assumption. Nothing more."

Little T fussed, threw the keys on the floor and stuck his fist in his mouth. "Teething," Lena said. She walked over to the refrigerator, pulled out a blue pacifier, and rubbed it on his gums. Then left it in his mouth.

Little T looked like a miniature version of his dad: caramel skin and jet black eyes with his mom's mop of reddish curls. The bigger T was a product of a white mom who wasn't sure Lena was the right woman for her son and a sweetheart of a Black dad who owned a body shop south of San Francisco. Both grandparents' doubts about my sister melted away when she produced Little T who, in general, was a happy guy who loved his Aunt Trisha.

"It's amazing what quiets him down," said Lena.

"What do you remember about Harrison when you were teaching him to swim?"

Lena closed her eyes for a second. "I've been thinking about that. Usually he was quiet and obedient, until he wasn't."

"What does that mean?" Terrel asked.

"Well, I remember this one time … he was frustrated, maybe angry. He stood at the edge of their pool, his skinny arms crossed over his chest, and said, 'I'm not swimming today.' His mother was nowhere around."

"That doesn't sound so strange," I said.

"It happens all the time. But there was something odd about this silent little boy. I said that was fine and I asked him to pick something he'd rather do. He gave me the sweetest smile and asked how long I could hold my breath and would I show him. I didn't think too much about it, so I jumped in. I dove down to the bottom and managed to sit there for about a minute. As I came back up, Harrison swam down toward me. I can still see that silly smile on his face. He put his feet on shoulders, then his hands on my head, pushing me down. I easily threw him off and took a few strokes to the side of the pool to catch my breath.

"When he surfaced, I told him to never do that to anyone in a pool again. 'Am I in trouble?' I remember him asking, and then he said, 'I was playing.' He climbed out of the water, grabbed a towel, and headed for the house." Lena stared out the window for a second, then shook her head.

"Maybe he *was* only playing," I said.

"That's what I thought at first, but later I felt he wanted to drown me."

"Oh, come on," Dr. T said. "He was only a kid."

"It wasn't so much his actions but that sweet smile that never left his face."

"Did you tell his mother?" I asked.

"She didn't seem too concerned. She did mention that his doctor had put him on some kind of drug. But she never said what kind or what it was for. After that, being around him made my skin crawl, so I stopped the lessons."

"He must have changed, because the two of you looked lovey-dovey at his father's memorial," I said.

"Frankly, I forgot about that whole event until a few days ago. He didn't seem so weird the other day."

"You two can continue talking when we're out of here. I'm involved with enough dead bodies at work," Terrel said, standing up with a firm grip on the content child sucking the pacifier with gusto. "I know that look in your eye, Trisha. The word 'why' is beginning to float around in that curious mind of yours."

"You can't blame me," I said to Terrel. "He came on like he saw his uncle drive their boat over his father. There was no doubt in his mind. But when I questioned him about it, all he could say was, 'Who else could have done it?' Like it was a done deal, because he wanted it to be a done deal."

"Yeah, okay," Terrel said, walking out of the kitchen. "Nice talking to you."

"So, it wasn't an accident?" Lena asked.

"I have no idea," I said. "I walked around the marina by the Golden Gate Bridge this afternoon and chatted with a few boaters. They remember the Coast Guard towing in the boat and EMTs wheeling a body off in a body bag. They don't remember anything about another man on board."

"But …" started Lena.

"Then he told me that his uncle had been having an affair with his mother."

"How does he know that?" said Lena.

"He said his father told him. I honestly don't know what to believe. Do you remember anything about his mother?"

"Not really. She was friendly. Always paid me after each lesson." Lena paused. "The only thing that stands out was she watched the lessons from inside the house through a window. I mentioned once that she was welcome to be outside with us. She seemed embarrassed that I noticed her. Her face turned bright red."

"She knew about her son's off kilter behavior. Maybe she was keeping an eye on him?"

"I don't know. But after that, she never came to the window to watch."

"Did she work?" I asked.

"Yeah, I think she did back then," Lena said.

"It might make sense for me to go over and see her," I said to Lena as I stood up and moved over to the front door.

An enormous smile spread over Lena's face. "Detective Trisha, back on the case."

"No," I said and pulled open the door. "Just have a few questions."

"Hah." I heard Lena snort as I shut the door behind me. "You made up your mind to figure this out."

"Is he paying you?"

"You bet."

Chapter 5

The meeting with the widow, Justine Barlow, didn't go the way I expected. I decided to surprise her. In retrospect, not a good idea. I coerced my sister to contact Harrison and invite him for a coffee date. When he responded with a 'when and where,' I knew this would give me an opportunity to see his mother without him around.

Pulling into their large circular driveway, I realized that when I was there for Andy's Celebration of Life, the scope of this massive house and land that fanned out along the rolling hills eluded me. Maybe it was all the mourners converging on the front steps and rippling through the overpowering double front doors that made things appear smaller. But now, with the floor-to-ceiling glass windows covered by shadowy curtains and the dominating front door, cheerless without its stream of friends and relatives, the house grew in size each time I took a step closer.

An upsurge of the jitters passed through me as I paused at the front door. Could I make a quick retreat to my car without being seen? I implored the voice in my head to disappear. It didn't, but I pushed forward. I don't know why I do this, I thought. It drives me crazy. I pulled back on the large brass door knocker and let it fall. A stillness smothered the house. I grabbed the knocker again and knocked on the door. Once. Twice. Silence.

"Mrs. Barlow?" I called out. Wouldn't a place like this have a housekeeper? I turned around to look across the hills stretching down to the valley below. Sticking out in the distance was the Marin County mini-mountain, Mt. Tamalpais, with its somber fir trees blending together as they reached for the sky.

"Hello?"

I wanted to retrace my steps back to the car. Instead, quietly, I opened the front door and stepped in.

"Mrs. Barlow? Are you here? Is somebody here?" Inside, the house was quiet. Vacant.

An opportunity? Or a mistake? Probably a mistake, but that never stopped me before. I took a step inside. "Mrs. Barlow?" I called out again. The house couldn't be emptier. Off to the left, down a wide hallway, was the room that housed the after-service buffet and the sign-in book. No one would have guessed that anything or anyone crowded this space a few days ago. An uneasiness crept up my neck and my heartbeat faster, echoing in my ears. Something was off but I wasn't sure what. That fight or flight feeling crept across my body. An unexpected intensity spread across this large, empty room. Someone was going to find me here and wouldn't be happy about it. I had to get out. Now. I usually liked pushing myself into places where I didn't belong. Not today.

As soundlessly as possible, I edged toward the wall of windows overlooking the pool below. Two large glass doors stood open, and I could hear voices clearly by the pool. There was Mrs. Barlow on a lounge chair facing the swimming pool, her long silver hair partially covered by a wide brim straw hat. Immediately, my breathing slowed down. Whatever I was worried about, probably someone finding me, melted away. Maybe I could redo my entrance and walk to the pool to talk to her.

"That's not possible," she said into the phone. "I don't have that much money. There's no way I can pay you back." She leaned over to the chair next to her. Then someone reached out and patted her arm. I couldn't see the profile, but it was a man.

"Please. You have to understand. We're bankrupt. There's nothing left." She sounded desperate. The air filled with silence. Then, "No. You can't. Please don't do that. My son is home. Don't come here." She looked at the man next to her, his arm still resting on hers. "He hung up. What am I going to do?"

Their voices lowered and then Justine abruptly stood up. She knocked over a book resting on a small white metal table, and when she went to pick it up, she slowly turned toward the house as if she knew I was there. I ducked behind a curtain, glued myself to the wall, and inched away from the windows until I came to the hallway. After a tiptoe sprint to door, I rushed to my old Honda, climbed in, and locked the door, trying to settle down.

I had to talk to her. Forget the stealth approach. Now I would be loud. I turned on the ignition, and with my foot firmly placed on the brake, I revved the engine. Louder and louder until my ancient car shook and spit gravel in all directions.

Before slipping out of the car, I pounded on the horn. Walking slowly toward the side of the house, I shouted, "Mrs. Barlow. Mrs. Barlow? Hello?"

"Yes," came faintly from the pool area.

I turned the corner and saw Justine Barlow standing between two lounge chairs I had seen from the window. The one next to her was now empty.

Justine was prematurely gray, but in her case, the silver hair hanging loose around her shoulders said nothing about age. From a distance, she could be mistaken for a much younger woman. But as I walked closer, she began to appear like a mannequin, stiff and glued together. Work had been done on her torso, that's for sure. Especially on her breasts. A black bikini hugged her curves. She pulled a towel around her waist.

"Can I help you?" she asked.

"Hi, I'm Trisha Carson. My sister Lena taught Harrison how to swim. A long time ago."

She looked blankly at me.

"We were both at the memorial for your husband. I am so sorry for your loss."

She looked first down at her feet, then up at the windows I was recently staring from. "You are truly kind. Can I help you?"

"Well, Harrison and I met the other day. I wanted to talk to him again."

"Sorry, but he's not here."

"Do you know if he'll be staying for a while? I'm sure he would be a help to you."

Justine sighed. "I don't know."

I glanced down at the small patio table between the identical lounges. Two glasses rested on the tiled top, half-filled with white wine.

Justine's eyes followed mine. She walked past the lounges, closing in on me.

"I'll tell Harrison you were here," she said gesturing toward the pool gate.

Instead of following her lead, I took a step toward her. She retreated, startled.

"Mrs. Barlow, I don't know to say this."

"Go on," she said.

"This is awkward, but Harrison thinks your brother-in-law killed your husband."

Her hand flew to her mouth. "Excuse me? He what?"

"He felt that his father's death wasn't an accident, that something happened on the boat when they were out on the bay."

"Of course it did. Andrew fell off the boat and was washed into the propellers. Trisha—that's your name, isn't it?"

I nodded.

"This is really none of your business. But if you spoke with Harrison, you know that he is upset about his father's death. And he tends to be high strung. His relationship with his uncle has never been strong. He's imagining things. Maybe looking for someone to blame. However, I don't see that this is any concern of yours."

She glanced up at the glass windows again. Then she walked past me. This time she didn't thank me for coming, but she moved next to the gate, held it open, and gestured for me to follow her. I glanced quickly around the pool area and followed her gaze to the glass windows. The curtain, the one that I hid behind, fluttered slightly.

⚬——•————•——⚬

I steered my car to the nearest fast food drive through I could find, then parked and gulped down a soda with mega hits of caffeine and grabbed a handful of french fries. I called my sister.

"Lena, you wouldn't believe it," I said into my cell phone chewing on the fries. "Her body looked like it was made of spare parts stuck together. And her boobs…"

"What are you eating? Sounds gross. And what were you doing looking at her boobs?"

"How could I not? The top half of her was mostly boobs."

"So, she had a lot of work done. What else?"

"She's bankrupt."

"Not possible," said Lena.

"Well, that's what she said. I overheard her talking on the phone to someone that loaned her husband money and wants it back. Like, right now. In fact, whoever was on the phone said they were coming to her house."

"How can they be bankrupt with that beautiful home?" mused Lena.

"There's something weird going on there. Did you meet up with Harrison?"

"Briefly. He didn't want to talk to me. Not really. You know he's a drama student? He landed the part of Macbeth at his university but now feels that his career in serious theater is over, since he's here."

"He's staying?"

33

"Seems like it. But he didn't say. Anything else weird, besides the mother's body?"

I described the scene of the pool and the house. "Someone was there. Sitting next to her while she was on the phone. It was a guy, and she didn't want me or maybe anyone to see who it was."

In the background, Little T was grumbling. "Just a minute." Lena's voice faded as she probably turned to look at her son. "Shush baby." Then her volume increased. "Well, it wasn't Harrison. Maybe it was the brother-in-law."

"That's what I thought. Could be he really is involved with the dad's death and the mom, like Harrison said."

"This sounds like a plot for a Grade B movie. Need to go. Little T has crawled into the kitchen." Lena clicked off the line. It didn't matter how I felt a week ago; I was now involved in this death. Could Harrison be right? Was it murder? I needed to talk to the brother, Marty, and his family, and I also wanted to see the infamous boat.

Chapter 6

Earlier this morning, I had asked Jon for a favor … locating the Nereus. It took him less than an hour to text me back the marina and slip number.

I consider Jon my sweetheart. It took me a while to realize that, but when I finally did, my life improved a hundred and fifty percent. We met about three years ago when I worked at Fort Mason on the San Francisco Bay waterfront. Once a coastal defense site during the Civil War, the long wharves that jutted out into the bay are now a national historic site and home to museums, galleries, theaters, restaurants, and offices, including mine. I once worked for a masters swimming organization with a photographic view of the Golden Gate Bridge. Jon used to patrol the grounds during the day. That's how we met.

The next morning after taking The Babe, the house bulldog, for a walk, I drove over to Gaspar de Portola Yacht Harbor, a two-hundred berth marina on the northern end of San Francisco. It was called Portola for short. Glamorous homes in the four million dollar range swept down to the vibrant boat basin's edge and glided up to the reclusive base of Ring Mountain.

I strolled by the small harbor master's office. Outside was a large whiteboard with information that any boater, whether the owner of a thirty-six-foot sloop or a two-person kayak, could use. Scrawled in black marker were the times for the maximum flood and ebb tide, tidal current, winds and potential gusts for the day, outside temperature, and water temperature. At the bottom was an enlarged view of the daily tide chart showing its moon-driven ups and downs.

I stuck my head inside the cramped office. Sitting behind a desk was the harbor master, or in this case, harbor mistress.

"Hey," she said with a smile, looking up at me. She held up one finger indicating she'd be off the phone soon. "I'll get back to you" she said to someone on the other end. "Now, how can I help you?"

Behind me, a family dressed out in boat clothes peeked around me. Their little boy, around four years old and munching on some salted pretzels, smiled up at me.

"Quick question," said the dad. "Sorry, excuse me," he said but never glanced in my direction. "Did my dock box get repaired?"

"We're working on it," she said.

"Think we can go faster? I have some valuable boat equipment stored away there."

"I'll do my best," she said with a smile.

He nodded, turned around, and the family of four moved toward the dock.

"One sec," she said to me while typing something on her laptop. Off to the side of her government-issue, gunmetal-gray desk, three large monitors scanned the goings and comings of local mariners. Heavy boat lines were coiled in the corner. Stacked along the length of the other side were white PVC dock edge bumpers. Boat photos and smiling sunburned faces—plus fish, lots of photos of dead fish hoisted up in the air by the proud fisherman—slathered the office walls.

"One more time," she said and sighed.

"The Nereus. Can you tell me the berth number? I'm supposed to drop something off and I forgot where it's docked."

She looked up at me skeptically, paused for a second, then said, "You said the Nereus? You know the boat owners?"

I nodded. "This must seem odd; I know there's been a death in the family."

She snorted. "A death? I should say so."

"The brother asked me to leave something on the boat." I patted my backpack and smiled. I hoped she believed me.

She went back to her laptop's screen and typed in a few words.

"Guess I could have texted them," I said to the harbor mistress. "Sorry for the intrusion."

"C Dock, Slip 253. Go to the right. Dock letters are over the gate," she said and returned to the screens in front of her. "I'll unlock the gate from here."

"I'm impressed with your video set up." The three monitors each displayed six views of the marina. "You can watch everybody coming and going."

"C Dock, Slip 253."

"Thanks," I said and moved slowly toward the door. With one final glance over my shoulder, I walked out. Although she seemed fixated on a diagram of the yacht harbor splayed across one monitor, her fingers remained frozen on the keyboard.

⁂

The dock was on the outer edge of the marina and the boat was tied up about halfway down the pier. A midweek quiet blanketed the rows of boats. Halyards clanked faintly against the metal masts of the sailboats, and a few seagulls squawked overhead. I strolled past the Nereus and meandered to the end of the wooden dock, pretending to enjoy the clean lines of the yachts buttoned up against the light winds. Would anyone be around to see me climb onto the Nereus? I needn't have been so careful. Except for the family that had stopped in the harbor master's office, now on the other side of the marina, not a soul walked the docks. I paused at the Nereus's berth and indifferently walked down the finger pier that separated the boat from its neighbors. Glancing at the water basin in front of me and still seeing no one, I walked closer to the power boat and pulled myself aboard. It rocked gently under my feet. I moved forward toward the enclosed cockpit and took a seat in front of the console, secure from prying eyes.

So, this was how it feels to be at the helm of a powerboat. The marina spread out in front of me like an army waiting for battle.

The boat was spotless. I ran my hands over the console, across, and stuck them between the white waterproof cushions. Not a crumb or a candy wrapper to be seen. The floor had been swept clean. Dock boxes were hidden underneath the bench seats. I saw padlocks on all of them. Narrow steps led down to a wooden door that led to the cabin. A padlock kept me out of there, too.

In the cockpit, I sat on one of the side benches and gazed around me. If this was the boat that Andrew Barlow was originally on, evidence would be hard to come by. As I sat there daydreaming and looking out at the bay, I heard a small voice.

"Hi," said the boy I'd seen in the harbor master's office. He was still munching on a bag of pretzels. "Are you going out?" he asked.

"Where did you come from?"

He pointed a pretzel at a group of people standing by the dock gate. "That's my mom," he said.

"I remember seeing you. I'm waiting for the owners, but I think I made a mistake. Maybe I had the wrong day."

The skinny kid wearing a zip up gray hoody didn't say anything for what seemed like ten minutes.

"Daria was here yesterday," he mumbled through a mouthful of snacks.

"Daria?"

"She goes to high school," he said.

"Is she the owner's daughter?"

"Yeah. She has a brother, Dawson. They're twins. Have you ever seen twins? They're funny."

"They like to go out on the bay?"

The boy laughed. "Not Daria. She doesn't like getting wet. She yells 'Stop that' all the time."

"Do you know Mr. Barlow?"

"He's dead," said the boy.

"He's what?"

"Dead. That's what my momma told me."

From a distance, I heard a woman's voice. "Lucus, come on we're late."

"Bye," said Lucas as he scampered down the dock.

This kid knew more about the family than most, and a bag of pretzels could get him talking.

I did another quick search around the boat. It still looked immaculate. Wish I could get into those under-seat boxes, or maybe down below. But each lock stayed securely in place.

While climbing over the gunwale, the side of the boat, I glanced at two kayakers paddling out and caught the leg of my pants on a piece of deck hardware.

"Ohhh." I fell, reaching out, grabbing at empty air. Would I fall between the boat and the dock? Would I crash onto the finger pier? The boat moved away from the dock as one of my legs buckled underneath me and the other stayed firmly attached to the boat. I was about to be ripped apart.

"I wondered why someone was yelling. Makes sense now," said a voice from the dock. In front of me stood a grizzled-looking guy with a beard, wearing a greasy white T-shirt.

"Help me please," I said.

"Sure thing," he said. He grabbed the side of the boat and pulled it closer to the dock. Then he took my arm and heaved me to a one-legged standing position. With me leaning on him, he stretched across to the boat and freed my pant leg. I pulled my now unstuck leg to meet the other one.

"Thank you," I mumbled, rubbing the inside of my thighs. As the wooden dock moved with our weight, he reached out to steady me.

"How'd that happen?" he asked.

"I wasn't paying attention."

"You looking for the Barlows?"

I stared at him, trying to come up with a plausible reason why I was on the boat of someone I didn't know. "Barlows? Is that whose boat it is? I'm on the wrong boat."

He guided me over to a dock box and I sat down.

"What boat are you looking for?"

"The Nereid in Tiburon Yacht Harbor."

"You're lost young lady. This isn't the Tiburon Yacht Harbor. This is Portola. And this isn't the Nereid. It's the Nereus. This isn't the marina you're looking for. The one you want is off Main Street in Tiburon."

"My leg hurts," I said, rubbing both of them this time.

"Come down to my boat. I'll make you a cup of tea. I think I have an aspirin or something. Might help."

My cellphone pinged. It was a text from Lena. *Call me*, it said. My sister would have to wait. This wizened sea salt might be an interesting man to talk to.

I limped down the dock, groaning slightly as I followed him to a large wooden sailboat at the end of the dock.

"Hatch," he said, his words blown away into the wind.

"Excuse me," I said.

"Hatch. My name is Hatch Grey."

"I'm Trisha Carson."

He climbed aboard and held out a hand, helping me on board.

"You sit here," he said motioning to the bench seat. There was a small table attached to the gunwale with a cup of coffee and a book resting on it.

"I'm so sorry I disturbed you. Don't worry about the tea. I need to go."

"No. No. You stay right where you are. Trisha Carson, you took quite a tumble. Look, you scraped your arm. It's bleeding. Now you sit there. I'll fix you up."

He climbed the steps down to the cabin and disappeared. I took the chance to answer Lena.

Me: *I'm on a boat.*
Lena: *??????*
Me: *I face planted trying to get off.*
Lena: *U ok?*
Me: *My legs, thighs hurt. Arm is bleeding.*
Lena: *What exactly were u doing?*
Me*: Tell you later.*

I clicked off and stuck the phone in my jacket pocket.

"What kind of tea do you want? I have herbal, green tea from an exotic region of China—or so it says on the package—and black tea," called Hatch from below.

"Green is fine. Thanks," I responded.

While the water was boiling, Hatch came on deck carrying a well-supplied first aid kit. First, he cleaned the wound, swiping some antibiotics on it, and then he covered it with a square of gauze and a large bandage. Then he repeated his actions on my knees.

"There you go. You'll be fine in no time. Gotta go get the tea." He carefully picked up the debris left and wiped the area around me. He was meticulous.

"Thank you."

"It was nothin'. Be right back."

While he clattered around the small stove below, I concocted a way to get him to talk about Nereus and its owners. But first a little chit chat.

A hand slowly projected from the cabin. "It's hot. Take care. Hope you don't mind, I put a splash of honey in it."

Although I didn't think I needed the tea and the thought of honey in green tea made my stomach churn, it tasted surprisingly good. Warm, relaxing, and sweet.

Hatch scrambled up the wooden steps holding a package of lemon cookies.

"Not sure how old these are," he said with a smile and put the cookies down on the bench. He sat next to them.

I took a long sip and then cupped the mug in my hand.

"I don't know how I made such a big mistake. Not only was I on the wrong boat, but the wrong marina. I didn't realize there was more than one marina in Tiburon."

Hatch remained silent.

I couldn't think of much else to say. "Do you live on your boat?" I asked.

"Sometimes," he said. "I switch off. Here. Home. Back and forth." He smiled.

"Home is somewhere here in Marin?"

"Yep. But originally from New England. The Boston area."

"You sailed there?"

"Oh yeah. Taught sailing for years on the Charles River."

"Do you miss it?"

"I miss the frostbiting."

"The what?" I had no idea what he was talking about.

"Sailing small boats in the winter. There's no winter here. Maybe rain, but no biting wind and snow," he reminisced.

I shivered thinking about sailing in conditions like that.

"I haven't been on many boats. My sweetheart sometimes delivers boats up and down the California coast and from one side of the bay to the other. I went with him once, from here to the Berkeley Marina."

"Down wind. Bet it was a quick ride," Hatch said.

I nodded and moved into what I really wanted to know. "That boat I fell off ...? It's pretty nice from what I could see. What kind of a boat is that?"

"Northstar 55," he said. "Expensive."

"Does it get used a lot?" I asked, sipping the tea.

"Fair amount."

"I hope the Barlows—that's what you called the owners, right? — won't be upset. I don't think I destroyed anything."

Hatch watched the water around us, eyes on a powerboat moving slowly into the marina. Then he glanced back at me. "The boat belongs to the family. Daw, the son—the one in high school—is the only mariner of the bunch," said Hatch. "I don't think he'll care or even notice."

Well, finally, news I could use. "That's a pretty nice boat not to care about," I said. "While I was sitting there, a kid came up to me and mentioned that the owner died."

"Want some more tea?" Hatch asked.

"No, thanks. But did the guy really die?"

"Terrible accident. Andy, that was his name, was in the Bay, swimming, I think. Somehow, he got washed into the boat's propellers."

I shuddered and hopefully appeared both distressed and horrified. "That's terrible. Did you say he was swimming? In the Bay? Who in their right mind swims in the Bay?"

"Andy did. All the time. Fashioned himself an open water swimmer. He was getting pretty good. Could handle the cold and was putting in the distance. His brother Marty often drove the boat while Andy was in the water."

"Was he driving, or whatever you said, the day he died?"

"Sure was. I was sitting here having a morning bun and a cup of tea when they motored out of the slip into Richardson Bay. I yelled to Marty and asked where they were going. Said something about the marina under the North Tower of the Golden Gate Bridge." Hatch paused and scratched his head. "I'm pretty sure they were both on board and Marty was at the helm. Now that I think of it, it could have been Andy. No, I remember Marty. Sorry, I'm having a senior moment."

I sat there sipping the hot liquid. So, they left together … if I could trust Hatch's memory … and only one returned. Maybe Harrison was right after all.

"I'm taking up too much of your time," I said. "I better go. My legs are really starting to ache."

He reached for the mug and the package of cookies and moved

them aside.

As I stood up, he reached for my arm and steadied me.

"Now take your time. Be careful. Step down to the dock. No more falling off boats," he said with a grin. I smiled and did as I was told. My legs burned and almost buckled under me as I stood on the dock. I grabbed on to the side of the boat and Hatch hastily grasped my arm again.

"You okay?" he asked.

"I am so sore," I said rubbing my quads.

"A warm bath might help," Hatch said. He gave me a funny look. "I know you."

"You do? I don't think we've met."

He took off his brown wool beanie and ran his hands through his thinning hair. "Yeah. We have, but I can't place where," he said, somewhat bewildered. He tilted his head and closed his eyes. "Nope," he said as he continued to scrutinize me. "It will come to me. I'm good at remembering people. Now you go rest those legs."

"Thanks again for all your help. I would probably still be sprawled all over the deck if you hadn't rescued me." I limped toward the gate at the end of the dock. I'd never seen this man before. I'd never been to this marina or visited anyone in the surrounding neighborhood. I held on to the railing, which now was beginning to resemble a ladder since the tide was going out. Low on the boat side, higher toward the parking lot.

The dock behind me swayed and loud footsteps followed me toward the gate.

"Hey, I remembered. The funeral. You were at Andy's Celebration of Life with some lady," Hatch called out.

"What?" I responded although I heard him clearly. "Thanks again." I waved and limped as fast as I could up the gangway, through the gate, and down the sidewalk to the parking lot. Before unlocking the car, I looked back at the sailor and waved. He stood there, hands on his hips, gaping at me.

How long would it take him to put two and two together and realize that I wasn't on the wrong boat in the wrong marina.

I slid into the car, jammed the key into the ignition, and made a run for the main road.

Chapter 7

"You want to tell me what you were doing on a boat," said Dr. T, "and how you managed to fall off it and not get wet?" Terrel was bringing me bags of ice to strap around my thighs and groin muscles to be held in place with ace bandages. "Here. Hold the ice. I'll secure it."

I was stretched out on Lena and T's couch, both legs resting on its arm. It was nice having an ER doctor in the family. He wasn't officially in the family since he and Lena weren't married, but they'd been together for a long time and little Timmy was the happy product of their union.

Although he liked to see me, or so I hoped, Terrel was skeptical when I dropped by. In the back of his mind, a neon red sign flashed "Danger, Danger! Danger! Trisha Approaching" each time I arrived unannounced. He saw me as someone who put Lena and occasionally Little T in danger, especially when I deliberated about a body … a dead body that was found in the Bay area. For that, I received regular lectures. He knew I'd solved crimes, more than one, but he preferred if I picked a different wingman or woman.

My thighs began to numb out from the cold, and I sighed. "That's beginning to feel much better. But my knees hurt. So does my arm."

I pulled up my pants legs and saw Hatch's attempt to patch me up.

"Trisha, you really did it to yourself. Let me clean that up for you." He walked into the kitchen and came back with warm water. Then he disappeared into the back of the house and returned with sterile cloths, gauze and more ace bandages. "Looks like someone did a pretty good job."

"Hatch did that," I said.

"Who's Hatch?" asked Dr. T.

"A guy who lives on his boat part time on the same finger pier as the boat I fell off of. He rescued me."

Dr. T had been totally absorbed in my battered knees and legs, or so I thought, but then he looked up at me over his black rimmed glasses and paused.

"Let's go back to my original question. How did you fall off a boat and not get wet? And why were you on a boat in the first place? And who is this Hatch person?"

"It's a funny story …" I started. "By the way, where's my sister and the baby?"

"Don't change the subject."

"Well, she called me and it sounded like she wanted to see me. Like right now," I mumbled.

"Trisha."

"Okay. Okay. As you can tell, I didn't fall in the water but on the dock. I got my foot or pants leg caught on some metal thingy on the boat and I didn't realize it. One leg kept moving and the other didn't."

"Why were you on a boat? Was Jon there?"

"Jon is out of town. He was sent to some sort of Park Ranger training. In Southern California, I think."

Dr. T grabbed a roll of gauze when Lena flew in the front door.

She gasped when she saw my legs. "How did you do that?" she said. Terra cotta flowerpots balanced unsteadily in her arms.

Terrel turned around. "What's all that?" he asked.

She leaned over to inspect my leg. "Ick," she said, screwing up her face.

Dr. T stretched up and gave her a kiss on the cheek.

"The lady down the street is moving, and she has more flowerpots than she can take with her."

"Your sister refuses to talk about what she was doing on a boat," said Terrel.

"Maybe I can pick up some pots on the way home," I said. "I'd like to put some flowers out on my deck." I thought if I kept talking, Dr. T would drop the subject of me and the boat completely.

"Oh no. That won't work. Lena's story can wait. Why were you on a boat?" Dr. T said.

"Maybe the question should be, why did you faceplant off the boat?" my sister questioned.

They both stared at me.

"Talk," said Dr. T.

"It's not such a big deal. I was trying to visit someone in the Tiburon Yacht Harbor. But I got the locations mixed up. You know how bad I am at directions. I ended up at the Gaspar de Portola Yacht Harbor, also in Tiburon. And the boat I was originally trying to find had almost the identical name to a boat at this harbor."

"The Tiburon Yacht Harbor?" asked Lena.

"No. Gaspar de Portola Yacht Harbor. It's not that far from the Richmond-San Rafael Bridge."

"I'm confused," said Lena.

"You're making all this up, aren't you?" asked Dr. T. "I don't care where it was. Why were you on the boat? The wrong boat from what you said?"

"This really is none of our business," I said, attempting to appear miffed.

"I know where you were," chirped Lena. "I bet you were trying to find the boat that Barlow was on before he got chewed up by the propeller."

"What?" said Dr. T.

"Well ..." I started.

"You're at it again, aren't you?" Dr. T glared at me as he finished his patch job on my knees. "What are you going to ask Lena to do this time?"

"Nothing. The only reason I'm here is that Lena wanted to see me." I pulled my legs off the couch and stood up too quickly. "Ow." I limped toward the kitchen. "What do you have to eat?" I asked.

"Did you find anything?" asked Lena, trailing after me.

"Don't get involved," yelled Dr. T.

"I'm only asking a question," Lena called over shoulder. "Can't I be curious?" Lena hadn't filled Terrel in, so we told him about the funeral and Harrison's theory.

"You don't think there's been a murder?" asked Dr. T.

"I go back and forth," I said. "But right now, there's nothing to worry about."

"Okay. No more questions for now," he said and wandered to the back of the house.

"Where is this lady's house with the pots?" I asked my sister.

"At the end of the block. She's lived here forever. According to her daughter, who was helping her pack, all of her mother's money is gone."

"Did she have a lot of money?" I asked.

"I don't know. She lived very modestly. Anyway, her daughter and husband helped her sell the house and now she's moving in with them. She's really unhappy about the whole thing. The mother, not the daughter."

"I would be too. I'm sure she didn't plan on living out her days as a boarder in her daughter's home."

Lena shrugged. "The daughter called and asked me to stop by. Her mom once told her that she only likes me in the neighborhood."

I applauded slowly and performed a dainty bow. "It's an honor to be in your presence, my lady. Why you?"

"I found her missing cat a while back, and I brought her over some food when she had the flu. I guess that makes us best buddies. She was beyond upset when I walked in. Crying, moaning, talking nonsense. Things like 'What will happen to me? Where will I live?' She was really over the edge. Anyway, I talked with her a bit. Helped her find the number of her financial advisor. I pinned it to a corkboard in the kitchen. Then I left."

"I hoped she wasn't scammed out of her money," I reflected. "What if she had an internet boyfriend?"

"I doubt it's that dramatic," said Lena.

"If she's on a limited or even fixed income, losing a ton of money could be more than upsetting. Is that why you wanted me to come over? Couldn't you have told me this on the phone? I'm going home. My thighs are aching and my knees still burn."

"There's one more thing." My sister walked out of the room and returned carrying a large brown envelope. "This came for you."

For some reason, I didn't want to take it from her hand. I backed up and shook my head. "What is it?" I asked.

"I don't know," answered Lena. "Here. Take it."

"Who's it from?"

She glanced at the return address and didn't say anything. "Might be a law firm."

"I don't know anybody in a law firm," I said, reaching for it. I glanced at the return address. "Somewhere in Illinois. This must be a mistake." I laid it on the kitchen table.

"Aren't you going to open it?" Lena asked.

I picked the envelope up again with my fingertips, afraid it would burn my hands. "Think I'll drop it in the trash."

"What is wrong with you? Open it," demanded Lena.

I didn't know why I was hesitating. I tapped it against my other hand. Then, without a word, I tore it open. On the letter head of Regent and Trumbell was a short note saying that they represented my husband, Bradley Carson, who I hadn't seen in almost five years, and that he was filing for a divorce.

"Brad wants a divorce," I said, staring blankly at Lena. "Why did he use your address? That's so odd, isn't it? He wrote to you. He should have …"

"Trisha, are you okay? You are deathly white."

"Nobody sends me mail here."

"Sit down."

Instead, I limped over to the entrance to the kitchen, stopping for a minute to adjust the ace bandages and cold pack on my legs.

"I'm going home," I said, not looking around. I dropped the electric piece of paper, wondering if it would catch the house on fire. I moved through the front door and zombie-walked toward my car.

"Trisha, come back." Lena bolted down the front steps two at a time and grabbed my arm.

"You can't drive like this. Come back inside. Sit down," Lena said and turned toward the house. "Terrel, come here. Now," yelled Lena.

"My hands are cold," I said, rubbing one against the other. My throat zipped close. "I can't breathe."

"Trish, look at me." Lena stood in front of me, but she appeared to be so far away. My gaze inched closer to her face. My hands flew up to my neck.

"Can't breathe," I gasped.

"Terrel! Hurry up!"

The screen door slammed against the side of the house as Terrel charged out the door.

"What happened?" he asked Lena as he scanned my face.

"She can't breathe."

"Trisha," Dr. T. asked, "what's going on?"

"Feeling dizzy. Want to go home. Need to take the dog for a walk. Dizzy," I said, reaching for the car door handle.

"No, no. You're coming back inside," Dr. T said. He slid one of his arms around my waist and led me up the front stairs.

"Lee, open the door."

Terrel laid me gently down on the couch again and the dizziness eased. Lena draped two quilts over me and a soft warmth expanded into my core. Then T disappeared and came back with a stethoscope.

"Just going to check your vital signs," he said as he listened to my heart and lungs and nodded. "Good," he said. Then he checked my blood pressure. "BP is low, and your heart rate is up," he said.

I blinked.

"How're you feeling?" asked Terrel.

"Tired," I said. "And my head is tingling."

"Tingling? That's a fine medical term. Just lay there for a few minutes. Don't get up. Lena?" He motioned her into the kitchen. "What happened?" he whispered so his voice wouldn't carry.

"Brad. A letter was sent to her. Here."

"I don't understand," he said perplexed.

"It's from her husband Bradley Carson. I told you about him. The guy went to work one day and never came back. That's when they were living in Colorado. His brother eventually called Trish and said Brad didn't want to be married anymore. He finally filed for divorce."

"I thought she was divorced."

Lena shook her head. "She rarely talks about him."

"This looks like a panic attack. The surprise must have caused a drop in blood pressure. She didn't fall or bump her head?"

"She fell off the boat, remember?"

"Maybe it's the combination of the fall and the letter," Dr. T surmised.

Terrel walked back into the living room. "How do you feel?"

I sighed. "Stupid. I feel stupid."

"You're not. Rest for a bit. Wanna tell me what happened?"

"Nothing much," I said.

"I beg to differ. A few minutes ago, you couldn't breathe. Any idea what caused this reaction?"

"Former, really curren missing husband sent me a letter. No, his lawyer sent me a letter. Here at your house. After all this time, Brad wants a divorce. I had pushed him out of my mind, so far out I forgot that he existed. But he still does."

I sat up and stared at Terrel's face. "Your glasses are dirty." I took a deep breath and let it out slowly. "I'd thought about filing for divorce but never got around to it. Mostly because I didn't know where he was. You know, he walked out. I'm sure Lena must have told you," I said.

From the back of the house, Little T fussed in his crib. "I'll tend to him," said Lena. But she didn't move.

"Can I go home now?" I asked my almost brother-in-law.

"How about Lena drives you? I'll pick her up later," he said.

"I'm okay."

"I am being cautious. That's what doctors do."

"I'll be all right."

I stood up. Tall, lanky Dr. T stood up next to me.

"You've got to change your T-shirt," I remarked, scanning him from the waist up. "There's baby goop all over it and your glasses need cleaning."

"You already said that. Okay, you can go home," he said. "When you start criticizing me, you're fine."

I nodded and headed once again to the front door.

"Wait," he called after me.

"I'll be fine. Really."

He put his hand on my arm firmly and stopped me. "Trisha, I think you should talk to someone."

"I'm talking to you."

"No, a mental health professional. This sounds like a panic attack, and from what Lena tells me, it isn't the first time."

Staring over his shoulder, I glared at my sister. "Traitor," I mouthed. She turned and left the room.

Chapter 8

This horrible pressure in my chest would pass, I thought, looking in the car's rearview mirror. I took a few deep breaths and a sip from my water bottle. Panic attacks, as Dr. T alluded to, regularly kept me company a few years ago. But they faded when I learned how to breathe deeply. Today's event was an exception.

After hearing from my runaway husband, I fell right into that familiar bottomless pit. Why should I react that way after no contact for almost five years? My mind took off on that hamster wheel as I struggled to bring it back under control. I finally remembered the breathing techniques to lead me to the here and now. That always worked. Breathe in, two, three, four, five; hold, two, three, four; and out, two, three, four, five, six. A few of those calmed down my full-speed mind.

Didn't Lena come in with flowerpots? Go find the flowerpots. I scanned the sidewalks as I drove slowly away, checking out the front yards. In the distance, I saw a moving truck and people scurrying back and forth. This must be the home of the flowerpot lady. I pulled into an empty parking space close to the corner and walked back. The anxiety episode, whatever it was, faded.

"Hi," I said to a bulky man in a pair of grease-stained jeans and a no-color T-shirt. A rolled-up rug was balanced on his shoulders. He squinted as he glanced up, cutting the glare of the sun.

"Can I help you?" he asked. At the same time, he threw the heavy rug into the back of a truck, sending up a curtain of dust. The man in front of me gasped for air while I slapped my hands over my mouth and coughed.

"Sorry about that," he said, wiping the dust and dirt from his face. "Come over here," he said, walking onto the perfectly cut green grass. "Now. Can I help you with something?"

"I'm Trisha. My sister was just here. She lives down the street … has an eighteen-month-old baby?"

"Evan," he said and shook my hand. He pulled out what used to be a rag of some sort and tried to wipe his face again.

"Sorry," he said. "I must have been packing the truck."

"She picked up some flowerpots. I wondered if your mom…?"

"Mother-in-law," he corrected me.

"Mother-in-law had any more she was giving away."

"She does. I just put them into my van. But you can have them."

"Are you sure?"

"Not a problem. They were forced on me," he said, laughing. "Wait here."

He walked over to a white van that was partially blocked by a wooden dresser, two intricately decorated Japanese lacquer screens, and an old-fashioned cherry wood pie safe. I could see a few letters on the van, but I stayed focused on the furniture.

I walked toward the narrow, spindly antique that was used for storing pies, bread, meats—anything that needed to be protected from mice, rats, and any other hungry creepy critters.

"I haven't seen one of these in years," I said, running my hand along the polished veneer. "My grandmother had one in her pantry. Your van makes a perfect backdrop. All you'd need to do was block out the 'M A R' on the van and you'd have an outdoor showroom."

The man walked around the furniture, leaned into the back of the van, and pulled out some pots.

"Here you go."

As I reached over to take them, an angular woman in rolled-up denim overalls walked across the grass, a dusty red kerchief tied around her head Rosie the Riveter style.

"I'm Hildie. I overheard some of your conversation. Do you know my mother?" she asked, putting out her hand. Then she pulled it back. "Sorry, I'm really dirty."

"My sister, she lives down the street and was just here … knows your mother. She gave her some flowerpots. I stopped by hoping there might be a few more."

"Your sister is Lena, right? Chatty?"

I nodded. "That's my sister. Has she started running your life yet?"

"No, but then I don't live here. It's just my mom. But I have met her. I remember she mentioned that she had a sister. You were living in Colorado. I think she said you're the youngest."

"Ah, no. I'm the oldest by eight years. She lives in our parent's home. We both grew up down the street."

"Sorry. I probably mixed it up. One of you, I guess it must be you, brought the other up."

"Indeed, I did."

Those days seemed so far behind me. As Hildie continued talking, I drifted back to the time when Dad abandoned us. Our mom was wasting away from lung cancer. Both my sister and I knew she'd recover since she never smoked. But that didn't happen. My high school graduation was only months away. My plans included college with a major in criminal investigations.

When that diploma rested safely in my hands, Dad walked out the door, leaving me to raise my elementary school sibling alone. I promised myself, no matter what, Lena would never enter the system. Petty crime like shoplifting school clothes, especially the hottest sneakers, food from the best grocery stores in Marin (Lena was fond of sushi), and renting out the garage to so-called friends with stolen goods allowed us to stay in our parent's home. A part time job in a local pharmacy helped. Lena smothered her anguish and grief in the pool and pounded out lap after lap, winning medals at every meet she entered. Colleges recruited her. Representatives from top universities with the best national swim teams offered her free rides. Once she made her choice, I finally relaxed. I'd done it. My sister's future was secure. More than twenty-five years passed before I saw my father again. He'd kept track of us through his old friend and now landlord, Earl. Lena's pregnancy drew him back to California.

Unfortunately, that's when I began to mentally fight with the world. I approached my daily life with dread. Staying alone in my bedroom calmed me down. But as soon as I opened the front door, a swell of panic rippled through my body. Anxiety became my persistent sidekick.

"Trisha? Trisha! Are you okay?" asked Hildie.

"Sorry. I was lost in thought. Remembering what it was like to grow up here." I tried to smile.

"I said, there are more pots if you'd like them."

"I'm fine. Thanks. Lena said your mom was moving?"

Evan went back inside the house to begin another trip hauling furniture.

"Yeah. She lost all, and I mean all, of her savings. What's left to support her is this house. While it's being sold, she'll stay with us," Hildie said.

"How did she … I mean, I know it's none of my business, but what happened?"

"Bad investments," she said and turned to walk away, then glanced back. "I'm sorry to be so abrupt. This has been a difficult time for my mother. Everything that she and Dad worked for their entire lives is gone."

"Was this an internet scam? Like on a dating site? Where the guy promises love and a future … but, oh, he needs a little money. Just a little. And a little more."

"No. Not at all."

I stood there awkwardly waiting for an explanation. Finally, I realized none was forthcoming.

"I'm sorry to hear about this. Are you planning to sell her things? That pie safe is so charming. I could make an offer."

"Everything is going into storage until we figure out what to do next," Hildie said, shaking her head. "This is such a clusterfuck. My poor mother. She doesn't want to believe there's nothing left. She's sure the money will show back up. I never thought some so-called reliable financial advisor would rip off my mother."

"Someone local? I'd like to know the name so I stay away from this guy. If you don't mind me asking."

"Two brothers. I can't remember their names. Think it starts with a D or B. They were so caring and sweet when they talked to Mom. I sat next to her during the appointment. I knew, just knew, she'd be safe with them. I was so wrong. Sorry, but my mind's full of dust and things I have to do. Their name will come back to me, I'm sure," she said.

"No worries. I don't have any money to invest anyway," I said. "I'll leave you guys alone with your packing," I said, juggling the flowerpots and their saucers in my arms.

"If my mother decides to get rid of anything, we'll contact your sister," she said.

"Thanks." I flung open the Honda's trunk, wrapped the pots with extra sweatpants and a sweatshirt I always keep with me, and stuffed them in. Then I slammed the trunk shut, got in, and drove away.

Through my rearview mirror, I saw Hildie and Evan stop and look after my car as I turned the corner.

Chapter 9

Dad and Earl were in the midst of a heated discussion about the baseball teams in the run up to the World Series when I got home.

"That team is going nowhere. All of their pitchers stink," said Earl, his gray ponytail swaying from side to side the more agitated he became.

"But they have the hitters," said Dad, sitting on the couch He took a sip of his beer and then pointed the green bottle at Earl, who nodded. "Yes they do."

"But the Twins are clutch. You wait. You'll see," said Earl as he stood up and stretched.

"Hey Trisha. Where you been?" asked Dad.

"Over at Lena's house. Can you help me with some flowerpots? They're in the trunk."

"Sure thing, sweetie." He followed me out the door to the car.

"Where'd you get all these?" he asked, picking up an armload.

"Lady down the street from Lena. Evidently, she lost all her investments. The only thing left is her house, and she has to sell it to have money to live on."

Dad stopped. "Say that again."

"Well, the flowerpots ..."

"No, the part about her investments."

"Whoever was managing her investments screwed up. All her

money's gone," I said, picking up the saucers and slamming the trunk shut.

"Well, I'll be. The same thing happened to one of my buddies who volunteers at China Camp Park. Once his investments disappeared, he had to sell his house. Then he moved to Arizona to be closer to his kids."

"That's too bad. Hope that doesn't happen to you," I said nudging him with my elbow.

"Never gonna happen," Dad said.

"Why is that?" I asked, fumbling to open the door to the house.

"Don't have any investments. Hardly have any money. For sure no stocks or bonds."

Earl heard the last few comments as he walked over to hold the door open. "You doing some investing?" he asked

"Not me," said Dad. He stopped and looked at Earl. "Do you remember the guy who helped out on the pier? He had an old Ford truck?"

"I think so. Really knew his way around wood. Antonio, right?"

"That's the guy. Used to be a furniture maker."

"Yep. Did he ever show you those chairs he made?" asked Earl, now leaning against the door.

"Earl," I said.

"No," said Dad.

"Workmanship up the wazoo," remembered Earl.

"Dad, what does this have to do with the lady who lost all her money?"

"Right," said Dad. "Forgot for a moment. Do you recall before he moved, he said that all his investments went belly up?"

"You're right. Doesn't say much for his financial advisor," said Earl.

"Trisha met a woman who had the same thing happen to her. That kind of thing doesn't happen very often, does it?"

Earl shook his head. "Do you know who handled their money?"

Both Dad and I shook our heads.

"Even if I had any money, I wouldn't invest it. Too risky," said Dad. "Now, where do you want these?"

"Upstairs. On the deck by my bedroom. And, if I ever have any money …"

"Well, we know that's not going to happen," laughed Dad.

"Thanks for your encouragement," I said. "Just take them upstairs."

"On my way," said Dad, juggling the terra cotta pots. My phone shimmied and buzzed in my pocket. I sat down on the staircase and pulled out the cell. Work was calling, which seemed strange since the baseball season was over. I'm in Guest Services for the San Francisco Giants, winners of three World Series rings. I even had a replica of one I wore on a gold chain at the ballpark.

"Hello. Hey hi, Molly. What's up? Thursday? Sure. In uniform, right? Okay. See you then."

"Trish, are you coming?"

"Yeah. That was the Giants. Some venture capitalist company rented most of the park for an employee party. They need people to work the event."

"Sure wish I went to employee parties like that," said Dad, who had decided to try to balance a flowerpot on his head.

"Watch it!" I yelled. "It's going to fall and break."

"Spoilsport," said Dad, reaching up for the pottery just before it leaned a little too far off kilter.

The flowerpot lady and the volunteer wood worker were soon out of my mind. I needed to get back to the Barlow family. I had an idea. I texted Harrison.

I want to talk to someone in your uncle's family. Can you help me with that?

The next day, I met Harrison outside Mt. Tamalpais Academy. We were waiting for his cousin to walk out the front door of the small prestigious high school tucked into a Marin hillside.

"She should be out by now," Harrison said, checking his watch. He pulled out his phone and texted her. She immediately responded. He clicked a response and stuck the phone back in his pocket.

"She's at water polo practice," he said, letting out a deep breath.

"Let's go wait for her at the pool." I started to get out of the car. Harrison told me to wait.

"They practice somewhere else. No pool here. Come on, let's go find her."

Harrison was quiet during the ride to the local high school.

"Can you tell me a bit about your cousin?" I asked, trying to come up with a conversation starter.

"No. We're not close."

I let out a frustrated sigh.

"Have you talked with her since … you know … since your father died?"

"You mean since he was killed."

"You don't really know that, Harrison. And frankly, the police disagree with you."

"They don't know what they're doing. I'm one hundred percent sure, make that one hundred and fifty percent sure he was murdered. That's why I asked for your help," he said, glaring in my direction. "But frankly, I'm not so sure you're the right person."

I saw an exit ramp away from this whole family and drama. "Well —" I started.

He cut me off. "But I still want you to try. My father's dead. My uncle is still alive. And he shouldn't be."

Harrison wanted revenge. When he talked about his dad's death, his pale skin bloomed a deep red. In his mind, the wrong person was dead.

⚬———•————•—⚬

Cousin Daria strolled out of the pool surrounded by three other girls that looked like her: straight wet hair, swimsuit still on, plaid pajama bottoms pulled up over the suit, and a backpack with a damp towel poking out slung over their shoulders.

High-pitched squeals echoed across the empty lot to our car.

"That's her, right?" I asked Harrison, pointing to the blonde in the middle. "I saw her at your dad's Celebration of Life."

"Yep, that's the spoiled rich bitch Ms. Daria. Hey, cuz!" yelled Harrison. "Over here."

The spoiled rich bitch Ms. Daria rolled her eyes, sighed, and mumbled something to her friends who broke into a rash of giggles. Then she walked our way. Slowly.

"What's up, cuz?" she asked. "Is this the lady you want me to talk to?"

"Yeah," he said.

"Well, I won't talk to her if you're around," she sniffed.

"Why not?" Harrison asked.

I sat there not knowing what to do. "How about we talk over there?" I said, pointing to a bench outside the pool building.

"As long as he's not coming," she said.

Harrison glared straight ahead, lips pulled into an unyielding, straight line. Slumping down in his seat, he rammed a pair of white earbuds into his ears.

I climbed out of the car and aimed her toward the bench. "Look, this won't take long. I promise."

"Oh okay. It's just that Harrison has become this douchebag since his father died. He thinks my father was involved, which is so not true," said Daria.

We sat on the bench, and she yanked her towel from the backpack and wrapped it around her head.

"Do you know what happened to your uncle?" I asked. I carefully watched her face. A shadow glided over her profile, and for a minute I thought she was about to cry. But then she pulled the towel from her hair, covered her face briefly, and eventually looked up.

"I don't know anything," she whispered with a shrug.

"Were you close to your uncle?"

She pressed her fingers to her lips. Staring blankly out to the empty park lot, she mumbled, "No."

"Do you know what happened that day your uncle was killed?"

She looked at me quickly, then dropped her gaze and twisted the ends of her long damp blond hair around her fingers. "Only what I was told. That there was a boating accident and he fell overboard," she said.

"Was your dad with him?" I asked as quietly as I could.

"My dad was not with him," Daria said loudly. "Harrison thinks my father killed his own brother. Stupid fuck! That's what he is. A stupid fuck. My cousin couldn't find his ass with his own two hands!"

She stood up. The tirade was over. "I have to get home." With that, she walked toward one end of the parking lot to the last remaining car, a black BMW convertible.

As I watched her scurry away, I went over the brief conversation in my head. Yes, no answers and no details. No eye contact. Either she really didn't know or she was protecting her father. Very hard to tell. Her story differed from Hatch's. I walked back toward Harrison's car, and two things stood out from the otherwise waste-of-time conversation. I'm sure I saw a brief look of fear when I asked about her uncle, and then she blew up when I inquired if her dad was on board the boat. She was protective of her dad. That made sense, but the brief moment of gloominess, unease, and heartache puzzled me.

"Well, what did she say?" said Harrison as I slid into the passenger's seat.

"Nothing. Not a thing."

"I told you it'd be a waste of time."

"I'd like to go back to my car." I looked out the window and watched the BMW across the lot pull away. "That's a very nice car to drive to school."

"She gets anything she wants," said Harrison as he started his car. He headed toward the other exit.

"Do you think her brother would have more to say?" I asked.

Harrison shrugged his shoulders. "Don't know. They have that twin thing going on. But you could try."

"Where's the best place to find him? Is he at the same school?"

"I'll send his number. Text him," he said, avoiding my question.

When I finally arrived back at my house, I grabbed a flavored water from my refrigerator. This may sound strange, having a refrigerator in the bedroom, but it's more like a suite of rooms with its own small kitchen. At one time, I think it was the maid's quarters. I used to have a high-tech smart fridge named Frida, but she turned out to be a Peeping Tom. One day, in a fit of rage, I attacked her and shattered her camera. A nice normal refrigerator took her place.

I powered up my laptop and put in the name Barlow. Just who were these brothers? The first stories were about the boating accident. Then there were pages and pages about the brothers and their financial company. The bios on their business website showed two smiling families enjoying Marin County. A few photos highlighted the Nereus. Both brothers attended top business schools; Andy went to Stanford University and Marty attended the Booth School of Business, University of Chicago. The Barlow & Barlow Fidelity Investments website oozed sophistication and money. Lots of money.

I combed through page after page of photographs from society events both in Marin and San Francisco. In the pictures, they looked happy, friendly, glamorous, and rich. So, what was the problem? Nothing could be this perfect.

Chapter 10

Daria's twin brother, Dawson, ignored my text. I tried everything I could think of. Being sympathetic about his uncle. Asking to meet him after school anywhere he wanted. Offering to take him to any restaurant he'd like. Finally, I mentioned the family boat.

Ten minutes later, he responded.

Meet u at dock. 1 hour.

I left immediately, my car spraying rocks and dirt into the air as I jetted down Earl's driveway. I wanted to arrive before Dawson did and watch. Was he friendly with the harbor mistress? Would he stop and chat with any of the boat owners? Would he seek out Hatch? I can tell any number of things by watching how a person walks, the expression on their face, and if they're happy to be where they are.

I sat on a wooden bench a distance from the wooden gangway that led to the metal gate and the finger piers. Dawson came up behind me and tapped my shoulder. "You Trisha?"

I nodded. "Thanks for meeting me. I know talking about your uncle isn't much fun."

"Let's go down to the boat," he said. Walking toward the gangway, he said something like, "There's nothing much I can tell you." A brisk wind blew down the waterfront, masking his words and all sounds except for the halyards clanking against the masts.

When we reached the boat, I looked further down the gangway.

Was Hatch sitting in the cockpit? From my point of view, his boat was empty. Dawson climbed on easily. He put out a hand to me and guided me over the winches and deck hardware. "Let's go below. Get out of this breeze."

For a teenager, he had an ease with adults. And boats.

Inside, the cabin was molded in warm rich teak. Deep blue cabin cushions leaned against the bulkheads. A table secured to the floor made a cozy little nook. Dawson pulled out a thermos from his backpack.

"Want something to drink?" he asked, unscrewing the thermos and avoiding looking at me.

"No thanks." He moved abruptly from the small galley forward to a bedroom under the foredeck, and then back to the main cabin where I sat watching him. He flitted around like an anxious bird sensing the pressure of a predator.

Finally, he stopped moving and rested against the gimballed stove. "I don't know anything," he muttered.

"I understand that this is hard to talk about, but I heard that your father was on board that day. Would you know if that's true?" I asked.

"What day?"

"The day of the accident."

"How could I know that? I was at school. That's what my dipshit cousin told you? He wants to blame my father for everything. Why would my father kill his own brother? He had no reason to. This is Harrison, the drama queen, making things up."

"You may be right," I nodded. "But another sailor saw your dad and uncle together on this boat." I paused. "Did you know that?"

Dawson stared out of the cabin into the cockpit, eyes locked on nothing. There was no answer.

"Were you aware of that?"

He didn't answer. Both he and his sister were similar when it came to talking. They didn't.

"Can you tell me something … anything about your uncle?"

"He was okay," said Dawson.

"Did he have any friends?"

"How would I know? He hung out with my dad from what I saw. He was training for an open water swim. Dad would drive the boat and Uncle Andy would swim. Boring, if you ask me," he said.

Boring is what this conversation is.

I didn't know any more than when I climbed on board. He confirmed that the brothers were together. That's where the boating conversation stopped. And, oh yes, neither he nor his sister liked their cousin.

"Why don't you like your cousin?" I asked. "He doesn't seem that bad to me."

"You don't know him. Everything to him is OTT."

"OTT?"

"Over the top."

"Like what?"

"He always wears black and capes and black boots. He looks like a vampire."

"I think he's trying to be theatrical."

"You don't know him. He was jealous of my father. Always has been."

"Why is that?"

"Something to do with money, I guess. But I'll tell you something I bet you didn't know."

My ears perked up. Maybe he actually had something to say.

"My uncle was a studly mcstud stud."

"A what?"

"A cuntquistador. He liked the females. And according to Dad, he liked them young."

That was something I hadn't heard before.

"You sure about that?" I asked.

Dawson turned back to me. He shrugged. "It's what I heard."

I leaned over to look at him. "Tell me what you know."

His turned his back to me mumbled, "I don't know much."

"I am so tired of hearing that. I'm trying to help you and your family and your dad. Anything about your uncle might be able to help."

Dawson stood up and stretched his arms straight up and out of the cabin. Then he climbed up two steps into the cockpit and sat down on the top step.

"Well, I once heard my uncle talking on his cell to someone. It was the way you'd talk to a girlfriend," he said.

"Well, it could have been his wife."

"Nah. Dad told me they weren't getting along and Uncle Andy was thinking of getting a divorce."

Harrison never mentioned that.

"This phone call you heard." I stopped, not sure how to frame the rest of my thoughts. "How could you tell it was a girl, not a grown-up woman."

Dawson ran his fingers through his hair. He sat there, mouth shut for a few minutes.

"You couldn't tell, could you? You're just repeating what your father may have said. Or maybe he didn't?"

Dawson ducked down into the cabin. "I could tell. He mentioned meeting her after school."

"Do you know where he was going to meet her?"

"I'm not sure. He said something, but I couldn't hear it. His back was turned to me."

"Where were you?"

"Here on the boat, patching some fiberglass. Uncle Andy was out on the dock walking back and forth. He stopped a few boats down and I couldn't hear anything else."

I pushed past him and climbed into the cockpit.

"Come here," I said. "I want to show you something."

He climbed halfway out of the cabin and I pointed to Hatch's boat.

"Do you remember if he stopped at that boat?"

"I think so. That guy's always here, and Dad and my uncle spent a lot of time talking to him. Are you done yet?"

"Just a few more questions. Did you ever go out on the boat with your dad and uncle when they were doing a practice swim?"

"Sometimes."

"Where did they go?"

"Well, it depends. Dad would walk down to the boat … We live just up there." He pointed to a group of houses on the hill. "Sometimes Uncle Andy would meet him here. Other times, Dad would drive the boat to the marina underneath the north end of the Golden Gate Bridge and pick him up there."

"You mean the place with the Coast Guard station?"

"Yeah."

"Do you know what they did that morning?"

Dawson shrugged his shoulders and shook his head. "I'm meeting some friends. I gotta go."

When we were both in the cockpit, he buttoned up the boat and put the lock on the cabin door. Then he stepped onto the dock. As it rocked from side to side from his weight, I held on to a stanchion and climbed over.

"One more thing," I said, walking rapidly, trying to catch up with him. He stopped.

"Why would Harrison think your father killed his father? For what reason?" I asked.

"How would I know? Ask him," he said. Then he jogged to the end of the dock, climbed the gangway, and hurried through the gate in the direction of the parking lot.

I followed slowly, trying to make sense of all that I'd heard. Harrison's dad was a womanizer if I'm to believe Dawson. And he had his sights set on a schoolgirl? Really? I found the whole thing difficult to believe.

Chapter 11

I texted my sister and asked her to meet me at China Camp State Park. The picturesque park with its hilly trails and picnic areas edged San Pablo Bay. My family brought me and Lena here as kids. Now my dad and Earl spend most afternoons volunteering here, restoring the long pier and what's left of a thriving Chinese shrimp village from the 1800s.

I planned on apologizing to Lena for calling her a traitor. My blood pressure peaked every time I thought about her talking to her doctor sweetheart about my reactions in stressful situations. It wasn't that bad. And besides, it's nobody's business but mine. Somehow, I had to make that clear.

As I drove the windy road to China Camp, I caught glimpses of the bay, now a deep ocean blue through the tall oak trees. The winds tumbling through the Golden Gate had dropped to a whisper on this side of the bay. Even the fog slipped away. The afternoon felt like a warm, comforting blanket.

I headed down the hill into the parking lot and slipped into a spot at the edge of the beach. I could see Dad in that faded yellow T-shirt he liked to wear, bent over at the end of the pier, working on a pylon. A few minutes later, Lena rattled down the hill and pulled into a spot right next to me.

"Lee," I said, walking over to the passenger side and looking in.

"Hey Little T, it's so nice to see you."

"Mish, Mish," said the little boy. I picked him up, swung him around, and buried my head in his sweet-smelling neck. A lengthy sigh escaped from my lips.

"Sweet boy. I'd rather him call me Trish than Mish," I said as I handed him back to my sister.

"This kid has four words in his vocabulary. Da, ma, fruck for truck, and Mish. Be glad you made the cut." She reached over and unsnapped him from his car seat and pulled him out. We strolled over to a picnic bench. She unrolled a San Francisco Giants blanket, gave Little T a bright red bucket and shovel, and plopped him down in the middle.

"So, what did you want to talk to me about?" Lena asked.

"I want to …" I started.

"Hey look, there's Dad. Dad," she yelled. "Over here." She waved as he glanced around, and he gave her a tip of his baseball cap and then held up one finger, letting us know he'd be here soon.

The need for an apology faded away.

"I met the twins. Did you ever teach them to swim?"

Lena shook her head. "Never met them before. I saw them at the memorial service, though. Did they have anything to say?"

"Not really. There's no love lost between Harrison and his two cousins. The cousins are angry that Harrison blames their dad for his father's death."

"Did they have any reason for Harrison's suspicions?" asked Lena.

"If they did, they weren't telling me. But I did learn that Andy, according to Dawson, was thinking about divorcing his wife. And that he likes to date younger women."

"How young are we talking about?" asked Lena.

"School age."

"Please don't tell me he's a pedo and likes elementary school age girls?"

"No. But maybe high school or college. Dawson overheard a

lovey-dovey conversation where the now dead dad had said something about meeting a girl after class."

"Did you ever think it could be a teacher or a professor?" asked Lena.

"You know, I didn't."

"Great detective," said my sister.

"Okay, so what else did you find out?"

"Nothing was said. But his sister, Daria … and I'm not sure about this … seemed worried, concerned, maybe even a bit afraid to talk about her uncle."

"Duh. Of course, she would. That's it? That's all you know?" asked Lena, who stood up, took Little T by his hands, and helped him walk over to his approaching grandfather.

"Well, hello there, little man. Have you come by to help your old grandpa fix the pier?" Dad leaned over, picked up the toddler, and threw him in the air. Little T shrieked in delight.

"Nice to see all three of you," he said. "Are you here for late afternoon sunshine?"

"Dad, the other day you were talking about the friend who worked here that lost his money. Do you know any more about him?"

"He moved. To be with his kids, I think. But I told you that." He handed Little T back to Lena and she carefully sat him down again on the blanket.

"Is there anyone here who knew him? Really knew him?" I asked.

Dad stopped for a minute to think. He surveyed the weather-worn pier until he saw a man walking toward us.

"Him. Howard, that guy there." He waved at the portly man with the sunburned face. "Hey, Howard, come over here a moment."

Howard pulled out a blue neckerchief and wiped his hands on it. Then pressed it against his forehead. As he approached the four of us, he stopped. "Not going to shake your hands. I'm filthy."

"Howard, meet my girls, Trisha and Lena. This is my grandson, Timmy or Little T."

Howard nodded.

"Trisha asked me some questions that I can't answer. Remember when Antonio moved away?"

"Yeah, I do," said Howard. "Why?"

"Dad told me that he lost all of his investments," I interrupted. "I just met another woman, an older woman, who lost all her money too. Do you happen to know who he invested with?"

Howard put one hand on his chin and rubbed the fast-growing stubble. "You know, I think he told me, but my memory's not as good as it once was. Sorry. I'm not coming up with a name. If I do, I'll let your dad know."

"Thanks," I said.

Howard walked toward his car. "Gotta go get this sawdust off of me. Nice to meet all three of you. Bob, you have a fine looking family."

Lena shaded her eyes with her hand and looked out at the serene waters. "Could you watch Little T for about thirty minutes? I'd like to go in for a swim."

"Trisha, you go too," said Dad. "I'll watch my little champ for a bit. Maybe let him put his feet in the water."

"I don't have a swimsuit," I said.

"Fear not," said Lena. "I have extra suits, goggles, everything in the car."

I followed my sister up to her car. She chatted continuously about her next trip to the flowerpot lady's house.

"I found out from her daughter that the mom came from a very wealthy family in Marin. She grew up somewhere in Belvedere. Dad did something with importing and exporting. She had a lot of money invested. And now it's gone. Poof! All gone. Money doesn't guarantee anything."

"Right," I mumbled, having zoned out. Then I stopped and touched Lena's arm. "Did you know who she invested with?"

Lena paused. "No. I wouldn't ask a question like that."

"Why not? You ask all kind of questions."

Lena ignored me. She popped the trunk of her car and pulled out her swim bag. After rummaging around, her hand emerged with a black suit, bright red cap, and a pair of tinted goggles.

"Ew," I said, taking hold of the black strap with two fingers. "What is this white goop?"

"Probably sunscreen. It won't hurt you. It'll wash off in the water."

"You need to take better care of your things," I said, walking over to the changing rooms.

"You need to take better care of your things," mocked Lena in a sing-song, high-pitched voice. "I'm going in the water. I'll meet Her Majesty there."

"So annoying," I said as she walked away. My apology wandered to the back burner.

I quickly changed and walked down to the water's edge.

"There goes your silly aunt. She swims in cold water like your silly mother. Let's go splash water on them. Now take your pail and shovel," instructed Dad.

"Don't you dare splash me. I need time to get used to the water," I said as I tiptoed over the cracked oyster shells on the beach. Not much sand here, and the sooner my feet were wet, the better.

I inched myself into the water. Cool but not ice bucket cold. In fact, in early fall, the San Francisco Bay water was as warm as it ever was. Maybe in the mid-sixties. I took a deep breath and let it out slowly. My shoulders released and relaxed. My heart didn't leap into overdrive, but my fingers were tingling. Water dripped down my face, on the inside of my arms and the back of my neck. Lena's outstretched arm was pointing to a cloud when a pail of cold water hit me in the back. As I spun around, another wallop of salty water smacked me in the face.

"Stop that," I sputtered, wiping my eyes. At the water's edge, my father and Little T stood laughing, now scooping up water with their hands and shoveling it in my direction.

"Hey, knock it off," I said, trying to sound stern, but I couldn't hide my smile. I reached down and scooped up two handfuls of bay water and tossed them back at my attackers. Little T screamed. He soon grew tired of the 'splash aunt Mish Mish' game and, while sitting in the shallow water, he began smacking it with his shovel and giggling.

"Come on Trish. Let's go. We don't have much time," said Lena as she dove under the water and headed out for the round white buoy not far from the end of the pier. I will never be as comfortable or as graceful in the water as my sister. Within a few strokes, she had steadied into a symmetrical rhythm. I belly flopped into the water and followed her, feeling like an elephant kerplunking through the Bay.

Lena looked back at me and swam around the buoy, going right toward McNears Beach, another park not quite a mile away. Off to my right, the tall oak trees crowded their way up the hill next to the two-lane road I drove in on. To my left stretched the calm water crossing a shipping channel used by massive container ships moving toward Stockton. The distant East Bay hills promised a completely different landscape devoid of water and moving tides.

I followed Lena, who aimed between two sailboats anchored out in the deeper water off the beach. Stroke, head turn, breathe, stroke, head turn, breathe. The murky water cooled off a few degrees the farther I moved away from the shore. Lena passed the sailboats and swam parallel to the coastline, moving away from me. As I approached the two boats, I flipped over onto my back and floated between them. The water gurgled beneath me, holding me up like a comfortable mattress. I thought of meeting Dawson earlier and the questions I should have asked him. Preparation had gone out the window. Maybe Lena was right. My detective skills were on vacation.

The tide had pushed me back almost the length of the two boats. I took a few quick strokes and then treaded water, trying to get a better view of the boats that were on either side of me. With only my head above water, the front of the slick white sailboat looked much higher than I could have imagined. I realized how hard it would be to get back on board without a ladder or a helping hand. I stretched my arms up and couldn't grab hold of anything. They slipped down the side of the white fiberglass hull. I sunk under the murky water and surfaced, spitting out a mouthful of bay. I tried again. The second and third attempts left me breathless. Without a ladder or a helping hand, I couldn't climb into this boat. Is that what Andy Barlow experienced? Did he try to climb on board? On a powerboat, the easiest place to get on would be aft, if he couldn't reach the gunnel, the side of the boat. The tide pushed me back and I looked at the stern of the vessel. Yes, it was not as high. But even if both hands could grab hold of something, I doubt he would have the ability to pull himself up without help.

I swam forward, struggling against the tide. Small waves slapped against me, created by a powerboat moving across the water by the shipping channel. I grabbed on to the anchor chain and looked up. Something stopped at the white pencil buoy. Black and shiny, it could be a seal or it could be my sister. Then it turned around and waved. My sister now headed in my direction. I let go of the chain, kicked and stroked, but the current kept me in one place. Finally, I moved forward. Very slowly. But I had to keep swimming, using more energy than I really wanted, or I would drift backward. Lena, pushed by the current, quickly approached like she was on a conveyor belt. It took her half the time to reach the boats than it had to swim on.

She stopped swimming, but the current pushed her past me and the sailboats. "Let's go back in. Aim toward the shore or the tide will carry you beyond the beach."

I did as I was told, heading straight for the shoreline. Without putting in much effort, I glided closer to the beach, mostly traveling sideways like a crab. The wind picked up and tried to push me out toward the deeper water. But the current continued to carry me parallel to land. My heart rate zoomed upwards. Was the current stronger and faster than I could swim? Would I slide under the pier? Past the pier? As the beach came into sight, I headed straight in, kicking as hard as I could. As I inched closer to the shoreline, the strength of the current weakened. I finally put my feet down in oozing mud. Although the bay water still swirled around me, I had stopped moving. I stood up and walked toward the beach, the water choppy around my waist. Lena had made it to shore and wrapped herself in a towel that Dad brought down to the beach. Little T used the picnic table to pull himself up and waved at me.

"Mish. Mish," he called. My father, the towel caddy, stood at the water's edge holding a towel.

"You okay?" he said as I walked out of the water. "I thought you were on your way to Carquinez Straits."

"That's almost thirty plus miles to the north," said Lena.

"The tide and current. How is it possible to swim against that?" I asked both of them.

"You don't," said Lena. "The water can move faster than just about anyone can swim."

"Good to know," I said. "Next time tell me what's going on in the water before I get wet."

"Always check the tides," said Dad, picking up Little T and handing him to Lena. "Gotta go back to work."

"Are the currents stronger in the central bay?" I asked Lena as we moved toward the dressing rooms.

"They seem to be sometimes. But I don't think so," she said.

Chapter 12

The next day, I met up with Harrison. He left his black flowing cape at home. Instead, he wore black pants, a black T-shirt, and black shitkicker boots. His blond hair was pulled back in a ponytail. A black and silver intricately woven thread bracelet circled his thin wrist.

We stopped in at the same café we visited when he first asked me to look into his father's death. Once seated, he leaned forward, arms resting on the table. He opened his mouth to speak, but I cut him off.

"Before we get into that, would you know if your dad ever took the boat out by himself?"

"Sometimes. Why?"

"Curious. That's all. Who usually went with him besides your Uncle Marty? Did he take out any friends?"

"Sometimes clients from work. But they just partied at the dock. Hatch, the guy at the other end of pier, went out with him a few times, trying to teach Dad how to handle the boat."

"This is going to sound stupid, but did your dad ever go out alone and then drop into the water and swim?"

"That is stupid. No one would do that if they were on the Bay. The currents would either take the boat or the swimmer and carry them away. Look, you said you had something to tell me. Did the twins admit their father was involved?"

"Not exactly," I murmured. "In fact, they didn't say anything that would incriminate their dad."

Harrison bolted back in his chair, his neck rigid, his hands beginning to shake. "Well, what did they say?"

"Daria, as I told you before, said nothing. But—and I'm only repeating what Dawson said to me—he thinks your father may have been unhappy in his marriage and may have been considering divorce."

"No way," said Harrison, almost shouting. "That fucker."

"There's more."

"Go on." Harrison glared at me. A couple sitting across from us glanced over. My face bloomed red and hot. I took a sip of water to calm my nerves.

"I'm not sure how to say this. So, I'll just say it." I said, hesitating. "Well … he said your father liked young women."

"What?"

"That your father …."

"I thought that's what you said," said Harrison, cutting me off. "They think my father is a pedophile?" Heads snapped in our direction from the diners around us.

"Not so loud," I said, hoping he'd get a grip on his emotions. Although if someone told me the same thing about my father, my reaction would probably be similar.

By now Harrison had pushed his chair back, half stood, and leaned aggressively across the table toward me. "You're fired."

"I was never hired," I said. "I'm only checking on some things for you."

He ran his fingers over his face and took a deep breath. "You were the wrong person to help me. The absolutely wrong person."

This was not what I wanted to hear. I needed money. My auto mechanic required payment. I hoped when Harrison finally paid me there might be enough left over for a deposit on a newer car. Could I convince him to keep me on? Did I reek of desperation? Probably. But so what? Years earlier, when I daydreamed about my future career, I knew, just knew, that I'd be involved with criminal investigation. My community college, only a few miles away, had the basic classes to get me started. After two years, I'd transfer to a California state university and finish my education. Or so I thought. None of that happened after my mother passed and my father abandoned me and Lena. Slowly, I'd built up a reputation for solving crimes. I thought this one could catapult me into the next level, with more money and a chance of a PI license.

"I'm the right person," I said firmly to Harrison. "But you have to be open to whatever I find."

"I'll take care of it from here on in," he said and patted his pocket.

"What does that mean?" I asked.

"My uncle killed my father. That's the truth, and he's going to pay."

The bitterness in his voice frightened me. "Harrison, what's in your pocket?"

He shrugged his shoulders.

"I don't know what … if anything … you have in your pocket. But don't be a moron. There is no evidence that your uncle killed your father. You don't even know if he was on the boat. Maybe it *was* a terrible accident."

Harrison's arms stretched flat against his sides, his hands now curled into tight fists. Was he going to hit me? I pushed my chair back as far as I could.

"You don't know anything," he said through clenched teeth. With that, he spun around and rushed to the front door. The people sitting at the nearby tables glanced at him and then in my direction one more time. Slowly, the undercurrent of soft voices began again in the café. Our fight became an incident they would tell their friends and families later. I laid money on the table to cover the coffees and headed to the door, not making eye contact with anyone.

Once outside, I inhaled the fresh harbor air and tried to decide what to do about Harrison. He threatened his uncle. Did he have an actual plan in mind or was he blowing off steam?

"Miss. Miss," said a voice behind me. I turned to see a high school student with a white apron tied around his waist. He jogged in my direction, wiping his hands on the cloth, and stopped suddenly in front of me. He took a step back as if reconsidering what he was about to say. Then, "You're right about his uncle and … um … girls, especially high school girls. He would bring them in here all the time, saying they were waiting for his niece who never showed."

"Who are you?" I asked, standing there bewildered.

"Friend of the family," he said.

"Which family?"

"I go to school with Daria. I gotta go back to work," he said.

I grabbed his arm as he turned away from me. "What else do you know about the uncle?"

He shook his head and took a step away.

"Please. I'm trying to figure out how he died."

"Ask Dawson. He knows everything."

"What do you mean? Did you ever go out on the boat with Dawson?"

"Yeah, a few times. Why?"

"Was his dad there? Maybe his sister and a few of her friends?"

"I see what you're doing here. I never should have talked to you."

"Please. Just answer the questions."

"Yes, Daria was there. Sometimes she brought a friend. But from what I could see, the uncle never tried anything. Okay? That's all I know," he said.

With that, he jogged back to the café. I watched him disappear through the back door.

To my right sat a wooden bench with two flamboyant red geraniums on either side. I hustled over and dropped down on it with a thud.

It sounded like dear Uncle Andy's interest in younger women was common knowledge. And what did Dawson have to do with it? Could he be more involved with his uncle's death than I thought? I pulled the tablet out of my backpack, went to the Andy Barlow Propeller Death file, and added an ecard for the café worker. In the past, when I began to work on a case, I jotted all my notes down on 3x5 cards. Lena couldn't stand to watch me use such old school technology. One day I came home and there was a tablet.

"Join the modern age," was all she said. That tablet became my constant companion.

The wind dropped to a whisper, and the clanking of the halyards and high-pitched squawking of the seagulls stilled. For a few seconds, a suspicious quiet embraced the Sausalito waterfront.

I wanted to walk away from the Barlow family, the gruesome death, the salacious rumors, the battling cousins. Harrison already told me to stay away. But this had grown to be something more than helping a grieving son. I wanted to know if Andy Barlow's death was a horrible accident or a planned killing. Did Andy's interest in young girls have anything to do with it? What about Dawson? Did he and maybe his sister plan their uncle's death? Let's face it. The case intrigued me, but bottom line, I needed money. I planned on billing Harrison for the time already spent, and he better pay me. I needed to talk this out with my favorite sounding board: Jon Angel, my sweetheart.

Chapter 13

Jon and I have had our moments. I kept him at arm's length until I reluctantly let my guard down and opened the door to his love and attention. That was a good decision on my part.

Jon's car was sitting next to Dad and Earl's cars when I pulled into the driveway.

"I thought you were out of town at a ranger's meeting," I called out.

"And 'hello' to you too," he said with a smile as he leaned over the railing. "How's my best girl?" As I walked up the front stairs, he took my hand and pulled me into a hug. My goodness, he smelled good.

"That was a one-day thing. So, what've you been up to?" he asked as he held open the door and we walked into the comfortable living room.

Should I tell him? Maybe not? Last year, I promised not to open each conversation with a rundown of my current working crime.

"Not much," I mumbled, trying to think of something besides my last conversation with Harrison and the busboy from the coffee shop to talk about.

"Hey Trish," said my dad from the deck. "Look what I can do." Earl had given him the controls of his drone, and Dad was treetop surfing La Cruz Canyon. "Look, there's a little dog on the path. Wonder if he ever saw a drone before?"

"Don't do it," I said.

With a push of the lever, the drone dipped down slightly ahead of the dog, and he flew it down the path. Barking and growling, the dog followed the flying quadcopter, his owner jogging after him. Dad turned the drone around and flew it back until it hovered over the head of the owner. The dog raced back in the other direction and jumped up and down, almost knocking his owner over.

A chubby twenty-something guy encased in a too-tight pair of jogging shorts and a snug bright blue T-shirt looked up and spotted Dad leaning out over the deck with the controls in his hands. "Hey mister, stop that. You're driving my dog nuts."

Dad realized that he was the only one having a good time, so he flew the drone back up to the deck and landed it carefully on the couch cushion. "Sorry," he yelled down. "Got carried away." The man waved and Dad turned around, placing the controls on the table next to the couch.

"Guess, I need to be more careful," he said.

"I'd say so," said Earl with a nod. "Chasing dogs with a drone will not make me popular with my neighbors."

"I agree," I said.

Jon wandered into the kitchen, followed by me. "You want to tell me something. I know you do. What's going on?"

A massive sigh escaped from deep inside me. "I'm not supposed to tell you."

"Who said that?"

"Well, I thought that's what you wanted. I can solve my crimes but I need to leave you out of it."

"I never said that."

"You did too."

"No, I didn't. What I wanted was to have a normal conversation now and then that had nothing to do with disappearing people or bodies floating in the bay."

I took that as my cue.

"Remember the funeral I told you about? It was for the father of one of Lena's swim students, years back. There was some kind of boating accident on the Bay and the boat's propeller chewed him up. I even have some pictures. Wanna see?" I pulled out my phone and began scrolling to find the gruesome pics of a mangled body.

"Thanks for the offer. Maybe some other time." Jon pulled some beers from the fridge for him, Dad, and Earl. He turned toward my father. "Does she ever just sit down with the two of you talk about a TV show she saw?" He handed them the cool bottles.

The two men shook their heads. "She's been like this since she was a little girl," said Dad. "Once she has something on her mind, nothing else in the world exists."

"Well then I might as well get it over with," said Jon as he stared at me sitting on the edge of the couch next to Dad.

"Okay. I'll listen, but how about we put a time limit on what you're about to tell me?"

"That should work," said Dad.

"Would you like to place a small wager on whether she can stop talking once she reaches high gear?" said Earl.

"I don't talk in high gear. You have me confused with Lena, the local chatterbox," I said, now standing with my hands on my hips.

"Twenty dollars?" asked Dad.

"It's a bet," said Earl.

They both sat back in their respective seats and stared at me like I was a wide-screen TV.

"Go ahead," said Dad. "Talk."

"I will not," I said. "Come on Jon. Let's go sit outside, maybe walk down into the canyon." I grabbed Jon's hand and pulled him toward the front door. Then I turned around and gave both Dad and Earl the finger.

I heard them erupt into laughter as we left the house for the trailhead. The brown dirt path packed with dry, solid earth rambled past tall, peeling Eucalyptus trees scattered between gigantic redwood trees reaching to the sky.

"Let's sit here," said Jon. "Now, as your father said, 'talk.'"

"Well, the dead father's kid Harrison, who got me involved with this in the first place, fired me. I wasn't giving him the information that he wanted."

"That's it?" Jon asked.

"No. He said something like 'he would take care of it.'"

"That doesn't sound so bad. To me it says he's going to look into it, do his own investigating."

"Seriously? That's all that comes to mind. I think he's talking about revenge. He's planning to do something to the uncle who he suspects as his dad's killer."

"Oh, come on Trisha, give the kid a break. He just lost his father and can't believe it. If he's like the rest of us, of course he wants to make sense of it all."

"I don't buy that. He's angry and he's looking for an excuse to do something, I don't know what, to his uncle."

Jon sighed and shook his head.

"I'm right about these things. You know I am," I said. "But there's more. One of the twins told me their dead uncle was unhappy in his marriage and that he had a roving eye. He particularly liked young girls." I leaned back, stretched my arms out, and put my feet up on the barrier protecting hikers from the drop off. "What do you think of that?"

"Trish, don't be so melodramatic. Maybe the twin didn't like his uncle. They're kids. And they are going through a tough time in their lives … all of them."

"I tried to broach the subject with Harri—"

"You what?"

I stopped talking and looked at Jon. "Not a good idea?"

"Think about it, Trisha. You tell a grieving son that his dad was a pedophile. How did you expect him to react?"

"You have a point," I said. "Except that it might be true. And I think he should know. Harrison and I met at this café down by the Sausalito waterfront. He stormed out when I mentioned his dad's potential interest in younger girls."

"Smart kid."

"He was almost screaming at me when he left. Everyone in the café heard him and stared both at him and me. I was really embarrassed."

"I think you brought that on yourself," Jon said.

I told him about the busboy and what he mentioned to me.

"You've got nothing. Maybe he was a good uncle. Maybe he'd met his niece's friends before and he was helping them with … with … I don't know, homework or something like that." Jon stared out at the trees, thinking out loud.

I heard a faint buzzing over my head and looked up. Within arm's distance was Earl's drone with a note attached. I reached up and grabbed the note, and the drone hovered in place.

"What does it say?" said Jon, snatching it out of my hands.

"Hey, stop that," I yelled. "It was meant for me."

"No way. It has my name on it," said Jon. He flipped it open, laughed, pulled out a pen, and wrote something on the note. Then he refastened it to the drone, which then headed straight up through the trees.

"Are you going to tell me what he said?"

Jon tried not to smile. "Your dad wanted to know if you stopped talking yet."

I clamped my mouth shut. But it didn't stay closed for long. "That's so rude. What did you reply?"

"I said, 'what do you think?'"

"My sister is the talker. Not me," I said, tapping my feet on the barrier.

"I have to admit that, although you had a lot to say, you were more controlled than in the past. Anyway, let's go. I'm driving south to Muir Woods National Monument to talk to an administrator. I'll walk you back."

I nodded, stood up, and moved onto the path, not saying a word.

"Don't you want to know what I really think about all this?" Jon asked as he caught up with me.

I didn't answer. I walked faster and then started to jog.

"Hey, slow down." Jon lagged behind me.

We finally made it up the hill back to the road. My breath came out in spurts.

"Okay, what do you think?"

"You're on to something. I don't know what. But none of this feels right. The more you talk to people, the weirder it gets," said Jon.

Chapter 14

A few days later, I drove into the vast parking lot at Town Center Corte Madera. I prepared myself for meeting Martin Barlow, Andy's brother. I needed to find out if he was on that boat.

For the occasion, I dug out my casual but professional-looking clothes: dark stone washed jeans, an impeccable white button-down blouse, and a tailored jean jacket. My brown hair was pulled back and into a high bun. Not bad, I thought as I looked into the mirror, and then reapplied some mascara and lip gloss. I remembered Justine Barlow at her husband's memorial being comforted by Uncle Marty. At one point, he looked over the crowd. Did he see me? Probably not. He had his hands full with Justine and Harrison. I'd have to take my chances.

Barlow & Barlow took up a corner of a commercial property, three stories high with a glass front. A small fountain surrounded by a blue tiled base sprouted water to the delight of a few children trying desperately to get their hands wet. I took the elevator to the second floor, found the glass double doors. Two gracious high back wing chairs in a subtle gray and white print sat across from a comfortable gray couch. Business magazines were spread out on the low glass coffee table between the two. Instead of peaceful landscape paintings, a wide-screen TV stretched across the wall. Two business pundits riffed off each other as a tickertape of stock prices traveled across the bottom of the screen.

I sat in the waiting room alone. Then I stood up and walked toward the dim hall off to the side. Was I in the right place? I walked back to the couch and glanced up at the TV.

"Ms. Carson," said a woman, entering through a door behind her desk. "I'm so sorry, but Mr. Barlow is running a bit late."

As if on cue, Martin Barlow hurried through the glass double doors, clearly out of breath. "Please excuse me. Traffic, you know." I reached out to shake his hand, but he had already turned toward the hall. "Give me a minute. Won't be long."

He scooted down the corridor, turned right, and disappeared while I stood there awkwardly.

"Why don't you have a seat?" said the receptionist, or at least I thought that's who she was. Leafing through a magazine, I watched Ms. Receptionist look at her computer screen. Then she smiled at me.

"I'll be right back," she said, leaving the office through the door I had walked through, heading toward the elevator.

Coming here seemed like a good idea two days ago when I made the appointment. Now, I wasn't so sure. From down the hall of the office, I heard the muffled sounds of Martin Barlow yelling. I scanned the waiting room and the hallway leading to his office. Still empty and quiet. I noiselessly slipped down the dim passage toward the inaudible voice. It grew clearer as I approached.

"There is nothing I can do yet. The insurance money hasn't come in. I will pay you. You have my word," said Martin. "Look, this is my brother's debt." There was a slight pause. I took a step closer to the door, trying to hear. "I know you expected the money … I'm sorry. There's nothing I can do about that except wait." Another pause. This one longer. He cleared his throat. "There's something coming up. It should ease the money problem." Pause. He must have walked further away from the door since his voice became indistinct again. "Expecting … bankroll …" was all I could hear.

Then the room glided into silence. I moved away from the door, bolting toward the reception area when the door to Martin's office opened. He took a step back when he saw me.

"Didn't mean to startle you. I was looking for the lady's room."

"Outside the office. In the hallway. To your left."

"I'll be right back," I said and bolted the rest of the way down the hall and out the door. I made a beeline for the lady's room and stopped in front of the mirror over the sinks. What was that all about? Insurance money not in yet? What was this bankroll? I took a paper towel, ran it under the water, and patted it on my face and my neck. Pull yourself together, Trish. Find out what's going on.

I stood up straight, looked at myself in the mirror, nodded, reapplied the lip gloss, and headed for the office once again.

Martin Barlow waited for me next to the empty receptionist's desk, a phony smile lodged across his tanned face. From the look of him, he spent plenty of time on his boat. His brown hair was cropped close to his scalp, and the deep wrinkles by his eyes indicated too much boating without sunglasses.

"Let's go back to my office and you can tell me about your grandfather … or was it your father? I've got your notes on my desk."

I followed him to a large enclosure with expensive teak office furniture. On one wall was a floor-to-ceiling mural of a towering ocean wave about to break. The window alongside his desk stretched across the other wall and overlooked the courtyard with the fountain.

"This is lovely," I said, sitting in a comfortable chair across from him but away from the breaking wave. It made me nervous.

He never lifted his eyes from the papers in front of him as he began to talk. "So, tell me, what can I do for you?"

"Well, my father," I started.

"That's right. It's your father," he said.

"He'd like to invest the money he has. It's not much, but he thought —"

Martin cut me off. "You look familiar. Have you been to my office before?"

I decided to tell him the truth. "No," I said. "I was at your brother's memorial service. My sister taught Harrison how to swim many years ago, and he asked that we both attend."

"Oh. Okay. That was a tragedy," he said, glancing out the window then back at me.

"I'd heard it was a boating accident," I said.

"Yes. Awful. Terrible accident."

"Lena—that's my sister, the swimmer—mentioned that he was training for an open water swim."

"What?" said Martin. "Sorry, but I was lost in thought for a moment. I don't really like to talk about it."

"Lena likes open water too. Do you swim in the Bay?"

"I do. Now, about your father?" A weak smile slid across his face.

"I've done some open water swimming, even a race or two, but nothing in the Bay. Is it really as cold as everyone says?"

"If you go out enough, your body will acclimate. Your father?"

"I've always wanted to do that." I stopped and smiled as sweetly as I could. "You two were out training and he fell off the boat?"

"Let's talk about your father and his potential investments."

"Of course. I'm so sorry about your loss. I can't image how you must have felt." I paused hoping he would pick up the thread. But the conversation about the accident was over. Done. Finished.

I cleared my throat. "Well," I began, "I think he has about ten thousand to invest, and he doesn't know anything about the market. I was hoping you can help." My father doesn't even have a hundred to invest.

"Where is his money now?" asked Martin.

"I'm actually not sure," I said.

"Do you have any of his bank statements, things like that, with you?"

"Getting them from my dad has been difficult," I said, shrugging my shoulders with an embarrassed smile.

Marty Barlow tilted his head to one side, took a deep breath, and in a bored voice said, "Didn't you say he wanted to invest?"

"Well, it's really been me bugging him. See, he's getting older and I'd like him to have something for the future."

"I'm going to give you a little homework," he said. "Sit down and talk to him about investing. What does he want to do? You have good intentions. But he's the one that needs to come in and talk to me."

"I'm not sure he will," I said.

"Try again. I have some pamphlets that might explain things clearer than you can. I'm going to be frank with you." The fake smile returned. "The money he has to invest … well … we handle much bigger amounts. I'm afraid we wouldn't be able to take him on as a client."

"That's disappointing," I said. "Could you think about it?"

He reached into a drawer and pulled out some pamphlets with happy looking people talking to someone in a business suit. "Show him these. They might help." He stood up and walked around me and held open the door to his office. This is what my father called the bum's rush.

As I moved past him, I said again, "I'm sorry for your loss."

He nodded and shut the door quietly behind me.

Chapter 15

Instead of driving home, I swung past my sister's house in San Rafael. She was in her bedroom that doubled as an office, locked into her computer, like a lion about to pounce.

"Hey," I called from the bedroom doorway. She exploded from the chair and then plopped down on her bed.

"What the fuck! Don't you know how to knock?"

"I did. But you never heard me. You were in the zone."

"What's up. Why are you here?"

"It's nice to see you, too." I walked over and gave her a hug.

"Oh, sorry. Let's get out of this room. The walls are closing in," she said, bolting from the bed, past me into the hall.

"Where's Little T?" I asked, not hearing the whimpers or giggles of my nephew.

"With the G'ma and G'pa. They took him home to the South Bay for a few nights to give me and Terrel a little 'us' time."

"I hope you're spending some of that time together. From what I can tell, Dr. T spends his extra time in the San Francisco Emergency Room. Probably to get away from you."

Lena picked up a pillow from the couch and threw it at me. "We're fine. In fact, we're going to Mendocino for a few nights as soon as he comes home."

"Fun. There's something I want to talk to you about."

"The guy caught in the boat propeller?" she asked.

"Yeah. I just talked with the brother. I wanted to find out from him if he was on the boat or not that day."

"Was he?" Lena asked.

"He wouldn't commit."

I walked around the living room in a circle.

"You're pacing," said Lena.

I stopped. "The problem is, I think he's really involved but I have no way of proving it."

"What did you want him to say? I purposely drove over my brother?"

"Well, no. Not exactly."

"I overheard him say something that bothered me."

"Eavesdropping again?" she asked.

"He said something about the insurance hasn't come in yet. Someone on the phone was pressuring him to pay them back."

"Was their investment business in some kind of financial difficulty?"

"No clue," I said. "Let's walk down to the market. I'll treat you to some ice cream."

Lena was out the door before I finished my offer. The old trees with branches that almost touched each other formed an umbrella of shade. Leaves dropped from the branches as we passed underneath. We strolled by the flowerpot lady's home, but the van was gone and the house looked forlorn and lonely. Three large waste cans rested against the curb.

I threw back the top of one for general trash.

"Trisha, what are you doing?"

"I want to see if there are any more flowerpots." I didn't want to dig beyond the first layer of disgusting trash. "Nope." Then I flipped up the lid for recycled paper and cardboard.

"I don't believe you. Close that thing. Now. Okay? Right now," Lena said.

I stretched my arm into the deep container, underneath the egg cartons, magazines, and flattened cardboard boxes. My hand settled on a clump of papers and envelopes that I pulled out. Lena grabbed my elbow and propelled me down the street.

"You are unbelievable, sniffing around in someone's trash," she whispered while I went through each piece of paper as I scuttled along, trying to keep up with her.

"Ads. Mostly ads. Internet bill. Water bill. Doesn't she know anything about internet banking? Paying bills online?" An elderly couple walked down the other side of the street pulled by a husky and a small poodle. They nodded and smiled.

Lena cheerfully called out, "Hello," then under her breath, she snorted. "Put those things away or I'm going home. Forget the ice cream."

I stopped and stared at Lena. "Look at this," I said holding out an envelope torn in half.

"I am not taking part in your pilfering."

"Look," I said again and held the envelope up in front of her face. "Read the return address."

She took it from me and read it. Her mouth dropped open. "It's from the Barlow & Barlow Fidelity Investments. That's Martin and Andy's firm. Do you think she was a client?" asked Lena.

"Lee, when do they pick up the trash? I want to see what else is in there."

"Tomorrow morning. Around eight."

"Good. Plenty of time. While you're on your way to Mendocino, once it gets dark, I'm coming back."

⚬⟋⟍ • ———— • ⟋⟍⚬

I brought Earl's dog, The Babe, with me when I returned. When people were introduced to this bulldog, they assumed with a name like The Babe that he was a she. But he's named after the famous baseball player from the 1920s and '30s, George Herman "Babe" Ruth.

I pulled into Lena's driveway, made sure my many fabric grocery bags were stuffed inside each other, grabbed the dog's leash, and took a deep breath.

"Let's go."

Darkness hung over the neighborhood. I slipped on my LED headlamp that I'd stashed in my pocket and switched it on. A bright beam of white light stretched from my forehead out in front of us. Blackness surrounded our bubble of light, except for the occasional streetlight and the shrouded glimmer in the nearby houses. The Babe and I walked the streets alone.

I encouraged The Babe to stop and sniff at every recycling container we passed. The next house belonged to the flowerpot lady. I checked the sidewalks and house windows while we strolled next to the trash container. With a big push, I knocked the recycling can over and the papers flew across the sidewalk.

"Babe, what did you do?" I asked in a semi-loud voice. "Sit, pup. I need to clean this up."

I took a quick glance around me again. No one came to their front door or looked out the window. I reached into the big green container and scooped the rest of the paper and cardboard out. The headlamp made it easy to pick out what I needed. Handful by handful, I stuffed broken down cardboard boxes, magazines and junk mail back into the container. Then came the jackpot. The logo of Barlow & Barlow Fidelity Investments appeared on a stack of papers all clipped together. I hurriedly stuck them in my grocery bag. I was working in a circle of light that extended the length of my arms, but I could hear the jingle of dog tags coming toward me.

"Can I help you?" asked a gravely male voice.

"That's okay. I'm almost finished. My dog must have thought there was some food in here. He knocked it over." I glanced up quickly and smiled. "Really, I'm fine."

"Your dog chose the wrong container if he was looking for food."

I looked down at the pile of papers in front of me.

"He's not the sharpest animal around. I love him anyway," I said. Under my breath, I whispered to The Babe, "Sorry pup."

"Well then, if you aren't needing another hand, we'll be on our way." The man and dog carefully walked around us and continued down the street.

"That was too close," I said to The Babe. After sifting through a few more handfuls of paper with no luck, I stood the container up, flipped the top closed, and started walking back to my car.

I laid all the papers out on my bedspread and sorted them and their envelopes by date. Then I read from the earliest to the latest. The correspondence told a veiled tale of an investment firm in crisis. It took reading between the lines to understand that they were about to declare bankruptcy. The flowerpot lady must have called the firm to withdraw a substantial amount of money, about two hundred fifty thousand now, and in a month's time, she wanted to withdraw the rest, almost two million dollars and close her account.

"Two million dollars!" I said to the empty bedroom. I never would have guessed that she was worth so much. Instead of the cash being deposited in her account, she received a registered letter saying that two hundred fifty thousand dollars would be available in two weeks.

What kind of an investment firm was this? Two hundred fifty thousand dollars was a large chunk of change for me, but maybe not for most investors. Why couldn't they give her, her own money. The next letter I picked up referenced another call she made to her investors. The flowerpot lady was not happy. She wanted her money— all of it; two million, two hundred fifty thousand dollars—within one week. She asked that it be deposited into her bank.

After scouring the paperwork on my bed, I realized that there was no answer to her demand for all of her money. Maybe it switched completely to phone calls or email. I did find a receipt for a registered letter that this customer sent to her brokers, with a copy to her lawyer.

There was a form indicating that the letter had arrived and been signed for.

Why wouldn't they give her money? "I bet they didn't have it," I said out loud.

From downstairs, my father called out, "What don't you have?"

"Never mind. I was talking to the TV. I guessed the plot twist."

"Good for you," he yelled out. With that, I stood up, walked to the bedroom door, and shut it tight.

From what I could tell, the flowerpot lady never received her money. Instead, she received a notice saying Barlow & Barlow was bankrupt. What a shock that must have been. From what I could tell, she had retired and planned to live the rest of her life on that money. No wonder she had to sell her house and move in with her daughter and son-in-law.

Chapter 16

When a supervisor from the San Francisco Giants called a few days ago and asked me to come in and work an event, she didn't mention what was planned. It didn't matter. A few extra dollars during the off season would come in handy. My usual carpoolers were out of town, so I drove myself. On the way across the Golden Gate Bridge, a text popped up on my screen. It was from Jon.

Stop by after work. Dinner? My treat.

I'm not fond of cooking, so a free meal appealed to me. Plus, Jon would be the chef. I pressed the button on the side of the phone and said, "Absolutely." The spoken word magically appeared on the screen.

"Ready to send?" the female voice asked me efficiently.

"Send," I replied.

I soon received a heart emoji on my screen.

Unlike the colossal parties thrown by tech companies in the San Francisco Bay area at the ballpark, this was a small congenial memorial service for an influential fan of the San Francisco Giants. He wanted his ashes scattered in the outfield not far from his decades-long seat in the first row of the bleachers. Although he had the money to bring his family and friends to a game and host them in the luxury suites anytime he wanted, he liked sitting next to the rambunctious, enthusiastic fans, an outfield wall away from the action. Until he became too sick to attend, the ushers found him in his seat minutes after the gates opened, wearing his decades-old Rawlings catcher's mitt, leaning over the wall and trying to catch a ball during batting practice. Anything he caught, he gave to a kid standing near him.

At the memorial, long time San Franciscans swapped stories about the baseball fan, and speeches were made by his family and one of the guest services employees who worked his section for as long as the gentleman occupied his seat. The intimate memorial service took place in the Field Club Lounge, one of the nicest spots in the ballpark. A mural of a player running toward home plate stretched across one wall. Beneath the artwork rested a buffet of ballpark food: hotdogs, garlic fries, beer, and ice cream sundaes. Next to the food stood an enlarged portrait of the old fan, wearing a Giants baseball cap, his favorite team jersey, and a goofy smile.

My job was simple: stand at the end of the lounge by the closed doors behind the portrait and make sure no one walked out into the long hallway that led to the field. I smiled and nodded and made small talk with the mourners, who told the funniest stories about this dearly departed.

Two hours into the memorial, my supervisor caught my eye from across the room, pointed to her watch, and mouthed the word, "Break." I nodded and quietly slipped through the closed doors behind me into the eerie dark hall that stretched the entire length of the park. How different it felt without fans crowding the space and the yeasty aroma of beer and pungent garlic fries. I took one of the dark walkways out to the stands and sat down in the bright sunshine. Although a few staff members prepared for the scattering of the ashes by the centerfield wall, I was the only one sitting in the forty-two thousand seat ballpark. On the Jumbotron, photos of the fan through the ages flickered by.

"Well, would you look at that?" said an escapee from the field club lounge.

"Are you attending the memorial?" I asked, ready to shoo him back into his proper place.

"Yes, but we'll be out here in a bit. I wanted to see the ballpark without anyone in it. That grass really is green. Bright green. Think I could go and touch it?"

"Not a good idea. The grounds crew would not be happy. You really need to go back to the lounge. I'll walk with you," I said as I stood up and tried to gently lead him back into the cool, shady tunnel away from the field. He took a few steps, then turned back to watch the slide show of his friend on the Jumbotron.

"Did you know him very well?" I asked, inching ahead, hoping he would follow me.

"Yes, indeed. We spent more hours than I can remember in those seats," he said, pointing to the bleachers behind the small memorial. "I knew him only from the ballpark. We didn't run in the same circles, if you know what I mean."

I smiled and shook my head. "I have no idea what you mean."

"Not many people knew, but he was rich. I had no idea he was so rich. Nobody did. Too bad."

"Too bad nobody knew he was rich? Sounds like he was a humble kind of person," I said to the friend.

"Too bad about what happened to most of his money."

A bell clanged in my head. I closed my eyes for a moment. I knew where this was going. I leaned against the cool wall of the tunnel and crossed my arms.

"What do you mean?"

"Investment problems. That's what he told me when I visited him in the hospital. Not only was he in pain, but he couldn't believe someone would steal from him."

"Was the hospital in the City?"

"No. In Marin. He lived in Ross."

"That's a very expensive town."

"Whoever managed his money was either a moron or a crook. The man lost almost everything. He was in the hospital when he learned about it. That's what probably killed him. It wasn't the cancer but the shock of being financially unstable at his age. That's what pushed him over the edge," his friend said.

"Tragic. I live in Marin, too. Do you happen to know the name of the financial firm? I'd like to stay clear from them if I ever have any money to invest."

"Not really. Some brothers in Marin. One of them recently died. Couldn't have happened to a nicer fellow," he said with a grunt. "He had enough money left to pay for this." He spread his arms out, trying to grab the whole ballpark. "Last days of his life. They took away his security."

Not just his.

I shook my head. "Tragic," I repeated. "Let's get you back to the lounge." I gently took his arm and led him down the tunnel, into the cavernous hall, and back into the cozy memorial service.

"Nice talking to you," I said, as he disappeared into the crowd. The brothers in Marin. It had to be the same pair that defrauded the flowerpot lady and Dad's friend. From what I could see, several people had reasons to kill one of them. It's surprising that they didn't go for both.

After a few speeches by his adult children, the doors behind me formally opened and the group of mourners breezed out of the lounge to the left, down the cavernous hallway, into the employee area. Off to the side, a large truck pulled into the delivery driveway and stopped to let the group walk onto the field next to the memorial.

I trailed behind them, lost in thought.

"Trish. Trisha," said a voice behind me. It was my supervisor. "We've got it covered if you want to take off early." A little extra time with Jon sounded like a good idea.

"Thanks. Think I will. Do you know anything about the gentleman that died?" I asked the supervisor. Before she stepped onto the warning track that separated the electric green grass of the field from the stands, she tilted her head toward me.

"A big Giant's supporter, both financially and emotionally. He was an anonymous donor for the kids' program that supplied baseball instruction, bats, gloves, and a chance to meet some of the team. I've been told he dropped more than a million dollars as their benefactor. He and his donations will be missed."

"Do you happen to know who that man is?" I pointed to the gentleman I had been talking to. "He mentioned that they had seats close to one another in the bleachers."

"Sorry. I don't know him." She looked at a clipboard with names of the attendees. "There's a few of his ballpark friends listed here. Talk to me later if you'd like to narrow it down." She turned to hustle the stragglers mesmerized by the large ballpark in front of them. They had stopped in their tracks, paralyzed.

"It looks twice as big as on TV," said one attendee as he stepped gingerly on the orange-colored clay warning track.

"Let's all go on the field," the supervisor said to those who seemed to forget how to walk until they heard her voice.

As I traipsed back to the ladies' locker room, I texted Jon and told him I'd be there within the hour. I hit send and then I texted another message to him.

Need to talk to you about the Barlow brothers.

Chapter 17

A large sign hung on Jon's door.

"Be back soon. Leave the Barlow brothers outside."

Very funny. But Jon made his point. He wanted to see me but not hear about my latest conundrum. I didn't blame him. My tendencies leaned toward reviewing, rehashing, rethinking every step of a case out loud. That doesn't help a romance. In the past, it has kept me at a comfortable distance from anyone in my life, except my sister. With Jon, I attempted to step away from those tendencies. Sometimes I could do it; other times, not so much.

Jon left the door unlocked to his small apartment near Hyde Street Pier, home to historic ships and close to Ghirardelli Square. From his deck, I could see the top of the three-masted Balclutha, a nineteenth-century square-masted sailing vessel. Next to the window was an actual black-and-white photograph from the 1850s with the waterfront full of tall wooden masts and sailing ships.

Beside the picture was a map of the current San Francisco waterfront superimposed over the shoreline of the 1850s. Many ships from the Gold Rush days were buried in that original waterfront, and an outline of a boat marked each one. If I read this map correctly, Jon's apartment and all the other buildings leading up to the tall Transamerica Pyramid were built on landfill and covered up the ships left from the Gold Rush days.

Old ship's hardware decorated the walls, and blue and white director's chairs sat haphazardly throughout the living room. A bookcase stretched from floor to ceiling opposite the sliding glass door that led out to the deck. I leafed through books about the National Park, safety in rural areas, and an adventure paperback. Surfing gear took up the bottom shelf: a few bars of surf wax, a fin key that unlocks the fin on a surfboard so it could be replaced, a black ankle leash that connected the surfboard to the surfer, and a bulky folded up black surfboard cover. Three surfboards, all different lengths, stood erect like soldiers next to the bookcase.

Jon sprinted through the front door.

"Made it," he huffed. In two steps, he sprang across the small living room, dropped his packages on the white counter, gave me a big bear hug, and lifted me off the floor.

"What a greeting," I could barely say.

"Hope you're hungry. I went to North Beach for some of the best cioppino to be had in the city. Plus, their famous house salad and sourdough rolls."

"Jon?"

"Yep?"

"If you put me down, I'll help set the table."

"Sure thing. It just feels good to have you here. You never visit." He lightly set me down.

For some reason, my face bloomed a bright red. Although Jon and I had been a thing for more than two years, anytime he complimented me, I still blushed and felt about twelve years old.

I pulled out the dishes from the cabinet. Then he grabbed some silverware from a drawer, butter from the fridge, and glasses left to dry on the counter.

"What happened to all your furniture?" I asked. "All you have are fold-up director's chairs, surfboards, and a bookcase."

"I don't like stuff," he said. "Don't need it."

We ate, chatting about some of the hilarious and not-so-hilarious tourist run-ins he had during the week, and I kept my mouth shut. Somewhere in the middle of a story about a local swimmer off a beach right outside the Golden Gate Bridge swept away with the tide, he stopped talking.

"You've been very quiet," Jon said.

I responded with a tight-lipped smile.

"Do you have something you want to talk about?"

"Well, I had a strange experience at the ballpark." Instead of jumping into the story, I looked down at my hands that were resting in my lap and clenched them into fists.

Jon sighed and then nodded.

"It's connected to that dead brother found in the Bay, isn't it?"

I nodded and clenched my hands tighter. My nails dug into my palms.

"You look like you're going to explode if you don't say something. So, say something."

The words came pouring out of me. "At the ballpark. Today. This memorial service. The man who died lost money just like the flowerpot lady and Dad's friend through their investments with two brothers, one who recently died in Marin. It must be the same brothers, right? Marin isn't that big."

Jon was staring at me.

"Who is the flowerpot lady? And your dad's friend?"

"That really doesn't matter. The point is these guys are ... were frauds. And that's probably why one of them is dead."

"Who killed him?"

"I don't know. Harrison, the son of the dead guy, said that his dad basically told him it was going to happen."

"Really," said Jon as he pushed back his chair, crossed his arms, and tried not to smirk.

"These brothers must have been running some sort of scheme and it got one of them killed. The other is waiting for insurance money to come in, or so it sounded like when I ..."

"Don't tell me if you did something illegal."

"I had an appointment with Marty that didn't turn out very well. He wouldn't talk about his brother's death, which now that I think about it makes sense. If something happened to Lena, I wouldn't talk about it to some strange person," I said.

"You went into his office under false pretenses and asked him about his brother?"

I nodded.

"You got balls, girl."

"I didn't learn much about the brother. But I did overhear him talking to someone that must have been asking for money. Marty Barlow kept telling him that nothing had come in from the insurance company. But he also said something about a bankroll that could ease the money picture."

"What kind of bankroll?"

I shrugged. "I couldn't hear. But it sounds like he's expecting money."

Jon stood up and began to pick up the dirty plates.

"Let me do that. You were the provider," I said with a smile. Jon watched me as I took the plates from his hands and headed for the sink.

"Dead guy, defrauder discussion is over, right?" He put his arms around my waist. "The dishes can wait, Trish. I have other plans," he whispered in my ear.

My heartbeat jumped up a notch. I carefully laid the dishes in the sink and turned around. Jon's brown eyes, flecked with gold, looked at me with a smile. Then his hands came up and pushed my hair back.

"Jon, I don't think you were really listening to me."

"And why do you think that?" he asked, kissing my neck and then my cheek. I forgot what I was talking about and closed my eyes, enjoying the warm rush washing through my body.

"I want you to tell me all about it," he said, taking my hand and leading me into the bedroom. I didn't know how I got there. I don't remember walking into the room, but I didn't care. It was where I wanted to be.

I let out a huge sigh, and then he kissed me. An electric current flooded my body as I pressed myself against him.

"Anything else you want to talk about?" whispered Jon.

"No more talking," was all I could say.

⁂

When I woke up in the morning, I found a note on Jon's pillow.

"Early start today. Sleep in. Relax. Miss you already."

From Jon's bed, I could see the same view as from his living room: the top of the Balclutha's masts, plus a narrow swatch of white fog streaming low across the San Francisco Bay. This wasn't the first time I'd spent the night here. Each time I stayed, I became a little more relaxed. The first night was a disaster. I left about 2 am with Jon wondering what he'd done wrong. Now I could comfortably … almost … wake up in his bed. My next step would be to invite him home for the night. I wasn't sure about that. Maybe there would be a night when Dad and Earl were gone.

My phone pinged. If it wasn't Jon, I didn't want to talk to anyone. All I wanted was to stay in this comfortable bed and watch the drifting fog cover the bay. The pinging stopped. Then it started again.

"Oh, all right," I said with a sigh to the quiet, comfortable room. "Hello?"

"Trisha, did you hear?" said the male voice.

"Who is this?"

"Harrison. Did you hear?"

"Hear what?"

"My mother ran off with my uncle and got married."

I bolted straight up in bed. "She did what?"

"Yesterday or the day before. They went to City Hall in San Francisco and … and … and now they're married. That fuckass weasel. He killed my father and now he's married to my mother."

110

"Where are you?"

"At my mother's house."

"I can be there in an hour." I hung up and walked closer to the window. The breeze had picked up and small, angry white caps rippled below the fog. Maybe Justine had turned out to be the bankroll Marty talked about.

Chapter 18

Harrison must have heard my car pull up, since he shot out of the house and walked the last few feet while my car was still moving, talking all the time.

"They're gone. My mother left me a note. She and my uncle are on their honeymoon. I don't know when she's coming home."

I carefully tried to avoid hitting him when I opened the driver's side door.

"What am I supposed to do?" he asked, running his hands through his hair. "My family is destroyed. I'm leaving. That's what. Going back to England."

He started for the front door, and I jogged after him and grabbed his arm.

"How do you know all this?" I asked. "Did your mom tell you? Was it a note? A phone call? What?"

We stood by the open front door. Harrison kept looking everyplace but at me. Then he moved into the hallway and sat down on a bench.

"My mom wasn't home last night. I was, and I had a couple of drinks … well, more than a couple … from my dad's liquor cabinet and fell asleep. It was late morning when I opened my eyes. She was shaking me, telling me to wake up. Then she stuck her hand in my face to show me her new ring. 'I'm married,' she said. 'You're a widow,' I said. She shook her head no. 'Not anymore. Your uncle and I got married this morning in San Francisco.' I couldn't believe it. I kept saying 'No, no you didn't. How could you do that? Dad's barely dead a month.'

"'We're leaving now on our honeymoon,' she said. 'Now? Where are you going?' I asked. 'The Philippines.' I asked her why the Philippines."

"And what did she say?" I asked.

"She started to giggle and said something like 'to visit Marty's money,'" said Harrison. "Then she said something really weird."

"Like what?"

"She said, 'Your dad wasn't all you thought he was. I left you a letter explaining everything.' She walked out of the room. I could hear her opening drawers and closets in her bedroom. I went out to the hall while she rolled her suitcase toward the stairs. 'Harrison, I love you. Take care of the house.' She turned around, blew me a kiss, and waved. Uncle Marty was outside in the car waiting for her. How could she do that? Dad is barely dead."

Harrison slowly stood up and paced around the hallway, finally moving into the living room with me close behind.

"What did the note say?" I said.

"The guy's a scumbag. I'm going back to England," Harrison said again. While he walked back and forth in the living room, I foraged for the note. I located the delicate blue envelope on the table near the front door.

"Here. I found it," I called out, holding it in my hand.

"Not interested," he said.

"Okay if I …?"

Harrison waved me off.

I ripped the envelope and pulled out the embossed stationary. I'm not sure what I expected, a heartfelt note from a mother to her son still in mourning? An explanation for a seemingly out of context marriage? A deep dive into who her husband really was? It wasn't any of those. Instead of a note filled with emotion, it was a laundry list of chores

Justine wanted him to do around the house: a reminder to take the garbage out, the date and the time the pool cleaner was coming, that kind of thing. Toward the end, she disclosed that she had left on her honeymoon. It never mentioned when or if she would return. There was one more thing … a check for me. "Give this to Trisha Carson," the note said. "Tell her to keep investigating. This is her retainer." I slipped the generous check into my pocket.

Harrison stared at me. "Well?"

I felt for him. Couldn't his mom show the tiniest bit of compassion for her son?

"She left me a check so I could continue working for you. And she wants you to take out the trash." I paused for a second. "Did you have any idea that your uncle and your mother were … ah … close?"

"No. He was here all the time after my dad died. I thought he felt guilty for killing him and wanted to help my mother. Now I'm sure he killed him. But marry my mother? No way. How could he do that? How could she do that?" He sat down in an overstuffed easy chair and dropped his head into his hands. "I have no family anymore. Nothing. I have nothing left."

"I'm so sorry, Harrison," I said.

He stared at his phone. "I know I can get a plane out of here tomorrow, maybe even later today." He tapped a few keys and slid the screen up a few times.

"Don't do that. Please. Give me some time to figure out what happened."

"I don't care anymore. My mother is a … I don't want to say it. She and my uncle belong together. I'm not going to become stepbrother and sister to my cousins. That's incest, isn't it?" Harrison looked like he was about to cry.

"This is our opportunity. Your mother is gone, so the house, your father's in-home office, everything is open to you. And your father and uncle's office in Corte Madera will be empty. If you can get me in there, I can look through everything: his computer, his desk, files, everything. But you need to stay.”

“I have to get out of this house.”

“Harrison, please. Don’t you want to see this to the end? Don’t you want to find out who killed your dad? I know I would. This is a chance. I can’t promise you that I’ll track down the killer, but I’ll do everything possible,” I pleaded.

Harrison wouldn’t look at me. His eyes stayed glued to his phone, but his fingers had stopped moving.

He let out a sigh. “A week. That’s all you get.”

“That’s not much time.”

“A week. Then it’s goodbye, Marin.” Harrison stood up.

“Okay, a week, but you have to get me into your uncle’s office tomorrow.”

He nodded. “Let me check with my stepbrother, stepsister, cousins, whoever they are. I wonder if they know about this.”

“Good reason to call them.”

Harrison hesitated.

“Do it. Now,” I pushed. I had this feeling that if I didn’t convince him to act, it wouldn’t happen, and he’d disappear.

He held his cell up close to his mouth. “Call Daria.”

I heard the echo of his voice. The call went to voicemail.

“I don’t wanna talk to you. Not now. Leave a message,” said the female teenage voice.

“Hey cuz,” said Harrison, “did you know we are more than cousins now? Your father and my mother eloped in San Francisco and got married. Do you believe that? Did you know? You’re my half-sister and I need your help. Call me. Like now.”

“That should pique her interest,” I said. “Look Harrison, start going through your father’s stuff. Everything. Drawers, closets, desks. Check your mom’s room. There has to be something there that will tell us our next steps.”

Harrison’s reaction was hard to gauge. There was an internal struggle going on inside this young man. Should he run away or look for his father's killer?

"You owe this to your dad. If you think he was murdered, we have to find the killer. Look, I've learned a few things about their business."

"What do you mean?" he asked.

"Can I get something to drink before I go into all this?"

"Sure," he said and I followed him into the large modern kitchen. "You want a beer?"

"I don't drink. Ice water is fine, but help yourself."

He grabbed a beer from the refrigerator and filled a glass with ice and water for me. He reached into a cupboard, pulled out a bag of spicy chips, walked into the formal dining room, and threw them on the table. He sat down and looked at me.

"Talk."

"Did your father talk about his business recently?"

Harrison leaned back into the chair and balanced it on two ornate legs. Then he propped his feet up on the glossy twelve-person dining table. "Nope."

"Are you sure?"

"Well, he used to joke that his brother wanted him out of the business. But he was the front man. He could talk to anyone and sell them whatever he wanted to sell them."

"Why did your uncle want him out of the business?"

"I don't know. I once heard him say that as fast as he brought money in, my dad would make it disappear. Whatever that means."

"Did he spend a lot of money? Clothes, cars, vacations?"

"Well, he liked to go to Vegas."

"He was a gambler?"

"Oh yeah. Gambling and swimming—odd combination, but they were his passions. I think he'd rather to do either of those than work." He paused and sadly said, "I miss him so much. For an old guy, he was packed full of energy."

He pulled a chip out of the bag and took a swig of the beer. He pushed the bag across the table to me. "Why are you asking me questions about the business?"

"I have come across three investors who had money in the company that your dad and uncle ran. They lost all their money, from what I can tell. It was so bad, some had to sell their houses and move out of state or in with their kids. I'm talking about older folks."

"That's got to be a mistake. My dad and his brother didn't always get along, but they were dedicated to their clients. They said that all the time. Nobody lost money when they invested with them. Nobody," Harrison said, dropping his feet to the floor and slamming the chair legs down.

"Unfortunately, that might not be true."

"You don't know anything about their business or their clients." A deep groove in his forehead became more pronounced, and his neck stiffened. "I'm not going to listen to this bullshit. I want you to get out of here."

"This is important," I said.

"There's the door. Leave."

"Harrison—"

"You can't come in here and bad mouth my dad and his business." He stood up, walked to the door, and opened it.

"I have proof. Letters that came from the office telling a client that …"

"Get out. You're a con. Big mistake asking you for help."

I gathered up my things and headed for the door. "Look, all I know is what I've been told and read and …" As I walked by him out the front door, he slammed it behind me. "And I'm not lying," I said to the slab of wood now staring me in the face.

"Harrison," I called through the solid entryway. "Don't leave. Okay? I need to get into your uncle's office."

There was no reply. I absentmindedly moved toward my car and leaned against the hood. Okay, so Harrison was angry. Made sense. His father died tragically. Then out of the blue, his mother married his uncle. His whole world turned upside down. I got in the car and backed out of the driveway. The mother thing was beyond strange. No matter what Harrison thought, I had to find out what was going on with this family. It was even worse than mine.

Chapter 19

I sat on the carpet with my back against the Barlow & Barlow Fidelity Investments office door. The night before, Harrison had a change of heart. He texted me that he located a key to the office and would meet me at nine. It was ten o'clock and he was an hour late. He didn't answer his texts, phone, or email. If I left, he might make good on his threat to fire me, and my mechanic and I needed the cash. The aroma from the cup of coffee I bought him evaporated into the sterile hallway.

"Jerk," I said to myself. I texted him again.

Where r u?

Ten minutes passed and still no reply.

"Okay," I said to the empty hallway. "I'm done." I'd take my chances on receiving a paycheck. I reached for the doorknob to pull myself up and the office door silently opened. A pale triangular patch of light from the hall penetrated the dark office.

"Harrison?" I called out, sticking my head through the office door. There was no answer. I tried again as I walked into the dark space.

"Harrison!"

I paused by the receptionist's desk, now empty except for a blank computer monitor and keyboard. No photos, containers of pens and pencils, or calendars littered the desk. This was an office not just closed for a stretch of time but shut down, maybe forever.

I slipped back to the door and closed it. Then I stood absolutely still and listened. Outside, the muffled engines of big trucks pulling up behind the buildings camouflaged any other sound. I skulked along the side of the hall that led to the two principles' offices, one right next to the other. I'd seen brother Marty's. Now it was time to inspect the brother's domain.

As I approached the door, I stopped. Indistinct voices filtered into the office from the outside hallway. Did Harrison finally show up? I had a few choice words to say to him. The Barlow & Barlow door opened and the voices of two men bickering could be heard. Definitely not Harrison. Opening Andy's office door, I quietly stepped inside, closing the door almost completely.

"This is a fucking waste of time," said one man with a deep voice. "He said the insurance payout wasn't in."

"I don't believe him," said the other. "We'll never see that money."

"Where's his office?" said deep voice, growing closer as he walked down the hall. Would they notice the door was slightly open? The second man reached out for the doorknob and began to turn it. Directly on the other side, I held my breath and watched the silver knob move. I prepared to shove the door shut and lock it. But then what?

"No, not that one. That's the dead guy's. The one next to it."

I covered my mouth with both hands, slipped into a crouch, and let out a huge sigh of relief. As they walked into Marty's office, I did what I should have done in the first place: shut the door firmly, lock it, and look for a place to hide.

"Fucking waste of time," the deep voice guy said over and over.

"We gotta do this. I'm not tellin' the boss we didn't look," said the other, frustrated.

"Well, you do it. I'm not," said deep voice, who headed back to the front office.

"Give me five minutes. Just five minutes and we'll leave."

In the office next to me, I heard drawers open and shut, filing cabinets slam.

"Nothing there. Let's call the wife. Make up a story about the insurance," said the other man, walking back to the reception area. He paused outside Andy's office and his hand rested on the doorknob again. He absentmindedly turned it but nothing happened.

"This door's locked. Might be something in here. Do you have any picks?"

The hallway grew silent as I imagined a lockpicking set flying through the air.

"Got it. Now let's see what this guy is hiding."

As the picks scraped the interior of the lock, I dashed to the empty closet and pulled the door shut. Stupid move, I thought. But then I realized that another door stood behind me. I opened it and found myself in Marty's office. Silently I closed it just as the intruder opened his side of the closet.

"You're right. There's nothing here," said the voice on the other side of the wall. I listened as he repeated his actions of opening and closing drawers and filing cabinets.

"Nothing here," he muttered again to himself. "Need to call the wife."

"His wife's dead," said deep voice. "But the wife of this Andy guy must know something."

"How much was Andy into the company for?"

"That's the million-dollar question," said deep voice, cackling. "Make that two. The guy was a loser. A gambler chasing the last hand."

"Think he owed two million dollars?"

"Plus or minus," said deep voice. Their conversation grew distant as they walked out the front office door and closed it with a thud.

The office was oppressively quiet.

I kept my hand on the closet doorknob for security and inched into Andy's office. The two thugs had left the door open. I walked into the office hallway, just to make sure. Unsteadily, I eased back into the carpeted room. It was the exact duplicate of the one next to it, with a large window overlooking the plaza below. But this office had two floor-to-ceiling bookcases, a highly polished table to one side, probably for client meetings, and an L-shaped desk next to the window. Like the receptionist's office, the computer was missing. Two two-drawer gleaming wooden file cabinets on rollers stood next to the file cabinets. I sat down heavily on the desk chair and rolled toward the window.

"That was too close," I muttered to myself. I stared out the window and watched below as the two men emerged from the office building. They turned the corner, heading for the parking lot, and the view became clearer. Stocky and thick necked, the shorter man was bald and wore a black T-shirt. Did he have the deep voice? The other's dark slicked-back hair gleamed in the bright sun from gel that held every strand in place. His stomach sagged over the belt to his pants. His dark green polo shirt stretched across his ample belly and inched above his waistline, showing pale pink skin. They disappeared into the lot, and the corner of the building blocked my view.

Our dearly departed Andy had quite a reputation. He was a gambler with a debt of about two million dollars owed to a big-time money lender. I recalled overhearing Marty talking about insurance on the phone when I first visited this office. Maybe these goons decided that Andy was worth more dead than alive and stepped in to secure his insurance. Did Marty agree with them and take the steps needed to get rid of his brother?

As my heartbeat slowed to a normal range, I moved over to the low file cabinets the intruder had left open. The top drawer held supplies: legal sized pads, white paper for a printer, small square packages of sticky notes, and a large supply of pens and pencils. No client info. I closed the drawer and pulled open the one underneath. Empty. Swimming gear filled the neighboring file cabinet. The top drawer held three dark blue towels, orange and red swim caps, plus a neoprene cap rested on top of the towels. Two pairs of black jammers (knee-length male swimsuits), goggles with tinted lenses in their cases, a small bottle of lens spray, and two partially squeezed tubes of sunscreen rounded out the swim collection. A current tide table, like the cherry on a hot fudge sundae, rested at the very top. This man was a serious swimmer. I took out my phone and snapped a few pictures.

The bottom drawer held cold water gear: neoprene gloves, booties, and lined rash guards. A sleeveless full-length wetsuit folded into a drying bag took up the rest of the space. I snapped a few more pictures.

I wondered if this guy did any work at all. Or was he always in the water? No wonder he didn't pay off his debts. He spent more time swimming in the Bay than in his office. I stood there reviewing the small photographs on my phone when my phone pinged.

It was Harrison.

Sorry.

"I don't know who's the biggest idiot, him or me," I mumbled and headed for the entrance to the office building. Walking to my car, I nervously searched the parking lot, hoping to see something that would identify the guys who broke into the office. Four rows over, I noticed the two men hunched down in a white sedan, engrossed in something. Maybe they decided to text their boss? The green shirt disappeared when he leaned over. If I wanted to track them down, I needed a shot of their license plate. Probably the plates were lifted from a different car, but I considered it worth a shot. Moving from car to car and dipping down behind each car trunk, I advanced slowly, making sure I stayed invisible to them. With only one row of automobiles separating us, I snapped a few photos. The plain white California plate with blue characters almost screamed, "I'm phony."

Now was the time to walk away. Quietly. But did I? Ah … no.

I had to see why they were so preoccupied. Approaching from the driver's side, I peered through the window. The two men, immersed in the small screen in front of them, watched small balls bounce into each other. A kid's video game consumed them.

"Ah shit," said green shirt, tossing the phone into the back seat. His eyes stopped moving when he saw me. "Lady, what do you want?" Bald head turned toward me, he rolled down the window and hissed, "You watching us?"

I shook my head, "No. Sorry. I thought I knew you." I backed up to the car behind them, then turned and sprinted away. When I looked over my shoulder, green shirt pointed something in my direction. A jolt of energy surged through me. Was it a gun? I looked again. No. It was a camera. Complete relief. Why a camera? I jogged over to my vehicle, stood near the front bumper, and pulled out my phone. Their white car backed slowly out of the parking spot and drove in my direction. My heart jumped into overdrive as I began repeatedly clicking the camera button on my phone. Their car headed straight at me. No signs of turning. I jumped back behind the truck parked next to me and promptly fell and skidded on my knees. Brazenly, they rolled slowly past the front of my Honda, still filming me.

I stood up, my knees covered with bright red blood.

"I'm calling the police." I hit 911. Green shirt dropped the camera inside the car while sneering at me. Then he stuck out his hand, two fingers mimicking the barrel of a gun, and pulled the imaginary trigger.

"I know who you are," I yelled at the retreating car. I heard them laugh as they sped out of the parking lot.

Chapter 20

Two hours later, after a lengthy conversation with the local police, I left the parking lot. Before I drove off, my photos, which included the white car's license plate, moved from my phone to theirs. Did I mention I had been snooping around the empty office of Barlow & Barlow Fidelity Investments? It never entered my mind. Did I say that there was someone in the office with me and I thought it might be these guys? Negative. The cops initially thought the guys were nutcases patrolling the mall's parking lot scaring the shoppers. That conclusion worked for me.

Dad was the only one home when I reached my high-tech home. I walked past him, his head stuck in the refrigerator, and headed straight up the stairs to my suite of rooms. He didn't need to see my scraped knees.

"How's things, Trish?" he called out to me. "Want a sandwich?"

I didn't answer.

"Trish?"

"Everything's fine. And I'm not hungry."

"Well, excuse me for asking."

Dad, Lena and Jon, even Dr. T, would have unsympathetic opinions about my recent trespassing. And I didn't want to hear them. Slamming the door behind me, I headed for the bathroom, cleaned my bloody knees, and covered them with large waterproof bandages. My knees throbbed. After pulling two bags of frozen peas out of the freezer, I flopped down on my bed and rested the veggies on my wounds.

"I want calm," I said, and Earl's latest high-tech addition to the house took over. The white walls of my bedroom turned into a still, deep-green lake surrounded by snow-topped mountains. Last year, he added LED wallpaper in every room. At times like this, it came in handy. Watching the water ripple across the wall, I heard the click of the door. I froze. Then a white car with a sneering man flashed in front of my eyes. A tightness flooded through my chest. Each breath became shallower. "No air," I said to the calm, indifferent lake.

"Trisha, are you okay? Something bothering …?" asked Dad as he opened the door.

"What happened to you?"

"Can't breathe." The words came out in gasps.

Instead of panicking, Dad quickly walked over to the bed, helped me sit up, and quietly but firmly said, "Take a deep breath. Follow what I'm doing. Breathe in, one, two, three, four; hold one, two, three, four; and out, one, two, three, four, five, six, seven."

It took three rounds of breathing before my chest relaxed and the uncontrollable fear leaked out of every pore in my body. My father brought me a glass of water from my little kitchen.

"Better?" he asked. I nodded. "What's going on?"

"I don't know."

"Do you get these breathing spells frequently?" Dad asked, brushing back the hair from my forehead.

"Never before," I lied.

"And your knees? Did you fall?"

I nodded 'yes,' not wanting to explain.

"I think you had a panic attack," he said, holding my hand and putting the bags of peas back on my injuries. "Your mom started getting them when she was diagnosed with cancer. Come on downstairs. Let's get you something to eat."

Dad sat me down in the living room in the middle of a Costa Rican rainforest, the trees swaying gently in the electronic breeze. While he made me some tea and toast, I called out, "Seen any wildlife?" When he walked up the steps to find out what was wrong with me, he paused the old Humphrey Bogart movie, Casablanca, that he had been enjoying.

"What a strange background for that movie. Why not Morocco? Or something a little more desert-y?"

"Because deserts are hot. This forest is keeping me cool."

"The air conditioning is keeping you cool," I said, smiling at him as he placed a plate and mug on the hammock in front of me.

"Feeling better?" he asked.

"I am."

"Trishy, as your father, I suggest that you make a doctor's appointment. Panic attacks, anxiety, that kind of thing is manageable."

"Good idea. I'll think about it."

"Do more than that. Go see someone."

"Sure," I said, brushing him off.

"Your mother loved this movie," he said. "It was a classic even when we watched it back in the day. She was a big Ingrid Bergman fan."

"Really?" Dad didn't talk about his wife, our mom, that much. And now in the span of fifteen minutes, he mentioned her twice. Once cancer took my mother's life, Dad never got over the loss. He didn't want to be in our house anymore. Too many memories. He waited until I finished my senior year of high school and then he left, leaving me to bring up my little sister.

"Yeah. Her favorite. You know that Bergman died on her birthday of cancer just like your mom? I don't know why she never won an Academy Award for her role in Casablanca. She wasn't even nominated."

"What other movies did Mom like?" I asked.

"Important scene coming up."

The discussion about my mother hit a speed bump. I decided to change topics. "I want to talk to you about something. Would you mind turning off the swaying trees?" I asked Dad.

"Sure, toots."

Dad switched the floor-to-ceiling LED wallpaper to a library scene with windows that looked out over an empty green campus.

"The weirdest idea of why one brother killed the other popped into my mind. But first I want to know what you think."

Dad stretched his legs out straight in front of me and put both hands on the back of his head and leaned against the couch. For a second, he closed his eyes. "I look at it this way. There are two scenarios. One is he killed his brother. Two is he didn't kill his brother."

"I know that much," I said.

"But I don't think it's very organized in your head. You never were much on organization."

"Dad."

"Your backpack that you carried to school was a mess, remember? Papers were crumpled up in the bottom. You never could find anything."

"Dad."

"I think you need to get out a piece of paper and list reasons for each scenario."

"I'll do that. But I want to know what you think."

Dad sighed again. "Let's look at story number one. He killed his brother. Why would he do that? What did he gain? There must be a reason."

"There are plenty of reasons," I said. "Andy was draining their company of money. He was a gambler. Their firm was bankrupt and their clients wanted their money, which they didn't have because Andy had gambled it all away. Marty couldn't kick his brother out of the firm because they were co-owners. Or at least I think they were. And he was in love with Andy's wife. So, he killed him and married her. I think Harrison told me she comes from old Marin money. That she grew up in one of the county's richest towns, in Ross."

"What about story number two? That he didn't kill him?"

"Well, who did then? And why? Does Marty have to worry about being next?"

"Keep going."

"What about one of his kids? Did they kill their uncle?"

"Did they have a reason to do something like that?" my father asked.

"I really don't know the kids at all. The only one that seemed somewhat upset that her uncle died was the girl, Daria."

"You mentioned Andy was a gambler. How big were his debts?"

I shook my head again, deciding not to tell him about the thugs looking for the insurance money earlier today. "Since a bunch of people lost money when Andy took funds for gambling, maybe a former client killed him," I said.

"This is Marin. They'd sue."

"I don't know if suing would get them anything. From what I can tell, their investment firm was broke. Maybe the money they did get in from new clients was used to pay off debts or pay a client when they went to withdraw it," I said.

"You think they were running a Ponzi scheme? Like that Madoff guy?" asked Dad.

"Bernie Madoff? Could be. But that doesn't get us any closer to who killed Andy."

I stood up and gazed through the fake window out to the campus, then back to the shelves of books all around us.

"I have this outlandish idea that I want to run by you," I said.

"Go ahead," said Dad, nodding.

"What if they came up with this idea together, the two brothers?"

"Trish, I get that someone … someones … could coordinate a

death. But by propeller? That would be terribly painful. Who in their right mind would agree to that?"

"Well, maybe they were desperate. Not enough money to pay their clients, pay Andy's gambling debts, and pay themselves. I might consider it."

"Not me. And remind me never to go into business with you."

"I wanted to explore every possible motive. But yeah, I wouldn't offer myself up to the gods of the Bay just to settle debts."

I reached over to the environmental remote and snapped it off. We were now in Earl's comfortable living room. "I never really sat down and talked with one of their clients. That could help," I said.

"Sounds like they specialized in older folks like me," said Dad.

"If it comes to money, I think age didn't matter. If someone wanted to invest with them, they probably added them as a client."

"Remember when Bernie Madoff was in the news. He usually turned people down a few times before he took them on. That was part of his plan. Glad I never invested with him."

"What money do you have?" I asked him.

"I'm not telling you," he said and then smiled. "Consider doing some research on this Madoff guy. It might help you figure this out."

"That's what I intend to do."

Once back in my suite of rooms, I asked the wallpaper to put me in a forest. But it was too dark. "Put me in a forest with a setting sun."

Much better, I thought as golden light complemented the actual setting sun advancing across my floor. I picked up the laptop and flopped down on the bed.

I searched for Ponzi schemes and more than a million results popped up. Then I searched for Ponzi schemes and Barlow & Barlow Fidelity Investments. Only twenty-five results. I clicked on one, and Andy Barlow was quoted in an article saying that besides being illegal, Ponzi schemes were disrespectful to clients that trusted their investments with a particular firm. Oh Andy, you lying fraudster.

Then I logged into the My Community app.

My Community was a neighborhood social network. In the past, I've asked for recommendations for both a mechanic and a dentist. The mechanic worked out. The dentist, not so much. I clicked on the 'add a post' button, and in the subject line I typed Barlow & Barlow Fidelity Investments. How should I phrase what I wanted to say? Make it simple and believable was the answer that made sense.

I wrote, "Did anyone invest with Barlow & Barlow? Do you know what happened to them?" Then I pushed 'post' and stared at the screen for a few seconds. I always expected an instant response. Rarely happened, but I never gave up hope. I powered off the laptop and then took a giant leap from the chair to the bed and stretched out. My room, sensing movement, asked in a French accent, "What living wallpaper would you like?"

"None," I said to the sexy male voice from Paris. I loved that feature of my LED wallpaper. I could choose my English-speaking speaker from any part of the world. And I did. I worked my way through an old-school BBC-sounding female accent (I liked that one) and even an East London Cockney accent (sometimes hard to understand). I stayed with a twangy Australian cowboy accent for almost a year but settled on this smooth-talking Frenchman.

I rolled over on my bed and gazed at the treetops of La Cruz Canyon, growing tall outside my deck. Soothing, relaxing. Drifting off to sleep. Then my heart thudded an extra beat and thumped into overdrive. Husband … dub lub … divorce … dub lub … lawyer … dub lub. Each beat seemed to say, "What am I going to do?" I never answered the letter that came to Lena's address. In fact, I couldn't be certain where it was.

I sat up perfectly straight, like the rigid redwood beyond my deck.

As much as I wanted to ignore the whole thing, I knew I couldn't. With a worrisome sigh, I slid off the bed and surveyed my suite of rooms. Frankly, I didn't know where to start. I walked over to my small desk with the laptop, opened the drawers, and shuffled through the papers. Not there. A table with a bunch of bills stacked on top glared at me from across the room. Okay, next stop, the table. Under the bills were a few outdated coupons. I left them there. No energy to crumple them up and toss them in the trash. I stumbled into the small kitchenette. A box of cereal I didn't put away this morning lay on the countertop. Yesterday's dishes littered the sink. A faint odor drifted from the garbage can.

"Later," I said, knowing I could ignore it since no one really stopped in to visit except Dad and Lena. They both learned to keep their thoughts about my tidiness to themselves.

I couldn't find the letter from the lawyer anyway. I dug into the closet and my swim bag that Lena gave me, and I pushed around the dust bunnies under the bed. Sitting on the floor, I called Lena. Before she had a chance to say anything when she picked up, I pounced.

"Did I leave that letter from Brad's lawyer at your house?"

"Your manners get worse with each passing month," she said. "And yes, you did. You left it on the couch, and I stuck it somewhere on my desk."

"I thought I lost it," I said. "Actually, I hoped I did."

"Nope. It's here. Are you going to come get it?"

"Eventually. Did anything else arrive for me?" I asked.

"Like a second notice from this lawyer?"

"Yeah."

"Nothing. You should probably do something about it, don't you think?" Lena questioned.

"Eventually."

"What's Jon's take on all this?"

"Well …" I started.

"You did tell him, didn't you?"

"Not really. He thinks I'm divorced."

"What?" Lena barked into the phone.

I paused, not sure what to say.

"You're a jerk," my sister said and hung up.

Chapter 21

Why would someone leave a door open on a multimillion-dollar home? I expected Harrison or Justine to be inside watching me or a security system engaged and ready to scream when I walked through the door. But no, the Barlow house was accessible to anyone wanting to pay a visit. I texted Harrison that I planned on searching his father's office. His response was a curt, *I did that. Don't bother.*

That never stopped me before.

I headed for the pool area. "Hello?" I called out. I tried again louder. "Hello?"

No answer. I skirted the inviting patio leading down to the pool deck and walked up to the crystal-clear glass door with the windows peering out at me. I silently opened the door and walked into an empty room I'd been in at least three times now. No alarm exploded.

I moved toward the expansive hall and found the steps up to the second floor. "Hello?" I tried again. But the sound echoed around me. At the top of the steps, I could see the door to Harrison's room half open. I peeked in. The comforter spilled off the bed onto the floor. Four white pillows were stacked on the black sheets. Clothes and his dark cape dressed a nearby straight back chair. On the wall hung a large television. His state-of-the-art gaming system stood ready on a table beside it.

He had a great view of the pool. Automatically, I picked up his comforter and carefully folded it. Absent-mindedly, I kicked something hard under the bed. A portable safe about the size of an old-fashioned typewriter case scraped across the floor. Pulling it out, I rested it on the bed. The keys that went into a circular lock were missing. But like everything else in this house, the sturdy safe had been left unsecure. Inside I found a burner phone and a thumb drive. Of course, the phone was unlocked too. Digging into the settings, I located its number and called it from my cell.

It went to voicemail and a man said, "This is Andy. You know what to do."

I hung up but clicked around until I found a list of phone numbers he called before he died. I clicked on the first one. It went straight to voicemail with no identifying information. The second number proved more informative.

"Perry's Garden Parlor," a female voice said.

"Sorry, I think I have the wrong number. What is this?"

"A gambling establishment."

"Oh. Where?"

"Reno."

"Thanks. Sorry to bother you." And I hung up.

On the third call, "Who's this?" said a rough threatening male voice.

"A friend of Andy's. Andy Barlow."

There was a long quiet pause. "Whataya want?"

"Andy said you could help me," I said, trying to sound as pitiful as possible.

"Is that a fact? You know Andy's dead, don't you?"

"Yes, but I really need a game, a chance to win back some money I lost."

"Lady, go dig up your friend and ask him for it. He died owing me two mil. You pay me that and we'll talk."

He hung up. I bet that wasn't the only gambling debt Andy had.

I thought about keeping the phone, but in the end I left it where I found it. But I did take a picture of the numbers recently called. The thumb drive was another story. I stared at Harrison's laptop across the room. True to form, I didn't need a password to get in. Clicking on the external drive, financial files opened up in a spreadsheet. I pulled out a blank thumb drive from my backpack, inserted it into the laptop, and copied all the financial files. Then the phone and original thumb drive went back into the safe and under the bed.

My plans didn't include investigating Justine's room, but I happened to be here, so why not? Paintings of butterflies decorated the walls of her comfortable bedroom. Amber-toned side tables, a highboy, and a Queen Ann style traditional, full length floor mirror completed the feminine room. A flowered comforter draped across the bed. I did a quick scan of the drawers, closets, even under the mattress. Nothing looked out of place. No hidden safes here.

At the end of the hallway, one closed door remained to be opened. It wasn't a plush home office. Instead, I found a closet crammed full of sports equipment: skis, boogie boards, snorkels, a frisbee, and numerous baseball bats. Definitely not a workspace.

I headed back down the stairs, wondering where Andy's office could be. The large open floorplan couldn't go on forever. I walked through the dining room, a family room, a large living room filled with expensive furniture, even a library. Finally, I found the office. It connected to one end of the library.

A large mahogany desk anchored one end of the room. To the side was a floor-to-ceiling display case with maps, photos, trophies, and awards. Ankle-deep carpets covered the floor. Two plush chairs sat next to each other facing the desk. On the other wall was a huge stone fireplace next to a bar.

The desk was unlocked. I saw why when I pulled open the top middle drawer. It was empty. I opened the side drawers. All empty. I even pulled them all the way out, turned them upside down and shook them. Nothing but crumbs fell out. I switched on the computer next to the desk. It was locked.

Where would I keep something that I didn't want anyone else to find? I glanced at the bar and walked over to it and went behind. The set of drawers opened with a slight pull. The top had napkins, stirrers, and things needed to make drinks. I dug through it but found nothing. Then I pulled open the second drawer and uncovered some placemats and large, blue-tinted cocktail glasses. What a waste of time. If I still drank, I would have poured myself a bourbon from the well-stocked bar.

A small Chinese teapot with graceful lines and gentle curves caught my eye in the display case. Stuffed between plaques and awards, it seemed out of place in this manly room. As I turned it over to see what might be written on the bottom, I heard a jingle inside. Removing the delicate top, I pulled out a set of tubular-shaped keys. I rubbed the round steel between my fingers. These opened a small safe, probably the one under Harrison's bed. Did Andy hide his safe there while his son was away at college? Not very original. But maybe Harrison had stumbled on the safe somewhere else and concealed it in his room. I bet Harrison knew more than he let on about his father.

⁂

When leaving the house, I asked my phone to text Lena.

Could you look at some finance files? On a thumb drive. Coming over now.

Trying to watch both the road and my phone proved challenging. My eyes darted back and forth as I took the curves with too much speed, almost sending me into a white sedan coming the other way.

⁂

"Where did you get this?" asked my sister as I handed her the drive.

"It was under Harrison's bed."

Lena plugged in the thumb drive and clicked on one of the files. Rows of numbers came up.

"This looks like an old-time ledger, the way it's laid out," she said, peering at her monitor. "I really don't know what I'm looking at." She moved the first file off to the side and opened up the only other file on the drive.

"It's identical," I said, staring over her shoulder at the screen. The tabs up at the top were the same. The dates are the same. "Wait, look Lena. There are two running lists of numbers. What do you make of that?"

"I don't know." As we compared them to the numbers in both files, it took no time at all to see they weren't the same. "This doesn't add up," Lena said, enlarging what should have been the same list from each file.

"Unless ..." I started and then stopped.

"Unless what?" she asked.

"Scroll down a bit." She did until she reached the total on all three columns. "Nothing matches. But there is a lot more money on the first file."

"They're cooking the books," Lena said.

"That's what I think." I ran my finger down the monitor, comparing each number. "The first file that shows so much more money has got to be the phony one. The second file with two columns of numbers is the real one. Check out the totals. How much are they off?"

Lena enlarged the total amount on each file. "Almost one billion dollars. They're fraudsters! That poor flowerpot lady. She lost everything to a bunch of fraudsters. It had to be both brothers, right? You couldn't do this alone, could you?"

"I knew Andy was a gambler. I'm not a client or a family member or a coworker, so if I knew, his brother had to. I bet Marty spent most of his time cleaning up after this deadbeat brother."

⚬⟶•————————•⟵⚬

Later that evening, I finally got around to checking my request on

My Community. Almost a hundred and fifty people had responded. The gist of their posts said, "I lost everything." "Those brothers were crooks." "My retirement money is gone." Even a few non-profits had lost their investments.

I would have any number of people to connect with if they were willing to talk to me. I was looking over the list trying to decide who to email when another message popped up. It said, "Check your email."

I did.

It read. "I don't want to discuss this via email or in a public forum like My Community, but here is my phone number. You can call me and I'd be happy to tell you what I know. Vivian."

Without taking a breath, I dialed her phone number. Of course, it went to voicemail. A girl after my own heart. Never answer the phone if you don't recognize the number.

"Hi Vivian, this is Trisha Carson. I'm the person wanting to know about Barlow & Barlow Fidelity Investments. My dad was about to hand over all his retirement funds to them and they disappeared. Could we talk? Maybe go out for coffee?" Now I had to wait and hope Ms. Vivian would call back.

I did a computer search for Barlow & Barlow Fidelity Investments again, and what came up was mixed. According to one source, the firm was still in business but was closed for a short time after one of the brother's death. Calls were being answered and some transactions were taking place, including withdrawing some of the funds the clients had invested. But not all.

At this point, lawsuits hadn't been filed. But I bet they weren't far away.

A text popped up on my phone. It was from Harrison.

Did you find anything?

No

Told you so, he texted back. *I have a plane reservation to go back to England.*

When?

Tell you when I see you

Harrison was a jerk. Why couldn't he tell me now?

I started another text to my sister.

Please get me a boat so I can swim in the bay.

She answered quickly. *Not a chance. You're not ready. But that never stopped you.*

Truth be told, it almost stopped me many times. I could put on a good front, but when it came down to actually doing something, heart palpitations, tunnel vision—in other words, anxiety—often took over. Except for the two recent panic attacks, it had eased somewhat. Lena thought that having my sweetheart Jon in my life helped.

Maybe I'll jump off the Sausalito ferry and swim to shore.

Yeah right, she responded.

While I wondered what my next step would be, an email alert flashed on my cell phone screen. Two messages showed up. One from my employer, the SF Giants, and the other from Vivian, my Barlow & Barlow contact.

"Tell your father not to invest with these men," Vivian's message began. "Could we meet? I walk my dog every morning at the small beach near San Quentin. He's small and black with white paws. Would nine thirty work?"

I quickly responded, "Yes. See you then."

I walked over to the landing and yelled down to Dad, "I'll take The Babe for his walk tomorrow morning. That okay with you?" The Babe, hearing his name and the word 'walk' in the same sentence, skipped over to the front door and ran around in circles.

"Not now, Babe. Sorry to get your hopes up, but I'm not going O – U – T right now. We'll do that in the morning."

Dad appeared at the foot of the stairs. "You shouldn't tease the dog like that," he said.

"Didn't mean to," I said. "But it's okay if I take him … ah … with me tomorrow morning?"

Dad nodded. "Sure."

Chapter 22

The next morning, I loaded the excited bulldog into my car. To protect what was left of the seat covers, I'd put down a dark blue baby towel. Then the hefty seventy-one pound happy dog needed a lift into the car. For some reason, jumping into a car mystifies him.

The San Quentin exit, the last exit before merging on to the Richmond–San Rafael Bridge leading to the East Bay curved off to the right. Two quick right turns, and the northern end of San Francisco Bay crystalized off to the left, glimmering under a lacy haze. Eight blocks straight ahead, Main Street ended at the entrance to San Quentin State Prison. I grabbed a parking spot across from the walkway down to the small beach. The Babe barked and pulled and barked some more when he smelled the fresh salty air, then took off, towing me behind him to the path that lead down the wooden steps to the beach. All seventy-one pounds of him barreled down the sandy beach to a dog walker with five dogs surrounding him. I strolled in that direction, looking for a woman with a dog. I passed two more dogs and their owners playing catch in the sparkling surf.

"Who's this?" asked the dog walker as part of his pack came up to greet The Babe with wagging tails and sniffing noses.

"The Babe," I said.

"After Babe Ruth. George Herman Ruth, the Sultan of Swat?"

"You know your baseball," I laughed. "Have you seen a woman

with a little black dog? I'm supposed to meet her here."

The dog walker pointed to a small hill at the other end of the beach. On the top was a woman bending over a small pup. I couldn't see the color. Below her, crouched on a rocky ledge, were two fishermen, their lines taut in the shallow water. It was low tide and the ebbing water had left a dark ring circling rocks beneath the top of the hill.

"Come on, Babe. Let's go," I said to the dog now completely ignoring me. The hill was less than one-quarter of a mile away. How did she get up there? I strolled slowly in that direction, appreciating the warmth of the sun melting away the haze. At the end of the beach, I located a wooden staircase with massive succulents bordering the single flight of stairs. The Babe galloped down the beach toward me.

"Come on, boy. Up the steps." Which he did faster than I ever could. Then a steep dirt path led The Babe and I to the top of the hill. The Babe took off again, sniffing all the new smells. I stood there enjoying this unique view of the bay.

"Wow," was all I could say. To my right was the enormous parking lot for San Quentin State Prison. The massive prison, the oldest prison in California, stretched out behind an old white guard tower at the eastern side. To my left, the graceful slope of the Richmond–Bay Bridge slipped into light fog on its way to the east Bay. The Larkspur Ferry, sending out a wake that disturbed the quiet morning waters, headed for the landing.

The woman and her dog walked over to me. "I'm Vivian. Call me Viv for short." She looked at me carefully. "I know you," she said.

I shook my head.

"Barlow & Barlow. You had an appointment. And you planned to come back with your father."

"You're right. I do remember you. You worked the front desk."

"I worked the front desk only temporarily. Our receptionist left to have a baby."

I had struck gold. This woman held the keys to the kingdom, or at least the Barlow & Barlow history.

"Do you have time to sit and talk? I have so many questions."

"I bet you do," she said with a smile, a sad smile.

A weathered bench under one of the trees faced the bay. We walked over and sat down. Her little black dog jumped on her lap and licked her.

"I worry about Travis the most," she said, petting the dog.

"Travis? Who's Travis?"

"This little guy. I'm afraid I'll go to prison, and I don't know what will happen to him."

"Prison? You're kidding me. Just what were you and the Barlow brothers doing? When I visited Barlow & Barlow that time, the office looked a bit understaffed, just you if I remember."

"A few weeks later nobody would have been there," she said. "That's the FBI's doing. They came in … took us, Mr. Barlow and me, by surprise. Walked out with everything—the computers, the binders."

Viv, a small woman with snow white hair cut short around her ears, stared blankly out at the Bay. Her bird-like fingers picked at her dog's coat. Then she gently put him down. She crossed her arms and stuck her hands under her elbows. She shivered lightly.

"Oh look," she said, staring out at the channel markers. "There are a group of swimmers and someone on a paddleboard. I see swimmers all the time out there."

"Really," I mumbled, wanting to get her back on track. "My sister swims in the Bay, but I don't think she's ever been here. Viv, why did the FBI raid your office?"

"I don't know how they do it. It's cold. Doesn't your sister get cold?"

"I think she's used to it by now. But the FBI? That seems to me like overkill."

Viv avoided that question, too.

"You know, Mr. Barlow didn't want to take my dad's money. He doesn't have that much. But he really needed it to earn more than the banks would give him. But Mr. Barlow was firm. Dad didn't have enough to invest."

"Sounds like Mr. Barlow." Viv shook her head. "He was just playing with you. He would have taken his money. Gladly. But he liked to string people along, make them desperate to invest with them. I remember once, an officer from a nonprofit came in and was in tears when Andy said no to her. I could hear her pleading from the other room. He had her come back three times with the foundation's accountant, their books, everything. It was a big show. Of course, he would invest their money. But I think he liked feeling powerful, playing with people, their savings. His clients saw them as god-like. The returns they made for them were unheard of.

"My father used to say, 'If it seems too good to be true, it probably is.' Well, these clients didn't ask questions. And now, they're out. Their money is gone."

I listened in disbelief. "It's a good thing my dad didn't invest with them."

"A very good thing," she said. She squirmed on the bench. "It's time for me to go. Travis needs his breakfast."

"Can we talk again?" I asked as she stood up. The emerging sun glanced off the bay, settling into the worry lines on her face. She nodded.

"One last thing before you go. Let me get this straight. The Barlow brothers were involved with some kind of fraud, right?" She nodded. "And you?"

"I knew where the bodies are buried."

"Excuse me?"

"I was their accountant. I knew they didn't have any money left. Andy had gambled everything away. When we had that little recession a few years ago, clients came in and wanted their money. They withdrew everything. All Andy and Marty could do was take the new money that was coming in, like potentially your dad's, and give it to clients wanting to withdraw. After a certain time, they never invested anything. The money came in and it went right out."

"That's a Ponzi scheme, isn't it?"

"Yes dear, it is."

"But they did this, not you."

"I knew about it, but I was nearing retirement. I wanted to make sure that the money they invested for me was safe. And they did take care of me financially. Anyway, I kept their secrets to myself. And now I'll probably end up right over there," she said pointing to San Quentin. "My poor pup. What's going to happen to him?"

"I'll walk back to the beach with you," I said. Although she was small and probably close to seventy, if not older, she had a quick step and I had to jog to keep up with her.

"Come on, Babe. We're leaving," I said to the dog who'd sat by my feet while we talked. The dogs trotted ahead of us, their tails wagging with each step as we walked back down the wooden staircase to the beach.

"Can I ask you one more thing?"

Viv nodded.

"Why did you decide to talk to me? You don't know me. I could go to the police or the FBI with your information."

"I recognized your name on the My Community bulletin board. I did so many bad things, I wanted to make sure your dad's money was safe. You seemed nice and respectful. And I needed to talk."

A breeze had picked up and was blowing in from the west like it always did this time of day. The open water swimmers rounded the point and headed for shore, their bright orange rescue buoys streaming behind them, their cheerful voices and laughter floating toward the beach.

"I'm going to stay for a bit," I told Viv. She nodded and bent over to put a lease on her dog.

"We'll talk again," she said as she and Travis moved toward another set of stairs that would take them up to the street. A woman stopped to talk to her, but she waved and kept on walking.

Chapter 23

Driving home, a text popped up on my phone from an unknown number.

Can I talk to you? This is Daria.

What did Marty Barlow's daughter, the 'rich bitch' as Harrison called her, want with me?

Sure. In person? Or phone?

Come by the house.

I'm bringing a dog.

This half of the Barlow family lived in the hills not far from where the Nereus docked. The sprawling, spacious home overlooked the marina and San Francisco Bay across to the East Bay hills.

When she opened the door, Daria didn't look like the snotty rich kid I first met after water polo practice. Dressed in oversized gray sweats with her hair pulled back in a ponytail, she looked small and lost. We moved into the family room angled off to the side of the house. She collapsed on to the couch and pulled her legs up underneath her.

The Babe sat quietly next to me.

We sat there in silence for a few moments.

"I don't know what to do," she said, looking down at her hands. "I'm all alone and I'm scared."

"Where's Dawson?" I asked.

"He sleeps most of the time on the boat. He only comes back here to do laundry, maybe shower."

"You're really by yourself?"

She glanced up. "Yes. I am. Nobody is thinking about me at all. Dad is off with his new wife, my aunt, for fuck's sake. Dawson is down on the boat getting high. And Harrison doesn't like me. I. Am. All. Alone and I hate it."

"Have you heard from your father? I'm sure he'll be back soon. He has a business to run."

"He had a business to run. I think he's in some kind of trouble. That's why he took Aunt Justine and went to Thailand or someplace like that."

"What about other family members in the area? Are there any friends you can stay with? I can make a call to them for you if you want."

"No," she yelled. "Don't call any of my friends. They're mad at Dad for some reason. Or at least their families are."

I only had one way to keep her safe.

"Okay, look, pack a bag. Get enough clothes together for four or five days. Bring your textbooks."

"Where am I going?"

"You're coming home with me." I stood there, arms crossed, tapping my foot. "Move. Get your stuff."

"I'm not leaving this house," Daria shouted. She looked panicked.

"If you don't come with me, I'm calling Child Protection Services and they'll pick you up and dump you into foster care until this thing is worked out."

"You won't dare."

"Try me."

"You bitch."

"You're not the first one to call me that. Now get your things. I'm hungry. I want to go home and eat."

When she flounced off to collect her clothes and backpack, I called her brother. Voicemail. Doesn't anyone answer their phone anymore? I texted him.

This is Trisha Carson. Your sister is a mess. She's coming home with me.

I hit send.

From calling me a bitch to flinging herself into the passenger seat of my car took about thirty minutes. I rallied every bit of patience I had while waiting. I did not want her to come home with me. I never planned on being this involved with the Barlows.

"I want you to get my pops back. Can you do that?" she asked, starting to cry again.

I didn't know what to say. I felt for this girl who, for the first time, faced life on her own. It didn't matter that she had her own BMW, all the food she could eat, and an elegant home. She didn't have parents to help her manage this strange situation.

"I don't know if I can, but I'll keep trying. What's his number?"

She pulled out her phone and showed me her list of contacts.

"You've tried to call him?" I asked.

"Yes. Over and over. It goes to voicemail."

I punched in the numbers she showed me, and we both stared at my phone as somewhere in the world, perhaps the Philippines, it rang. And rang. And rang. Then it went to voicemail.

"Marty Barlow here. Leave a message." Then I heard the beep.

"Mr. Barlow, this is Trisha Carson. We met at your office. I'm with your daughter, Daria, and she's all alone. She desperately wants to contact you. She really shouldn't be staying by herself. She's underage. Please call her back immediately."

I hit the end call button. The confident teenager sitting beside me had melted away. In her place was a scared little girl with no place to go and no one to turn to.

"Let's try and find your brother."

I drove down the hill with a glum Daria at my side and parked in the marina.

"You stay here. I'm going to check out the boat."

As I walked toward the pier where the Nereus docked, The Babe decided to stop and sniff all the new smells, but I pulled him along. This was not a leisurely walk for me or him. Another boat owner opened the gate, and the dog and I scooted in behind.

I stood at the end of the Nereus's finger pier and called out, "Dawson? Are you on board?" There was no reply. No sign of the twin. I continued down the dock until I stood outside of Hatch Grey's boat.

"Hatch? Hatch Grey?"

A head popped up from down below.

"Well, if it isn't Trisha Carson. And who's that?" he said, angling his head toward the dog.

"The Babe. He's friendly. He doesn't bite."

Hatch nodded and said, "How're your legs?"

"Much better, thanks. My sort of brother-in-law is an ER doc and he checked me out. He said you did a good job."

Hatch tugged on this watch cap, then tapped his chin.

"You weren't looking for a boat in a different marina when you were here before, were you?" He nodded as he spoke.

"You got me," I said. "Sorry I lied to you."

"Not the first time a lady as lovely as you didn't tell me the truth." Hatch smiled. "What's going on?"

"Have you seen Marty Barlow?"

"Nope. His son's been on the boat, but not Marty. Is something wrong?"

"Yes. It's a long story but he's disappeared and left his kids high and dry. I have to find him and get him back here. Do you know any of his friends? Where he usually hangs out?"

Hatch shook his head. "Not really."

"Here's my phone number. In case he shows up, please let me know."

He looked down at the scrap of paper I gave him.

"You know, he didn't have anything to do with his brother's death."

"How would you know?"

"He wasn't on the boat when it left."

"You told me he was."

"Well, now, I'm telling you something different. I wasn't sure before. My mind sometimes gets a little fuzzy, you know. Hittin' those older years. Anyway, that morning, Andy was on the boat by himself. I asked him about it. Said he was going to pick up someone and then go swim for a bit."

"Who was he picking up?"

Hatch shrugged.

"Did he say where he was going?"

Hatch shrugged again.

"I don't believe you."

"That's the truth."

"Can you prove it?"

"Yeah, I filmed it. Was testing out the camera on my new phone. I could see him pulling out from the pier, so I started filming. I'll show you."

He reached for his phone, found the video clip, and played it. I watched over his shoulder. Sure enough, there was only one person on board.

"Watcha got there?" called out Andy as his boat passed by Hatch's boat.

"New camera," Hatch replied. "Where's your brother?"

There was an answer, but the words were garbled. I did hear something that sounded like "… pick up …" Then the phone camera followed the Nereus out of the channel into the Bay.

Hatch switched the camera off.

"Bet you didn't expect that," he said.

I stared at Hatch, wondering what else he knew but wasn't saying. I tried again. "Who do you think he picked up?"

"Don't know," he said. "Sorry, but I'm not much help." As he disappeared below, he paused, then said, "Those two brothers defrauded a lot of people. I heard all about that from the owners on these docks. They lost everything they had. Houses. Boats. I was talking to Evan Gunderson from Marin Marine and he told me the local boating industry lost millions."

He pointed to a woman on the next dock over. "See her. She works … ah, worked … for a church in Novato. They invested with the Barlow brothers. When their firm went belly up, they laid her off. Didn't have the extra money to pay her. She sold her house and is renting that boat so she has a place to live. Those guys were animals. Never thought about anyone but themselves."

He shook his head and disappeared below. This man's mind wasn't as fuzzy as he'd like me to believe. I stared at the empty cockpit, ready to climb in and throttle him.

"Come on, Babe, let's go home."

Chapter 24

Daria sat quietly during the twenty-minute drive to Earl's palatial house.

"I don't know what's happening to my dad. He never took off like this before. When my mom died, he stayed with us all the time. But now, he's never around. My family has fallen apart," Daria said. I thought she might start crying again.

"I know your life seems like it's topsy-turvy right now. Your dad will come back. I understand that you miss him and your Uncle Andy and …"

"No," she said abruptly. "Not my uncle."

What was that about? Time to find neutral ground.

"You know, my mom died before I graduated high school too. I became the mom to my sister. She's a lot younger than me. It was hard, but somehow, it worked out," I said.

"Really?"

"Yep."

When I pulled up in the driveway, Daria's mouth fell open. "You live here?"

"Yes, I do. The house belongs to Earl Cunningham. He's my landlord. Let's go."

She gathered her bags and stood by the car door, almost afraid to move. "I want to go home," she said defiantly.

"That's not an option," I said, climbing the front steps. Dad must have heard us coming since he opened the door.

"Well, hey, Trisha," he said giving me a hug.

Daria stood staring at both of us. "Are you Earl?" she asked.

"No. He's away for a bit. I'm Bob Shaver. Trisha's dad."

Daria looked confused.

"He lives here, too," I said. "Dad, this is Daria Barlow. She can't stay home by herself while her father is away, so I brought her here. She can stay for a few days, can't she?"

"Well, I don't see why not. Come in, Ms. Daria." He reached over and took her bags, even her backpack filled with books. "My goodness. The schools certainly load you kids down these days. Although now that I think about it, I carried a heavy backpack, too. When …"

"Can you save the stories until later? Where can she sleep?"

Dad paused for a moment. "You know, there's a couple of empty rooms down my end of the hall. She can move in there," he said, smiling at the teenager. "You'll like it here. Every little doodad in this house is smart, including the wallpaper. Trisha used to have a smart refrigerator, but it started eavesdropping on her, so we got rid of it. But everything else works through voice command," he said, leading her down the hall.

Daria looked back at me, not sure what to do.

"Go," I mouthed and shooed her down the hallway.

Cool fall air flowed through the room. I walked over to the glass doors out to the deck and shut them. Branches on the imposing redwood trees outside in the canyon swayed in the breeze. I dropped onto the couch. I had to find Marty or Justine Barlow. Someone needed to come back to the Bay area and take care of these kids. I texted Harrison.

Have you heard from your mom yet?

No, was the quick response.

Give me her cell phone number.

Why?

Just give it to me, okay? I want to talk to her.

He texted back the number. *Good luck with that.*

I called the number. Of course, it went to voicemail.

"Justine, this is Trisha Carson. You have to call me back. No one knows where you are. Daria and Dawson have been home by themselves. They're minors, Justine. That's against the law. Where are you? Harrison's ready to fly back to England. Please call back."

Dad came padding down the hall, Daria close behind him. "I'm going to take Ms. Daria on a hike down to the bottom of the canyon. Maybe walk over to the reservoir. That okay with you little lady?"

Daria tilted her head and looked up. "Sure, I guess."

"Maybe you want to tell your brother where you are?" I suggested to the young woman, who seemed both puzzled and pleased with her new surroundings. Being around my dad had calmed her down significantly. That was a gift he had that worked wonders on my sister and me when we were little and either scared or fussy. Interesting that he could still pull that out of a hat when needed. At least she didn't seem afraid of him, which I was originally worried about.

"I'll go get us some pizza," I said.

She stared at me blankly. "Okay."

Balancing a warm pizza, tempting with its gooey cheese and rich tomato sauce, I opened the front door to Earl's house. Music pulsed from the front room and I heard a girl's laughter coming from the deck. Dad was sitting on the couch, trying to find just the right wallpaper for a pizza dinner. He settled on the Trevi Fountain in Rome.

"Ms. Daria, pizza's here," called out Dad. Daria looked like a different person when she scuffled into the room. Relaxed and smiling.

"It smells so good," she said.

"Sure does," said a voice directly behind me.

Dawson. Daria's brother grabbed the pizza box out of my hands.

"Hope you got pepperoni. That's my favorite," he said, walking into the dining room. Daria followed him.

"I'm so hungry," she said.

"Can we change the wallpaper in here?" Dawson called out.

"Yeah. You can," said Dad.

"Wallpaper, turn into a roller coaster ride," Dawson said.

"No. I'm going to hurl. Change it," she yelled.

Dad walked in. "Wallpaper, Trevi Fountain, please." The surroundings calmed down, and Daria dropped her hands from her face and picked up a piece of pizza.

I pulled Dad's arm and dragged him to the hallway.

"You want to tell me what's going on?" I asked.

"Well, Ms. Daria did what you asked. She called her brother and told him where she was. Twenty minutes later, he showed up with a backpack full of his school things. I think all these kids have these days are backpacks."

"Is he staying?"

"Couldn't throw him out. He's a minor just like you said. Needs adult supervision. You sure there's no more kids in that family? Is anyone else arriving? It'd be good to know."

I watched the two teens sitting at the table, devouring the pizza.

"Hey, save some for us," I called out. In response, Dawson waved his hand, brush-off style.

"It's just the two of them," I said.

"Well, let's go eat," said Dad. "We'll figure out what to do later." He reached over, put his arm around my shoulder, and squeezed. "You did good, Trisha. They both need adults around them."

After our pizza fest—so glad I bought an extra-large—the kids started down the hall to their respective rooms.

"Did your dad or stepmom call back yet?" I asked.

There was another wave of the hand and a mumbled 'no.'

"What time do you need to get up for school?"

They looked at each other.

"I have water polo practice before school starts, so I'll be gone by six thirty," said Daria.

"I'm on a special travel team. We play all year round. The school lets us use their pool," she said.

"I don't want to wake up that early," said Dawson. "My first class isn't until two hours later."

"We only have one car between us," said Daria, her voice rising.

"Wait a minute," I said. "Where did that one car come from? I drove you here, remember?"

"Now Trisha, I'm letting Ms. Daria borrow my car until we can pick hers up after school tomorrow."

"Really?"

He nodded. I sighed.

"I have to go to practice," said Daria. "I don't know why you didn't drive. You have a perfectly good car at home."

"It's not my fault," said Dawson. "A friend dropped me off. But I don't have any clothes."

I cut him off. "What if I drive you home in the morning about seven thirty and you can pick up your clothes and car? Then I can drive in to the ballpark."

"Why you going to the ballpark?" asked Dad. "The season's over."

"They called me in to help with the employee party," I said, staring at Dawson. "Will that work?"

"It's still early," he grumbled.

"Be ready, in the kitchen, breakfast eaten—there's cereal in the cupboard—by seven thirty. Got it?"

"Yeah, yeah, yeah."

"Excuse me? Was that a yes or a no?"

"Yes! You're mean," he said.

"You have no idea. Don't you have homework to do?"

The teens and Dad gave me a "who does she think she is" look. Then Daria and Dawson continued down the hall to their rooms. I could hear them mocking me. "Don't you have homework to do?" whispered Dawson in a fake high voice. Daria giggled.

"Night, kids," said my father. Then he looked at me. "What's gotten into you? Patience, Trisha. Those two need some patience and kindness right now."

"I guess you're right. But I never planned on being a backup parent. This isn't what I want to do. I was only trying to find out if Andy Barlow was murdered or not. But now ..." I pointed down the hall toward the twin's rooms. "Their dad and his new wife don't seem to care what's happening to them, Harrison, and what's left of their business."

Dad bit his lips and tried not to smile.

"Well, get some rest. Sounds like you're going to need it."

Chapter 25

After I dropped Dawson off at his house, I joined the commuter traffic from Marin County to San Francisco. We inched slowly toward the Golden Gate Bridge. My 'lead foot' as my father called it spent most of the time on the brake. Off the brake for ten seconds and on the brake for ten. Even though cars surrounded me, the drivers seemed preoccupied with themselves. Next to me, one man in a business suit was having an animated conversation with someone, probably his phone. The woman on the other side used the lull in traffic to layer on her mascara. How she didn't stick that wand in her eye, I don't know. I spent too long watching her, so the driver of the car behind me skimmed her horn and it emitted a shrill beep. That ended the makeup tutorial for me. I hit the gas, then slammed on the brakes before I collided with the car stopped in front of me.

Dawson had said something that surprised me earlier. He spoke with his dad last night. That's all the teenager said. Not when or if his dad was coming home. I almost drove off the road when he mentioned that. I couldn't believe he didn't tell me earlier. "I'm glad I don't have kids," I said to the empty car as I inched my way closer to the Golden Gate Bridge.

My message to Justine must have sparked him into action. Maybe she called Harrison. As the traffic merged onto the bridge, I barely noticed the lack of wind that usually whipped off the Pacific Ocean into the bay. Lost in thought, I missed the beauty of the sun ricocheting off the tall white buildings in the business section of San Francisco.

⚬━ · ━━━ · ━⚬

The ballpark was empty except for a few of us brought in to stuff bags. I entered through the wide open service entrance, and I could see the empty field and the vibrant green grass in the outfield. The towering entrance shrunk into a dimly lit hallway that ballpark fans never saw.

"After you clock in," said a supervisor who stood near the time clock, "walk toward the Lefty O'Doul gate. There's a storage room off to the side. That's where you'll be working."

"Got it," I said, moving down the block long hallway. Without fans streaming by, the desolate concourse closed in around me. I walked faster, wanting to get out of the eerie walkway as soon as I could. Turning right toward the entrance gate, I heard muffled talking and bubbling laughter.

"Hey Trisha, glad you're here. We need all the help we can get," said my friend and coworker Charlee Ann. "So, what you been up to since the season ended?" she asked.

Before I had a chance to answer her, the man in charge said, "Pick up a plastic bag, walk down the line, put each thing in, and drop it in the box, okay?"

"Yes, sir." I saluted. "Not rocket science," I commented as I joined the five other employees moving efficiently down the line.

"Well," I said to Charlee Ann, who was working the other side of the wide table going the same direction as me.

"Don't tell me. You're investigatin' again," she said, shaking her head.

"As a matter of fact, yes. And you'll never guess," I said.

"Somebody died in the water," she said.

"How did you know?" I said.

"That's what you do. So, tell me all about it."

I started to talk, and within a few minutes everyone in the efficient assembly line stuffing bags was paying attention. Occasionally, they'd ask a question, but mostly they listened.

"Okay, this is what I know," I said, pausing as I picked up a Giants keyring. "Number one: Andy Barlow died in San Francisco Bay while training for a long swim."

"In the Bay? Isn't that cold?" asked Charlee Ann.

"Lots of people do it. The police thought it was a horrible accident. He was run over by a powerboat."

Their mouths collectively dropped open.

"Number two: Andy's son, Harrison, thinks his uncle Marty, his dad's brother, killed him—that he drove over him on purpose."

"Ew," the group of bag-fillers said in unison.

"I know," I said. "Harrison had been in London for college. He came back and hired me to check it out. He really wanted me to find evidence that Uncle Marty did it.

"Number 3: I talked to family members and co-workers and found out that their business ... they were financial advisors ... was in trouble. The dead brother was a compulsive gambler, and the money went out as fast as it came in. From the looks of his office, he spent more time swimming or gambling than working."

"What a scumbag," said Charlee Ann.

"Even some of the sailors at the marina invested with Barlow & Barlow. And the boating industry in Marin lost millions according to Hatch, who has a sailboat near the Barlows'."

"Number 4: I tried to find out who was on the Barlows' boat when it left the dock. Hatch first said he saw both men. Then a week later he said only Andy was on board and planned to pick someone up. He even showed me a video. I don't know what to believe.

"Number 5: A couple of thugs broke into the Barlows' office looking for insurance claims, I think. I know because I happened to be there."

I heard a couple of "Oh, reallys."

"Number 6: And this is the doozy. The remaining brother, Marty, married his dead brother's wife, Justine, and took off out of the country."

The noise in the room came to an abrupt stop. Everyone paused what they were doing and stared at me.

"I want to know who killed Andy and why."

The assembly line slowly restarted.

"I think it was done on purpose. This is no accident," said a spindly man with a receding hairline and a skimpy gray mustache working next to me.

"Me too," said the multi-pierced college student on the other side of the table. "And I don't care what that Hatch dude said, the other brother was on the boat."

The rest of the workers seemed in agreement and nodded their heads.

"I never thought Hatch would be lying," I said.

"Aren't investigators supposed to look at all angles? And besides, he already lied once. Bet he wouldn't think twice about lying again," said Charlee Ann.

"What do you mean?" I asked, picking up a Giants lanyard and placing it in the bag.

"You ever think this boat guy could be in cahoots with one or both of the brothers? Maybe he lost his fortune, too and wanted revenge."

"You think Hatch killed Marty?"

"I bet this Hatch dude is a serial killer," said the multi-pierced coed.

"You watch too many slasher movies, but maybe he helped plan it. Sounds like he knows boats as well as the people who were cheated," said the spindly man.

"Glad I don't have any money. No dinero," said the tiny middle-aged Latino woman.

The group laughed as they kept working.

"That doesn't feel right. But the idea that he was working with someone else … maybe who knows boats and had a lot to lose …"

"Like the industry guys you talked about?" chimed in Charlee Ann. "They could be involved."

I nodded.

"There's one more thing. Andy, the dead brother, had a liking for high-school-age girls."

"Horroroso," said the little Latina, and she crossed herself.

"Any other kids besides the college student?" asked the spindly guy.

"Twins in high school. Daria and Dawson. Since their father Uncle Marty is on his honeymoon, they're staying with me."

"Say what?" asked Charlee Ann.

"I couldn't let them be alone. They're minors."

"Don't they have any relatives?"

"If they do, they didn't tell me."

"What do they have to say about all this?" asked Charlee Ann.

"They don't think their father did anything. And they can't stand their cousin, Harrison, because he's blaming their dad. Dawson said this morning that he finally talked to his father. But he didn't say when or if he was coming back."

"You talk to him when he come back," said the little Latina.

"I think it's about money. The insurance money," said Ms. Multi-Pierced.

"You could be right," said a tall chubby white-haired woman who had been quiet up to this point. "Their investors want their money back. The thugs are looking for money. I bet the newly married couple decided to pool their inheritances to maintain their standard of living. And the kids … well, I doubt they were involved with the death, but they're old enough to know that their lifestyle could change. As the saying goes, 'follow the money.' Who needed the money the most?"

"I don't know," I said as I picked up a bobble head of the team mascot. "I think I asked all the wrong questions."

"Not wrong, But I think you overlooked some things. Go talk to this Hatch person again. Go talk to everyone again," said Charlee Ann.

Then the conversation switched to the potential players who my co-workers wanted on the team for next season. The stack of bags grew into mountains of bags that took over the room. My back ached from standing, stretching out, and leaning over. But we finished almost thirty minutes earlier than expected.

"Thanks everyone," said the supervisor. "We can clock out and go home."

Walking to my car parked in the empty ballpark lot, a text came in from my sister.

You're in SF, right? Meet me at Aquatic Park for some bay swimming.

Surprisingly, the prospective swim boosted my energy level and gave me something to think about besides the Barlow brothers and their kids.

Chapter 26

Aquatic Park sits on the edge of San Francisco and runs next to the tall ships from the Hyde Street Pier to the Municipal Wharf. Between those SF landmarks is a swimmable but normally chilly body of water. There's a string of buoys not far from the shore that a swimmer can follow like a trail of breadcrumbs. That's probably where I'd swim. I wasn't up to swimming the circumference of Aquatic Park or venturing out the entrance to the actual bay.

On the fifteen-minute drive from the ballpark through San Francisco to Aquatic Park, I kept thinking of Hatch Grey. How could I have taken his word as absolute truth? Because he helped me when I fell? Because he looked like an honest kind of guy, even after he lied to me?

My phone pinged. It was Harrison and the text read simply, *Well? Have you heard from your mother?*

No answer.

I bought my ticket to go to London.

Please don't. Not yet.

I had to get this case in order quickly.

I drove down to the foot of Van Ness Avenue next to Aquatic Park. "I'll never find a parking spot," I thought to myself. A warm blue-sky day in San Francisco, typical for fall, brought out the locals and tourists. The park overflowed with walkers and cyclists enjoying the sunshine. Off to one side, walkways led to the piers of Fort Mason, where I once worked and met Jon. On the other side, a sloping green lawn bordered the walkway down to the beach. As I slowly patrolled the parked cars, one pulled out and I slipped right in. Walking down the path to the waterfront, I watched the swimmers moving across Aquatic Park. The tide was going out. As they headed in the direction of the Golden Gate Bridge, they caught a free ride on the current, probably swimming faster than normal. But for those pushing against the current and going the other way, they slowed down like they were swimming through Jello.

I climbed up the concrete bleachers, stretched out in the sun, and closed my eyes. Around me, swimmers were chatting, pulling on caps and goggles, and heading down to the water debating on how long they'd stay in. I sat up and checked an app on my phone for the water temperature. It was between sixty-three and sixty-four degrees. Not warm by most standards, but wetsuits were scarce among the swimmers.

"It takes getting used to," Lena had said over and over. Since I didn't have a wetsuit, I wondered what my body would think of the chilly San Francisco Bay.

Hatch came into my mind again. He did say that some people docked nearby had lost money they invested with the Barlow brothers. Was he one of them? Could this all come down to a disgruntled client? Could I get him to tell me what part he had in this?

"Hey Trish," yelled Lena, walking down concrete steps toward me, her arms full. "I have everything you need. I stopped by your house and picked up caps, swimsuit, goggles, and towels. And some snacks."

She dropped them beside me and stood looking out at the water. "Lot of people today. Must be the good weather."

"Where's the locker room?" I asked.

"You're in it," she said.

"What?"

"You have to deck change. Don't worry, I brought you a huge

towel."

I picked up the red striped towel, wrapped it around my waist, and wiggled out of my work pants. Then I attempted to put on my swimsuit without the towel slipping. Not so easy. I literally draped the towel around my shoulders, managed to take off my work shirt, and pulled up the top of the suit.

"This isn't all that easy," I huffed, pulling up the straps.

"You'll get the hang of it," Lena said. "How was work?"

"Very helpful. I told them what I was investigating and they showed me that I missed some major information."

"Like what?" asked Lena as she stretched out her cap and slid it over her auburn curls.

"I flat out believed Hatch … never questioned him at all. He could be the killer. He really could," I said as I attempted to pull on my cap. I split it in half.

"Here," said Lena, handing me a black neoprene cap. "Put this on first. Now these." She handed me some squishy ear plugs.

"Is it that loud in the water? Who's going to be talking to me? The seals?" I asked.

"No, silly. It keeps the cold water out of your ears. You're warmer that way."

I fitted the neoprene cap on my head, fastened the chin strap, and then put in the ear plugs.

"Now this," said Lena.

"What?"

"Put this cap on top of that cap."

"Say again."

She put her face next to my ear and almost yelled, "Put this cap on top of everything."

"Okay, okay. Sorry I couldn't hear you with all this stuff on." The bright red cap was the finishing touch for my open water swim outfit. "So how do I look?" I asked my sister as I stood up and did a little pirouette.

"Annoying," she said. "You look annoying."

"What?" I said, smiling.

"Oh, never mind. Come on." She grabbed my arm and pulled me down the steps, across the sidewalk, and onto the sand. We were at the water's edge.

"Now," said Lena. "The water's going to feel cold at first. Just expect it. Walk in slowly. Let each part of your legs, your ankles, calves, thighs take the shock. You'll get used to it. Stop at about your waist."

I did as she said. But I was walking on tiptoes trying to keep as much of me out of the water as possible. I'd stop and then walk a few steps farther. Stop again. Then walk on until the salty bay water was lapping around my waist. The bottom half of me didn't feel cold anymore.

"I think I'm numb," I said to Lena.

"Sprinkle some water on your face, your neck—especially the back of your neck—and up and down your arms."

I followed her orders to a T.

"This alerts your body that it's going to get cold, fast," Lena said. "Feels warm."

"Maybe for you. I haven't been in open water in about a year."

"You big baby," my sister said. "Now you have a couple of choices. You can dip down in the water right here and pop right up and you're all wet. Or you can gently lean until your chest is in the water and take a few strokes with your head out of the water. Or you can just go for it and start swimming."

I decided on the dip. I took a breath and dunked every part of me under the water. It was so shallow I ended up sitting on the sandy bottom. Then I sprang back up as fast as I could.

"It's cold. Cold, cold."

"Yeah, but wait until you start swimming," said Lena as she paddled out toward the white buoys.

I took a deep breath and plunged after her. The water felt warmer.

Not Hawaii or Florida warm, but warmer. The sun toasted the top layer of the salty water, and I enjoyed feeling its rays as I turned my face to breathe. Lena and I were moving against the tide that was still ebbing, so it took a while for me to reach the first buoy. Lena was already there, floating on her back, looking extremely peaceful. She straightened up when I approached.

"What do you think?" she asked, water splashing around her neck.

"I'm either used to it or frozen," I said, spitting out a mouth full of San Francisco Bay.

"Probably frozen," she said, smiling. "Let's swim to the far end buoy and maybe a little further. You can sightsee. Look at the tall ships moored there. Tide's going out so we won't be pushed into them."

"Glad to hear that. Those boats look huge from down here."

I tagged along behind her, stroking faster and kicking harder, trying to keep up. It didn't work; she glided through the water effortlessly. I fell further behind, but I enjoyed the cool tingling water slipping past me. There was nothing to see in the water, not even my hands. Too much silt concealed the underwater view. But if I turned my head a little further when breathing, I noticed a green lawn with people stretched out sunbathing. When I lifted my head to sight on the last buoy, the tall ships Lena talked about grew huge to massive to gigantic. I started to swim back the other way.

Lena had stopped at the last buoy and waved me on. "Come on. You're going the wrong direction." But Lena didn't swim parallel to the tall ships. Instead, she headed into the center of the Cove. I didn't question. I just swam, making sure I didn't lose sight of her. The tide pushed us at twice the speed we'd been going when we first started. She stopped swimming and began treading water so I could reach her. The wind had picked up, and little wavelets pushed against the tide going in the opposite direction.

"Look," she said. "Look around you."

I could see the entrance to the cove, and about one and a half miles into the bay was the craggy small island that housed Alcatraz Federal Penitentiary, now a national park. Salty water hit the back of my cap and dripped down my face. Under the water, my legs and feet moved in circles, keeping me afloat. I gawked at the Golden Gate Bridge in the distance; it appeared like a toy replica.

"Wow," was all I could say since the choppy water made it hard to speak without swallowing mouthfuls.

"How you doing?" asked Lena. "We've been out close to twenty minutes. That might be enough for the first time."

"Getting tired. Arms feel like lead. Going in."

"I'm going to swim to the other side of the Cove opposite the Maritime Museum," Lena said.

I nodded and headed for shore, all the while thinking of Andy Barlow out in the middle of the bay. How long had he been out? Was he tired? Cold? Did he want to get out of the water?

I swam in until my feet touched the bottom, then headed toward the concrete steps. Draped in a towel, I pulled off my suit and slipped on the sweats Lena had brought for me. Then I started to shiver. The sun glared in the sky, but its heat didn't reach me. Stretching out on the warm concrete and letting its warmth filter through me helped. My whole body tingled, feeling both tired and exhilarated.

With my eyes shut, I saw Andy Barlow in the choppy water. Depending on what the tides were doing, the current either pushed him away from the boat or toward it. Whoever piloted the boat had to have water knowledge so he could keep the swimmer close but not too close. Hatch Grey might be that person.

"Well, that was refreshing," said a dripping Lena after skipping up the concrete steps toward my prone body. She stood over me and shook her strawberry-blonde corkscrew curls like a dog.

"Hey, cut it out." I sat up, shielding the sun with my hand.

"What'd you think?" Lena asked.

"I liked it. But it's taking a while to warm up." I looked past her out of the Municipal Pier. "You know what I was thinking?"

"Why didn't you try this before?" guessed Lena.

"No. What was Andy Barlow feeling when he was swimming? Only today did I realize how strong the tides and currents are. Is it possible that someone couldn't swim forward against a strong tide?"

"You bet," said Lena. She already had a towel draped around her and slipped off her swimsuit underneath.

"If that was the case, the culprit could have used the tide to his advantage. All he would have to do is make sure the rear of the boat faced Andy. Then let the tide do the rest."

"It sounds too easy. I would hope that any good swimmer could dodge the back of the boat," said Lena.

"But what if the driver put the engine in reverse and hit Andy, possibly knocking him out?"

"You have a vivid imagination," said Lena, now fully clothed and munching a handful of almonds. For a few seconds, we sat there quietly. The wind blowing in from the west picked up even more, and the flags near the historic ships slapped and snapped.

"Trisha? Trisha Carson? Is that you?"

The male voice came from the side. When I looked up, I was staring directly into the sun. His features were black against the brightness. All I saw was a silhouette.

Lena gasped. "What are you doing here?" she asked, moving between me and the faceless figure. I pushed to one side to take a clearer look. My mouth hung open. It was Brad, Bradley Carson, my runaway husband.

Chapter 27

"What are you doing here?" I choked the words out.

"In town on business," he said quietly and took a seat beside me. "When did you start swimming in the Bay?"

"Brad, you need to leave. Go back from wherever you came," said Lena.

"Hello to you too," said Brad, not even looking at my sister.

"I haven't signed your divorce papers yet," was all I could think of saying. My mouth felt caked with sand. Swallowing made me choke. For a moment, I forgot where I was.

"That's okay," he said. "Look, I want to talk with you."

"Well, that's not going to happen," said Lena with her hands on her hips. "Let's go."

I didn't move.

"Trish, come on."

I shook my head. "You go." I stared at Brad. "I think I better stay."

"If that's the way you want it," she said and picked up her towel and wet swimsuit and marched down the concrete steps without a look back.

Tentatively, I reached out and touched his arm. "It really is you."

Brad smiled. "Yep. I'm real."

"How did you know we were here?" I asked.

"I called your dad. He told me."

"Brad, where did you go? You never came home from work. I called the police, your job, all your friends, and finally your brother."

"Trisha."

"You know what he told me?"

"Trisha, please."

"He said you didn't want to be found."

Brad sighed. "I'm sorry. I wasn't …"

"I was your wife and you disappeared. You walked out."

"I'm sorry," he repeated.

"Just walked out."

He now had gray hair sprinkled in his sideburns like grains of salt. Reaching out slowly, he took my hand.

"It was a mistake," he said. "I thought I didn't want to be married. That I wanted freedom. But all I've done for the past few years is think of you … what you were doing … how you were … if you'd found someone else. I even dream about you." He stopped. "Have you … found someone else?"

"It's none of your business," I said, glancing out to the water in Aquatic Park. The wind blew harder now, pushing sharp grains of sand across the beach.

"You're not here on business, are you?"

"No. I wanted to find you and try and explain. I was a thoughtless idiot back then. But no longer."

"Okay you explained. What else do you want?"

Brad pulled his hoodie close to him. "It's cold here. Can we go somewhere else? Get out of the wind?"

I pushed my towel and the soggy swimsuit into the plastic bag Lena had brought me.

"I'm going home. I'll sign the papers and bring them to you."

"Trisha, please stay. I don't want you to sign the papers. I never stopped loving you. That's why I'm here. I want us to be us again."

I looked at him in amazement. "There is no us anymore."

"Please. All I want to do is explain what happened to me. Give me some time, okay?”

I stood up, ready to walk away and go back to the life I now had. My head buzzed. Where had he been? His eyes pleaded with me. I took a few steps away.

“Trisha. Ten minutes. That’s all I want, please.”

I turned to watch a swimmer walk out of the water, up the beach, to his girlfriend on the bleachers next to me. She waited with a towel that she lovingly wrapped around him. Then I turned back to Brad.

“Thirty minutes. That’s all you get.”

***

“This way,” Brad said as we walked up the remaining white concrete steps toward the Maritime Museum. “I’m staying at an Airbnb in that big apartment building at the top of the block.” He carried my plastic swim bag and the grocery bag filled with my work clothes.

“I’m cold. Not used to swimming in the Bay yet.” My teeth chattered. “I’m colder now than when I was in the water,” I tried to say, but my mouth wouldn’t let me form any words.

“Come here,” he said, and he stepped closer and put his arm around my shoulder. “We’re almost there.”

He stared at me as we walked. My body stiffened with each step, especially my legs. “Are you okay?” he asked. “You keep bumping into me.”

“After drop,” I mumbled. “Lena said you get colder after you get out of the water. Didn’t expect this.”

My balance was off and I walked like I had too much to drink. Frankly, I wasn’t sure this was after drop or just shock from seeing Brad appear out of nowhere.

***

His Airbnb was an elegant two-bedroom condominium with a wall-to-wall view facing the bay. I could see Aquatic Park and outside of the curved Municipal Pier, San Francisco Bay covered in angry little white caps. Alcatraz looked like a forbidden rock, a desolate spot for a prison. I could even see the Marin shoreline. Brad dropped my bags on the couch and ran into the bedroom while I stood there shaking, my teeth chattering. He yanked the bedspread off and folded it around me.

"I'll make you something warm to drink," he said, disappearing into the kitchen. "All there is is apple juice. Can I warm that up?"

The question, the tone, the voice pushed me back into the past. The good past when we talked to each other, joked about what was edible and what wasn't.

"Why not? That sounds good." Within a minute, I heard a beep from the microwave and Brad walked in with a coffee cup filled with warmed apple juice.

"That's all that's in here?" I asked.

"What? Sure. What else would I put in apple juice?" He reached out and gave me the cup.

"I had a bad experience with a date rape drug not too long ago," I said, taking a sip. The warm liquid washed through my body.

"You what?"

"Old news," was all I could say. The comforter and the apple juice connected for an agreeable combination. Holding the cup, my hands stopped shaking. With eyes closed, I drank a few more sips.

"Much better," I said. For the first time, I realized where I was. "Where did you go?"

"Costa Rica."

"Like in Central America?"

"Yeah."

"Why?"

"This is hard to say, but I'd been seeing someone, online."

"And she was from Costa Rica?"

"Yes."

"Okay, this all makes sense now." I stood up. "I'm going."

"I want you to listen." He sat down beside me, and I moved to the other end of the couch.

"Don't come near me," I said.

"Okay. Listen I have to …"

"Confess? Why don't you keep it to yourself? I don't care anymore."

"You gave me thirty minutes … now closer to twenty-five. Listen please."

His story was as old as time. Bored with life and wife, he struck up an online love affair with an exotic Latina. True soul mates who could never be together because he was married. He sent her money, almost all of our savings. But he took out enough for himself to buy a roundtrip ticket to San Jose, the capital. She met him there and they drove to the central coast about an hour from the airport. Brad thought she lived in or near an American ex-pat community called Playa Herradura. Not quite. She didn't live on the ocean. She lived in a small village outside Playa Herradura and worked at one of the resorts to support her two kids and parents. She used the internet when she worked. Her village didn't have internet access. In fact, it didn't have much at all.

"I realized I made a mistake as soon as I saw the tiny house her family lived in. I'd already given her most of my … ah, our money. I figured out pretty quickly that I would have to work. And this wasn't anything like minimum wage," he said.

What a jerk, I thought to myself.

"I picked up a job working on a fishing boat. The owners took American tourists and ex-pats out sport fishing for the day. Although the owners spoke some English, they wanted me to translate everything they said into English. I wanted to come home, be with you, but I was so embarrassed."

"You followed your dick," I said dryly. He stared at the carpet and started talking again.

"I lasted about nine months, not even a year. Then I flew back.

You'd left. Gone back to California. I moved to New Hampshire and lived with my brother and his family. That's where I've been. Finally got a job and my own apartment."

"So why are you here? It isn't for business, is it?"

"No." There was a long pause. "I came to find you. Can we try again, Trisha? Can you ever forgive me? We can start fresh."

I never answered his questions. I stood up, dropped the comforter on the couch. "I'm sticky from the salty water. My hair feels like straw. I'm going home. That's what you need to do. I'll sign the papers. It's over between us."

"Please don't go," Brad said. "You're the only thing that matters to me."

I held my breath as he slipped his arms around me, pulling me in close. His cheek brushed mine and I slowly exhaled.

And then he kissed me.

• • •

It was six thirty in the morning when I returned home to Marin. The Babe and my father walked in ten minutes after me. The twins were already getting ready for school.

"Where have you been, Trisha?" said Dad. I looked from face to face. Dawson started to smile. "Your sister said you met up with your ex-husband and wouldn't leave."

I glared at him.

"Now you've got to do the walk of shame," said Daria giggling. "What's in that bag? Your underwear?" She reached for the plastic bag and almost pulled it out of my hands.

"Stop that," I said.

"Trish, what are they talking about?" asked Dad. "Were you with Jon?"

I shook my head and headed for the stairs.

"Time for the walk of shame," hooted Dawson. Together the twins began chanting, "Walk of shame, walk of shame, walk of shame" as they left the house.

"Do you think she even remembers how to do it?" I heard Daria say heading for her car.

I slammed the door, took out my phone and texted my sister.

I fucked up. Literally and figuratively.

⚬——• • ⚬——•

Lena didn't want to hear about it. In fact, she didn't answer my text or even my calls.

The whole time I spent with Brad, there was no Jon. He didn't exist. I only thought about him when I drove through the Robin Williams Tunnel. Reality slapped me in the face. What had I done? But more importantly, why? Brad said he wanted to see me before he left. But that wasn't going to happen. "One for the road" sex was over. Completely. I hoped.

I managed to shut the mental door on both Brad and Jon. Instead, my thoughts fixated on Hatch Grey. Before another trip to the marina, I contacted Harrison. *I think I found the killer,* I texted.

His reply was a thumbs up emoji. And then, *I plan to go back to London at the end of the week.*

Have you heard anything from your mother?

A short cryptic reply. *No*

Couldn't this woman have waited a bit to remarry? Maybe a month or two? Until her son had time to grieve for his father.

I stripped off my work clothes that had seen double duty, as my young high school roommates told me. The 'walk of shame' clothes were tossed into my clothes hamper. I headed for the bathroom, and at the entrance, I pressed the button that warmed the bathroom floor and the towel racks. I turned on the shower and stepped into a cloud of steam. Hot water washed away my sins from last night. Should I tell Jon? Probably. Would I tell Jon? Another question all together.

Chapter 28

I had a text from Lena when I got out of the shower:

The flowerpot lady is here and wants to talk to you.

When I entered Lena's home, she managed to greet me but not look at me at the same time. She carried Little T and smiled at two women on the couch holding glasses of iced tea. Hildie, her cutoff jeans and Rosie the Riveter scarf replaced with dark blue leggings and a Beach Boys T-shirt, sat next to her mom. A small, plump woman with curly white hair and rosy cheeks, her short, chubby legs didn't touch the ground.

"Ladies, this is my sister, Trisha Carson. Hildie, I think you've met her before. She's taken an interest in what happened to Barlow & Barlow," Lena said with a sweet smile. Then she finally turned toward me. "Trisha, this is Mrs. Gunderson and her daughter, Hildie, who you met."

Lena took a step closer to me and shifted Little T to her other shoulder at the same time, coughing and whispering "skank" in my direction.

I moved away and faked a smile. "Your daughter was nice enough to give me some of your flowerpots. Lena said you wanted to talk to me?" I sat down on the chair next to the sofa.

Mrs. Gunderson nodded, and Hildie hemmed and hawed until her mother said, "Just tell her."

"I think you know my mother's story. The Barlow brothers went belly up. I thought they declared bankruptcy, but Mom received a nice letter from the brother who's still alive apologizing for the problems their company has been having and asking for patience until he sorts things out. He also asked her to consider making further investments with him. I told her to drop him like a hot potato."

Mrs. Gunderson sat up straight, lifted her chin, and said, "The Bible says to give people second chances." Hildie lifted both hands, palms up, as if to say, 'See what I'm dealing with?' and shook her head.

"Mom, the guy's a thief. A crook. A friend of mine said this was another Ponzi scheme."

"I don't know who Ponzi is or what it is," said the little woman now surrounded in a cloud of huffiness.

"I brought her here so she could talk to you," said Hildie.

"Me?"

"Your sister said you were investigating this whole mess."

Lena walked out of the room, grinning at me. "Need to change the baby," she said.

"She's mistaken," I started to explain. "I am helping the son of the brother who died."

"Oh," said Hildie, somewhat confused. "From what she told me …"

I cut her off. "I can tell you that reinvesting with Barlow & Barlow would be a bad idea. A really bad idea. Their financial company, if it's still a company, is … ah … let's say unstable."

"Who is Mr. Ponzi?" asked Mrs. Gunderson.

"The original?"

"Yes, please."

I pulled out my phone and typed in Ponzi scheme. "I want to make sure I get this right. Okay, on investors.gov from the Securities and Exchange Commission—and they're the experts—'Ponzi scheme is an investment fraud that pays existing investors with funds collected from new investors. Ponzi schemes are named after Charles Ponzi.'"

"He did it first?" asked Mrs. Gunderson.

"Yes. He got caught and they named this type of fraud after him."

"So, for this to work, the company needs fresh blood, all the time. Kind of like a vampire," said Hildie.

"So to speak. Only the blood is money. If the company can't get more money or if clients want to withdraw their money at the same time, these things tend to collapse. Because they never invested anything, they don't have any money to pay out," I said.

"Where did it go?" asked Mrs. Gunderson, completely confused.

"Based on this," I said, pointing to my phone, "Ponzi schemes offer returns that are too good to be true. In reality, if many clients want to withdraw large amounts at the same time, that money would come from new investors. Barlow & Barlow never invested those funds in the first place. When they ran out of money, they were bankrupt."

"How could they run out of all that money?" asked Hildie.

"I think Andy Barlow was using Barlow & Barlow as his own personal bank account to pay his gambling debts," I said.

"Oh my," said Mrs. Gunderson.

"That's why I think this very nice letter from Mr. Martin Barlow is not worth your time. He needs your investment to get back on his feet. I think it's to pay himself, if you want my opinion."

"Oh," said a deflated Mrs. Gunderson. "I wanted to help him out."

"I'm no financial advisor, but I don't think you'd ever see that money again."

"I told you so," said Hildie. "He cheated you, mom. But you weren't the only one."

"It looks that way," I said. "I'm sorry. I'm sure they had many clients like you that have been left high and dry."

"Remember I told you, Mom? Evan—that's my husband," she said to me and Lena, "lost some of our savings. So did a big chunk of the local marine industry."

"Well, I don't know what to say. And it's all because of this Mr. Ponzi?" Mrs. Gunderson asked.

"Come on, Mom, let's go. We've taken up enough of Trisha and her sister's time."

Hildie took her mother's arm and lifted her gently to her feet. A deflated balloon had more pizazz than Mrs. Gunderson.

"All of my money really is gone," Mrs. Gunderson said, finally accepting the horrible fact that she had been scammed, hoodwinked, duped.

"Mom, let's go," said Hildie quietly, and they walked out the front door. I could see Mrs. Gunderson shaking her head.

Lena walked back into the living room, minus Little T.

"That poor woman," I said. "I hope her daughter can convince her not to give that defunct firm any more money."

"You already did that."

"From what I've learned, he lost the firm's money in Vegas. I'm guessing he borrowed too much money from some lowlifes, gambled it away, and now they want it back," I said.

Lena walked over and shut the front door. Then she fixated on me.

Here it comes, I thought.

"Dad called last night."

"Oh," I said, trying to sound nonchalant.

"He wanted to know where you were. He said Brad called looking for you."

I nodded and sighed. "Lena, I don't know how to explain what happened."

"Well try, okay? Give it your best. The last I saw you was yesterday on the concrete steps at Aquatic Park with that … that phony husband of yours. Then I heard you didn't come home last night. Even those teenagers living at Earl's house knew what you were doing."

"It was a mistake. I was angry at Brad. I really was."

Lena snorted. "Most people don't fall into bed with someone they haven't seen in years and are still angry with."

"Brad wanted to talk to me. Thirty minutes, he said. That's all. So, we went back to his place. It was actually pretty nice. Big windows overlooking San Francisco …"

"I'm not interested in your travel review. How could you spend even three minutes with that man, let alone thirty minutes?"

"I can't answer that. I was getting ready to leave and then he hugged me. The next thing I knew, all my clothes were on the floor and we were in bed."

"Oh, Trisha, I can't believe you have so little self-control. What about Jon? Did you ever think of him? Even once?" asked my sister.

"Honestly, no. I fucked up. There's Brad, and then there's Jon."

"Not a difficult choice, if you ask me," Lena said.

"I don't want to talk about it anymore."

"I'm going to tell Jon if you don't."

"Don't you dare."

"Well, I should," she said.

As if on cue, Dr. T walked through the front door. He glanced at me and then Lena.

"What did I miss?" he asked.

"You don't want to know," I said, pushing past him.

"Is the baby okay?" He was clearly concerned.

"Trisha has turned into a two-timing …" That was the last thing I heard as I closed the front door behind me.

<hr>

Before I pulled out of Lena's driveway, I called Hatch Grey and asked him to meet me at a coffee shop in Tiburon. Although surprised, he promised to be there in forty-five minutes. After a leisurely drive to the small waterfront town, I spotted him immediately when I walked in to 94920, the coffee bar named after the ZIP code of Tiburon. He sat toward the back of the café wearing a ratty navy blue wool cap and a heavy black sweatshirt. His head nodded to the invisible music only he could hear through his headphones. I ordered and picked up my coffee, then walked slowly in his direction. I wasn't sure what I was going to say. I had to be careful. This might be Andy Barlow's killer.

"Hatch?" I tapped him on the shoulder. Startled, he looked up. Gray stubble grew on his chin, but his dark eyes were direct and clear. He motioned for me to have a seat.

"What's this all about? It sounded like you needed to see me."

"It's about Harrison Barlow, Andy's son. He's sure his dad was killed. That it wasn't an accident. I think it might be connected to the brothers' financial problems. Can you help me out? Do you know anything about the Barlow brothers and their financial company?"

The sailor sighed. "Well, I got to know both brothers. Never met them before. We didn't run in the same circles, if you get what I mean. They were out of my league financially."

"Were they the friendly type?"

"More silly than friendly. They didn't know the first thing about boats and yet they bought this big family powerboat. They thought it would be like driving a car. When they found out that it wasn't, they'd come down the dock and talk to me. I recommended that they get someone to teach them how to use the boat and what the rules of the road were on the Bay … things like that. They took my advice. Talked to the harbormaster and she suggested a guy I knew by reputation. He helped them a lot. The one son, Dawson, was a natural. He picked up terminology, tides, currents, boat handling in a jiffy. Both dads were competent but not the best sailors on the bay.

"Most of their time on the boat was spent tied up at the dock. Kind of like a party boat. Don't get me wrong. They weren't loud or drunk, but they liked to hang out and invite their friends on board."

I had to move this conversation, although interesting, to their business.

"You once mentioned that a number of people here invested with them."

"Yep, they did."

"Did you?"

"You think I have a lot of extra money?"

"I couldn't tell. For all I know, you could be a gazillionaire."

Hatch burst out laughing, a deep hearty laugh. "Not a gazillionaire. That's for sure. But I did invest a bit with them."

"Bet it was quite a shock when they went out of business."

"You could say that." Then he folded his arms across his chest and quietly watched me, almost daring me to ask another question. This conversation was ending if I read his body language correctly.

"Anything else?" he asked.

"Not really. I wanted to get a feeling for these men."

Hatch's expression didn't change.

"I was hoping someone who knew them might have an answer."

Hatch uncrossed his arms and leaned toward me. Started to talk. Then stopped. Then started again. "Andy had a reputation. Now, I don't often speak ill of the dead, but he liked money and girls. Not women, but girls, like his niece's age."

"Really? I heard he was a gambler."

The mariner took a deep breath and decided to tell me what he'd been thinking. "He once invited me to go to Las Vegas with him. That's not my scene, but I went anyway. Needed a break. And he paid for everything. Airplane, hotel, even food. He wouldn't let me pay, even for a beer. All he said was 'put it on my tab.'"

"From what I could see, he didn't win very much. He was always getting more money from a contact of his and losing it. Then trying to win it back. It was a sad thing to watch. I wasn't having much fun. I think gambling away money is ignorant, no matter how rich you are. And certainly not enjoyable. I left a day or two early. I think his firm's money was lost at the tables in Vegas and somebody wasn't happy about it. Maybe they took care of him."

"Took care of him, how?"

"Killed him."

"Any thoughts of who that might be?"

"I don't know. I never met the gangster types that funded him.

Maybe look at their list of clients.”

“Did anyone talk about getting even?” I asked.

“Nah. They talked about getting their money back. But no one really had a plan.”

“What about you? You said you invested with their company? You had to be upset when it disappeared?”

Hatch leaned back and crossed his arms again. A sly smile crossed his face. “I was just fine. I withdrew all my money after that trip to Vegas. I could see the handwriting on the wall.”

Chapter 29

Thanks to an overheard conversation, I learned that the wayward bride, Justine, returned home to Marin. While devouring breakfast this morning, Dawson mentioned that Harrison had texted him the news.

"Epic," said Daria, more interested in her waffles. "Is Pops back?"

"Dunno," replied Dawson.

Standing at the sink with my back to the twins, mini explosions detonated in my head. Justine had returned. When did she get back? Where was she living? Where was Marty? And why didn't someone tell me?

⁎

"Justine?" I called out as I thumped on her front door. "Open up! Now. Hello?" I pressed my ear to the front door, then leaned over to look in the tall front window. The quiet echoed downstairs of the large house.

"Justine, are you there? Please open up." The indifferent door coolly stood there and stared back at me.

"Hey! What're you yelling about?" said a female voice coming around the corner of the house. It was Justine. She stood there, her perfect hands on her perfect hips. If her face could sag, it would have. Exhaustion leaked through her façade. Her dirty knees complemented the streaks of mud across her cheeks.

"I need to talk to you. Please. It's about your husband. Make that your husband before your current husband. Andy."

"Come with me," she said and led me around the house toward the pool. Instead, we went off to one side where she had been gardening. She sat heavily on a white wrought iron bench and motioned for me to sit next to her.

"What do you want?" she asked. "And don't drag it out. I'm jetlagged and want to get a few hours' sleep before Harrison comes home."

I plunged right in. "How was your honeymoon?" I asked.

"Next question," she said sharply.

"You're married, right? You married Marty and left town for your honeymoon?"

"This is none of your business," she said.

"Where did you go?" I asked.

"Next question," she said.

"You left Harrison with nothing so much as a note."

"He's over eighteen," she said.

"His father just died. You marry his uncle and disappear. Please explain that to me." The intensity in my voice almost scared me. A warm flush crept up the back of my neck and spread across my cheeks. I felt dizzy. My pulse pounded in my ears. I leaned over and dropped my head between my knees, panting.

"Are you all right?" said Justine, her voice bending and stretching around me. I couldn't answer. Then a cold stream of water splashed across my face and down my neck. Another slap of water thoroughly soaked my T-shirt and hair.

I looked up at the woman with a garden hose in her hand.

"What are you doing?" I asked.

She shrugged. "I … you looked like you were about to pass out. What happened?"

I shook my head like a dog climbing out of a bath. "Too long to explain," I said. "Give me the hose. Please." She handed it to me and I put my face close to the water, drinking in sips until I felt my body fill up and return to normal. I splashed water on my hands, then on the back of my neck.

"There," I said handing her back the hose.

The frightened look on her face turned quizzical. "What just happened?"

"You disappearing like that triggered some old wounds of people leaving in my life. Sorry to scare you. Can we move over to the sun?" Shivers jolted through my arms. I stood up stiffly and walked to a lounge next to the pool.

"I'll be right back," Justine said. I picked up a towel draped across the chair and pulled it around my shoulders. The warmth calmed my body. Then I leaned back against the toasty lounger and closed my eyes.

"Here. Drink this. It's iced tea. I put a little sugar and lemon in it."

The amber drink gave me the boost that I needed. I sighed and sat up a little straighter.

"Thank you," was all I could say.

Justine collapsed in the lounger next to me. "Did you come to tell me what a bad mother I am?" she asked, shading the sun with her hand.

"I think so." I paused. "I wanted to ask you questions about Andy and why you married Marty so quickly after. But really, I wanted to know why you left your son."

A weak smile passed across my face.

"I'm sorry, but all this"—she swept her arms across the backyard —"has nothing to do with you. I think you should go home. Maybe we can talk later."

She grabbed my arm as I stood up and held it snugly as she walked me to my car.

"Are you sure you can drive?' she asked, watching me climb into the driver's seat.

"I'll be fine," I said, wondering if that was true. While I was backing out of her driveway, she walked along side of me and then stopped.

"Marty didn't come back with me."

"Do the twins know?"

She shrugged her shoulders. "Things didn't go that well between us. So, I came home."

"Daria and Dawson have been staying with me. But I think they belong with a family member. You and Harrison."

She threw up her hands and walked back toward the house. "Not now."

My mind buzzed on the drive home. Was Marty coming home, ever? If they married, did he leave Justine to clean up the mess from both brothers? Harrison must have told Dawson what was going on. And for sure, Dawson told Daria. Great. A nice little family network existed that managed to skip me. Had the twins moved into Earl's house for good?

I pulled into Earl's driveway with no recollection of how I got there. I couldn't remember one detail of the drive. Only the crunch of the tires on the stones outside the house woke me up. Dad once told me that what I just experienced was called highway hypnosis. My busy mind had hypnotized me, and I woke up at home. Perfect recipe for an accident.

The smart wallpaper was turned off when I walked into the tranquil living room. Whoever thought that painted walls, ordinary painted walls, could double as a tranquilizer? I veered off to the kitchen for a glass of cold water and then wandered back through the living room out to the deck. Long shadows snaked through the branches of the tall redwoods in the canyons. A visual paradise. I let out a huge sigh, sat down, and rested my feet on the deck railing.

Drip by drip, the adrenaline leaked out of my body. A nap was in order. My eyes closed, but instead of being soothed by the sweet singing birds in the canyon, I visualized myself yelling at Justine. "How could you leave?" I asked over and over. Maybe I should have 'Everyone leaves' tattooed on my shoulders. I thought I had worked through my mother dying when I was a teenager and my father walking out of the house after I graduated from high school, leaving me to raise an elementary school girl, and then Brad Carson, my now in-touch husband, one day heading off to work and never returning.

Obviously, I hadn't worked through anything. Justine's disappearance brought it all back. A hand pressed down on my shoulder. I gasped as I jumped up.

"Trisha? You okay?" said Dad. "You were snoozing away and then started mumbling in your sleep." He sat down in a chair opposite me.

"Things have been better," I said. My thumping heart quieted and moved into a steadier rhythm.

"Wanna talk about it?" asked Dad.

"The twins' father is still out of town, but their aunt … stepmother, I don't know what to call her … is back. I went to see her." Then I shut my mouth. More than once, Dad had tried to make amends for his disappearance. Bringing it up now (although that's what I wanted to talk about) would only make him feel worse. Again.

"And? Are they moving in with her?" he asked.

"I don't know."

"Here's my two cents. Let them stay here as long as they want. If this seems strange to you, can you imagine what they're going through? Why didn't their father come back?"

"She said things didn't go very well."

Dad tapped the side of his cheek. "Look at it from the kids' point of view. They know their aunt is back but not their father. Their whole lives have been turned upside down. We have a nice stable family here. Let them tell us when and where they want to go."

"Makes sense," I said. I leaned over and kissed Dad on the cheek. He smelled like sawdust and sweat with a touch of the sea.

"Were you at working on the pier at China Camp?" I asked

"Yep. My muscles are sore. Gonna take a shower," he said as he patted me on the head and meandered down the hall.

I texted Lena.
I'm losing my mind.
Her response.
Nothing new there.

Chapter 30

For dinner that night, the twins holed up in Daria's room and ordered delivery from a nearby Mexican restaurant. I wanted to go talk to them and find out what they planned to do, but Dad stopped me with a stern glance and a quiet but firm, "Leave them alone."

I couldn't ignore them if I stayed under the same roof, so I pulled on my running shorts, put The Babe on his leash, and called out, "Going for a run. Be back soon."

We headed down into La Cruz Canyon on the packed dirt path. The sky turned a deep yellow tinged with orange stripes as we disappeared down the hill. I decided to take a side path.

Plod. Plod. Plod. Each time I put my foot down on the path, small puffs of brown dirt flew off to the side. What an exhausting day. Learning that Harrison's mother was back home without her new husband. Almost passing out at Justine's house. Hovering behind that, my indiscretion with Brad, and finally the moral question of what to do about Jon.

I never saw the half-hidden branch connecting to one of the trees surrounding me, and I ran right into it. The force knocked me down right on my backside. I sat there a few seconds trying to take in what happened. I lifted my hand to brush away my hair. Both my hair and my hand were wet. With blood. It dripped down my face. The Babe came over and licked the blood off my face.

"No, don't, dog," I said, fumbling around in my shorts pocket for a tissue. What I found was grimy, downright nasty, but I pushed it onto my wound and held it in place. With my other hand, I pushed myself to a standing position with a groan.

"Let's go home, Babe," I said, walking unsteadily along the side path. Would I make it to my house before I passed out? My head pounded with each step. We reached the main path and I leaned over, trying to catch my breath before I started up the hill. I took the tissue off and a flow of rich, dark red blood trickled down my face. The tissue went back on.

"That should teach me," I said to the empty woods around me as I walked heavily up the trail. "Stay present," I muttered with each step. As The Babe and I reached the top of the hill, he took off, flying toward the house's front steps.

"Well, you're back soon," said Dad, leaning over to pet the dog. "Where's Trisha?"

I turned the corner to the house. "Here I am," I said. Dad straightened up and his face turned into a mask of concern.

"What happened to you? Your face, your shirt is covered in blood. Sit here," said Dad as he led me to the front steps.

"It's nothing. Really," I said. "I think the bleeding stopped." I reached up and patted my forehead. My hair stuck together, caked in drying blood. I reached for my phone as it started to ring. Lena was Facetiming me.

"Good God," she said, peering into her screen. "What happened to you? One of the criminals you've put away jumped you, didn't they?"

"Nothing that dramatic," I said, staring at the little square that was my face. I could see why everyone was alarmed. Streaks of rich red blood had dried on my cheeks, chin, and my T-shirt. I looked like the poster girl for an axe murderer movie.

"I was out running with The Babe and didn't pay attention. I ran straight into a tree branch. It didn't move, but I did. I landed flat on my ass."

"It looks pretty scary from this side," said my sister, her face now an inch away from her screen. "T, come here," she called, looking away from the phone.

"What happened to Trisha now?" I heard him say, and the two of them, cheek to cheek, peered into the screen.

"She has a hole in her head," Lena said, smirking, "But what's new about that?"

"Shut up. That's not funny. The blood's all dried up. And my forehead …" I pulled back my hair and felt the cut. Bright red blood coated my fingers. "I think I'm still bleeding and it's a lot deeper than I thought. Dad went to get me a washcloth." I turned around as he scurried down the steps with a basin of water, a cloth, and a towel.

"You need stitches," Dr. T said.

"You need to pay attention to where you're going," said Lena.

"I was distracted. A lot of things happening right now," I mumbled from behind the warm, damp cloth.

"Please tell me you weren't in a car," said Dr. T, moving his head back and forth to get a better view.

"No car. In the canyon with The Babe."

"Go get stitches," Dr. T said and then he disappeared.

"She'll call you back," Dad said.

"Wait," Lena yelled.

But Dad pulled the phone from my hand and said again, "She'll call you back," and hung up. "Now you sit still." He gently patted my face and rinsed the blood off, then rinsed again and again. Finally, he said, "Much better. Here, dry your face," and he handed me a towel.

"Why don't you run over to urgent care and see what they say?"

"Just put a Band-Aid on it. I'll be fine," I mumbled. But when I pushed aside my hair again, I saw a large flap of skin hanging from my forehead. "You might be right."

"Don't move." He walked to the kitchen and came out with a glass filled with ice cubes. "Hold them to your head. Here's some napkins."

I pressed the ice cubes to my forehead.

"Ouch." I winced.

"Want me to come with you?"

"No. I'll be …"

"Get in the car. I'm driving."

⁕

"Dad, could you speed up? At this rate, the clinic will be closed when we get there."

I watched out the passenger side windows as cars drove up behind us and then veered left to pass.

He ignored me. "Do you know where Harrison's mother and new stepdad were?"

"Thailand? The Philippines? Maybe?"

"Will Philippines return a criminal to the US?"

"I never thought of that," I said.

"Maybe he's going to let his new bride take the fall for the fraud he and his brother committed. I read somewhere that the firm of Barlow & Barlow declared bankruptcy. There are some very unhappy people left with nothing, especially if they're seniors and aren't working anymore."

"And they're from all over the Bay area. Not just regular people but businesses. I bet you're right. He's going to let Justine take the blame. She must be able to get out of it, don't you think?" I said.

"She'll need a good lawyer and money."

"Bet she can find both."

We were on the busy street that housed the urgent care clinic.

"Left turn coming up," I said to Dad.

"I know. I know," he said. The rhythmic clicks of the car's blinker sounded as Dad slowed down and then stopped, letting the traffic going the other way pass. I checked the passenger side mirror.

"Dad. Dad. Car coming up fast behind us. Heading our way. About a block away. But not slowing down."

Two bright lights grew closer and larger with each second. Dad looked in his rearview mirror.

"They're not stopping," I cried out, my heartrate spiking as the car grew closer.

Dad pressed the horn determinedly and it bellowed across the dark landscape. He flipped on the emergency blinkers. He stepped on the gas lightly.

"Stop! What are you doing?" I yelled out.

"Trying to get by this incoming traffic in the next lane."

"We'll be broadsided." I reached my foot over and clamped it down firmly on the brake.

"What are you …?" He took a quick look in the rearview mirror. "We're going to be hit. Nothing to do about it. Three seconds to impact. Push yourself against the seat," he said.

Three, two, one. Another second passed. I held my breath. No impact. No sound of breaking glass. Instead, a white sedan flew by almost close enough to touch.

"Missed us," I yelled, grabbing my phone to take a photo of the license. Dirt covered the California plate. But it didn't matter. I was too late. The car disappeared down the road and exited onto the highway going south.

Dad's face was pale. "Are you all right?" I asked him.

"We're safe," he said, looking at me. "I bet that person was talking on his phone."

He pulled into the driveway of the clinic and found a parking spot. I inhaled deeply and looked at my father, who was breathing heavily.

"That was on purpose," I said. "I know that car. I saw the guy, face covered with a surgical mask and hoodie around his head. I didn't see a phone. He stuck his hand out the window and pretended to shoot. He knew what he was doing. I know that guy, Dad. He pretended to shoot me before. In a parking lot."

"Why would he do that?"

"It has to do with Andy Barlow."

"Wait. Are you saying someone was really trying to scare us?"

asked Dad.

"Me. Not you. Someone doesn't like what I'm doing."

Chapter 31

Once home, I dropped some more ice cubes into a plastic bag and held it to my forehead as I climbed the stairs to my room. The twins had texted me that they were staying at Harrison's house for the night. The cell rang. It was Lena.

"What is it about you and hospitals?" she said.

"This wasn't a hospital. It was a clinic."

"Doesn't matter. Dr T thinks you're accident prone," my sister continued.

"Did you talk to Dad?"

"Yeah, and he told me all about your near accident."

"It wasn't an accident. Someone was trying to scare me," I said.

"Maybe somebody doesn't want you talking to people connected with Barlow & Barlow," said Lena.

"I told you that Justine is back, but Marty Barlow isn't."

"Where is he?"

"Probably where his money is," I said.

"And that would be?"

"Maybe Thailand? The Bahamas? Cuba? Who knows?"

"Do you still think that Andy Barlow was murdered?" my sister asked.

"More and more. Here's my scenario. Both brothers were very successful. Made a lot of money. Indulged themselves and their families. Maybe Andy lived way, way above his means."

"Okay."

"But Andy's real problem." I paused. "Gambling. He crashed his whole company because of his addiction. Add that to a minor recession and the well dried up. The money disappeared. I'm thinking that a client or maybe a group of clients banded together and decided to take out their revenge."

"But they would have to know about his personal life. His swimming," said Lena.

"He never hid that from anyone. So, it's possible. If it wasn't someone local, I'm betting his death had to do with the money lenders in Las Vegas. And I can almost guarantee you that these Vegas thugs tried to run Dad and me down tonight."

I paused and looked out at the blackness blanketing the trees growing in the canyon. In the distance, the 'whoooo' of an owl echoed across the expanse.

"Trish. Trish? You still there?"

"If the company is bankrupt and they committed some type of fraud, shouldn't everyone—meaning Marty and Justine—be panicked about losing their houses? The boat, the fancy cars?" I wondered.

"You'd think. If I was about to be thrown out on the street, I'd be in orbit," said my sister. I could hear Little T babbling in the background.

"I need to talk to a few more people. I'm missing something. It's like they have lost all their money, and nobody seems to care."

"Except those who killed Andy," remarked Lena.

"I think their longtime accountant/secretary, Viv, holds the key. I need to talk to her again, if she's not in jail."

***

The next morning, I took a chance.

"Babe, walk?" That's all I needed to say. The bulldog scampered over to the front door and steamrolled around in a circle. With good luck, Viv would be walking her dog at the San Quentin Beach again. I parked on the narrow street and walked down the wooden stairs to the beach. The tide left seagrass at the tide line as it ebbed toward the Golden Gate Bridge and the Pacific Ocean. The Babe took off running ecstatically back and forth, chasing other dogs. Off to the right, the Larkspur ferry moved slowly through the bay as it passed the channel markers on its way to the Larkspur Landing ferry terminal. I glanced up at the little hill where I had met Viv before. Was that an outline of a woman sitting on a bench or were the branches of the trees shaped like a person?

I jogged down the beach and then up the other wooden stairway with The Babe leading the way.

"Viv," I called out.

The older woman turned around looking for the voice that called her.

"Yes," she said, shielding her eyes from the sun as she stared in my direction.

"It's Trisha. We met the other week."

"Oh yes. Such a wonderful place to walk a dog," she commented as she turned and looked out at the bay again.

"Well, I'm actually here to talk to you," I said as I moved over to the bench and sat down beside her. She greeted me with a sad smile.

"You're not in prison and your dog is right here with you," I said. "That's what you were worried about last time we met." She had that thousand-yard stare locked on the water in front of her. Then she turned toward me.

"I'm cooperating," she said.

"With who?"

"The SEC. The Feds, and with anyone else they want me to talk to."

"Can you talk about it?"

"No, not really."

"I'd like to ask you some more questions. But you let me know if I get too nosey," I said with an encouraging smile.

"I'm not sure that's a good idea." She stood up, ready to walk away.

"Please, this won't take long. I promise to respect what you can and can't talk about it."

"No." She took a few steps toward the path to the beach. I had to make this work. I had no one else to talk to.

"Did you know that Marty Barlow married his brother's wife?"

She turned quickly toward me, opened her mouth, and then closed it again. "Yes, I was told that."

"Where do these steps go? I asked, pointing to another set of wooden steps that faced San Quentin.

"A small beach that you can only get to when the tide's low," she said. Her little dog sprinted down the steps with The Babe following close behind. Viv took hold of the railing and we walked down the worn steps past succulents with fleshy green leaves the size of small plates. On this side of the point, a few houses cozied up to the rocky beach. Not more than a hundred yards away stretched the large, almost empty parking lot for the prison. I followed her carefully as she lightly trod on the now exposed mud over to a little cove with huge pieces of driftwood and a few water-scrapped tree trunks. Viv pulled a ball from her pocket and tossed it to her little dog, who was sniffing the seagrass and undersized crabs that had washed ashore. Both The Babe and her pup went flying after it.

"Why do you think they got married? That seemed so odd to me."

"Well, the Barlows, both brothers—especially Andy—were extremely competitive. And Andy was known to have a roving eye. Marty knew about it and tried to … how do I say this … comfort his brother's wife. When Andy died, maybe it gave them a chance to express how they really felt about each other. But I don't have any facts. It's only a guess."

"What was Andy like?"

Viv's face lit up. "Funny, happy, always happy. He loved people.

His family. His clients. His friends. And he was a wonderful salesman. He could sell anything to anybody. I would say over and over, 'You could sell ice cubes to the folks at the North Pole.'"

It was obvious she adored the man.

"He'd always say to me, 'For you, Viv, there's a discount.'" She paused and sighed. "I miss him. I really do."

"So, if he was such a good salesman, I'm guessing that he brought in the clients and Marty took over from there?"

"Kind of like that," she said quietly.

"Were Andy and Marty, for that matter, good fathers?"

"Yes, they loved their kids. But something, at least in the past five, maybe six years, was wrong. I'm not sure if it was the business or their marriages. Or something else."

"What do you mean?"

"Marty seemed to be working harder than ever. My appointment ledger was full of prospective clients. You'd expect both men to be thrilled with the influx of new money, but they always felt it was never enough. Especially Marty. He wanted Andy to …"

She stopped.

"I heard that Andy was a gambler. Do you think he used the firm's money to pay off his gambling debts?"

Viv shook her head. "I'm getting into an area that I probably shouldn't be talking about. Next."

"Okay. Sorry." I walked over toward the chain-link fence surrounding the prison parking lot.

"Harrison thinks his uncle killed his father." I stopped. That should elicit some response from Viv. But I was wrong. She quietly picked up the ball and threw it again, this time into the bay. Her little dog stopped at the water's edge, but The Babe leaped into the cold water, paddled out to the ball, picked it up, and paddled back. He reached the beach and shook, so that water flew everywhere.

"Are you asking for my opinion?"

I nodded.

"Why would he do that?"

"Maybe he was angry about the business … or maybe he wanted to have Justine all to himself?"

"I wouldn't know." She called her dog and began picking her way through the rocks that had been exposed as the tide dropped. "It's time for us to leave."

"One more question. Did they own their own homes?"

She paused as if deliberating what to say. "As far as I know, they did. Or maybe some kind of company did."

"What kind of company?" I asked.

"That's as much as I can tell you," she said. "I don't know anything else."

Chapter 32

Text messages flew non-stop to my phone. Harrison, Daria, and her brother. Even Justine. They all said the same thing.

Emergency. Get here quick.

If it was that much of an emergency, why didn't they call 911? I tried phoning all of them, but no one picked up.

A text came in from Daria.

Locked in the pool house.

I replied with, *Call 911*

Too dangerous, she texted back.

I didn't understand. How could this be too dangerous to call the police? I quickly looked through my phone contacts and clicked on the number for Detective Mark Hamilton, a police officer I met when my next-door neighbors turned out to be international hackers. It went to voicemail.

"This is Trisha Carson. Remember me? Please get the police to Justine Barlow's house. There seems to be a major emergency, but for some reason, they don't want to call 911. Maybe they can't. I think this might have something to do with her late husband Andy's gambling."

Although Daria thought a call to 911 would put her in peril, I didn't. I called them and repeated my message.

I jogged out to the car, taking The Babe with me. But someone needed to know where I was going.

I called Lena and left a voicemail message. "Seems like a major problem over at Justine Barlow's house. Going now. I called 911."

Road construction slowed down my trip, but eventually I drove up their pebbly driveway and beat the police. Parked off to the side was the white sedan. I knew who was inside. The big wooden double doors were wide open. Nothing looked out of place as I hurried up the steps, stopping to peer into the house through the windows. I hesitated crossing the doorway into the house. Were the men still inside?

"Hello," I called out. No answer. In fact, I could swear I heard an echo. "Harrison? Justine? Are you here?"

Behind me came the sound of feet running on gravel. The two men headed directly for the white car, never glancing my way. They hurtled themselves into the vehicle and sprinted down the driveway, throwing dirt and rocks into a dark cloud. I watched as they careened onto the main road, running down the Barlow's mailbox.

Only then did I slowly and quietly walk into the deserted open corridor. I'd take a few steps, then stop and listen. I moved over to the wall, pressed myself against it, and oozed forward, still not sure I was safe. Slipping into the spacious living room, I headed for the stairs.

"Harrison? Are you there? I'm coming up," I called out. The staircase stretched up to the second floor and grew with each step. Would I ever get there? A scent of fear drifted down the length of the dim hallway. All the doors stayed shut. I inched over to Harrison's room and haltingly reached out to the door handle, unexpectedly cool to the touch. It opened easily. I gasped at what I saw.

Harrison had been zip tied, hands together in the back. Legs zip tied at the ankles. Dull gray masking tape across his mouth.

"What happened?" I said, approaching the bed. His large dark eyes watered with fear. "I'm going to take the tape off. I'll be as careful as I can."

He nodded and closed his eyes. I carefully pulled the tape off his mouth, stopping if he winced or shuddered. Finally, the limp duct tape dropped to the bed.

"Harrison, where is your mother, your cousins? Are they here?"

He opened his mouth, worked his jaw back and forth, and gulped down a mouthful of air. Grabbing a pair of scissors from his desk, I sliced the zip ties into pieces. Harrison stared at me, strangely distracted, then down at his wrists.

"These men came here looking for Dad."

"Where is your mom?"

"They said he owed them money. A lot of money. Like millions."

"Harrison, look at me. Where's your mom?"

Harrison babbled on about the money his father owed. I ran out of the room into the shadowy hall, opening each door. Finally, I threw open the door to the master suite. Justine lay on the bed, duct tape over her mouth, zip ties holding together her wrists and ankles. Panic pumped across her eyes as she saw me, then alarm.

"It's all right," I said. "It's just me, Trisha. I'm here to help. You'll be free in a minute." As with Harrison, who now walked down the hall in our direction, I tentatively pulled off the tape covering her mouth. She exploded with, "Oh god. Where's my son? Harrison, are you okay?"

He flew through the bedroom door and flung himself at his mother, hugging her while I clipped through the zip ties. She grabbed him and sobbed into his shoulder.

"Are you okay? Tell me you're okay."

Harrison whimpered, "Why did they do that? I don't know anything about Dad's debts." The mother and son sat on the edge of the patterned bedspread comforting each other.

"Is there anyone else in the house," I asked, looking around.

"Daria, but I don't know where she's hiding," said Justine.

"She texted me that she was hiding in the pool house."

Justine looked up, not sure what I'd just said.

"Pool house? I asked again.

"Downstairs. Outside," said Justine.

A light breeze ruffled through the leaves on the trees next to the pool. At one edge was a small pool house with two changing areas on either side. I faced three doors decorated with sketches of whales and dolphins. Slowly and steadily, I reached out my hand and rested it on the door handle of the pool house.

"Daria," I said in a quiet voice. No response. A little louder. "Daria, are you in there?"

I paused, afraid to open the door. What if she was injured or worse, dead? Suddenly, the door flew open and Daria whooshed by me, holding a long rubber plunger.

"Don't come near me," she yelled, half crying.

"It's me. Trisha," I said, reaching out to her. She froze. The plunger dropped from her hand and bounced along the pool deck until it rolled into the water.

"Oh Trisha," she said, running toward me and grabbing me so tightly we almost tumbled over.

"Sit down," I said, leading her to a lounge chair. I grabbed a can of sparkling water from a nearby cooler. "Here. Take this." I watched as she downed the drink. She didn't seem hurt, just terrified.

"I ran out of the house when I heard the men yelling," she said between gulps.

"What men?" I asked.

"Two men. Gangster types from Vegas, looking for Uncle Andy."

"What did they want?" I asked, but I already knew the answer.

"Money, lots of it. They said that Uncle Andy owed some guy they worked for millions of dollars. And they were here to collect."

"He didn't know that Andy was dead?"

"I don't know. I heard him talking to Aunt Justine. Harrison kept butting in trying to protect her, but they pushed him and he fell. I stood right there listening to everything," she said, pointing to the side door. "When I bumped into the door, the guy yelled, 'Who else is here?' and started walking in my direction. I didn't know what to do, so I ran to the pool and locked myself in the pool house.

"Are Harrison and my aunt okay?"

It was less than five minutes before the police arrived. Harrison and his mother hunched together on the couch and tried to answer the officers' questions. But the story they told seemed so wild. Henchmen from Las Vegas traveled to quiet Marin to shake down an investor for the money he owed their boss. But Andy was dead, had been dead for a few weeks, and his wife and son knew nothing about his bills. Or so they said. It didn't matter to the henchmen. Their only job was to get the money, or someone would get hurt. They pressed the two about the insurance. Did they receive it? Did Marty have it? Eventually, one of the guys took pity on the pair and instead of breaking an arm or a leg, saw them for what they were … family members who knew nothing about the gambling debts.

Daria began crying when the police tried to question her, and she hadn't stopped yet.

They wanted to know how I happened to be there. I explained that before the men had a chance to tie everyone up, the family texted me to get here quick. I had called 911. For a change, I kept my mouth shut and only said I was a friend of the family.

Dawson, the missing brother who had been hiding on the grounds of the property, showed up some time between the second and third police car.

"Who are you?" they asked him. It took a while to explain. He sat beside his sister and took her hand. I heard him say, "Sorry I left you. But when you ran out, I headed for the back door, ran down the hill, and jumped into the hedges."

I looked over the group before me as the police chatter on the radio added to the confusion of the family.

"You're all related?" asked one cop.

"Yeah, we are," said Harrison. "This is my mom and these are my cousins."

"We're now stepbrother and sister," chimed in Daria, whose tears had finally stopped.

"Excuse me," said an officer. "I don't understand."

Justine began to explain the complicated relationship to the policeman. I walked over to the cop standing behind him.

"Is it okay if I go home now? I'm really a bystander. Not much more."

"Let me get your information so we can contact you," he said.

I almost ran out of the house. The flashing blue lights on the police cars cast long strange shadows on the trees. The blue lights reflected off the windows giving the scene a creepy 'fun house' appearance.

"Excuse me," I said to one of the policemen. "I'm going to pull my car out."

The policeman standing there glanced at me. "Have they let you go?" he asked. Then he looked again. "I know you. You just called me and told me to get over here," he said. "You helped … when was it, last year? … track down that hacking ring that wanted to shut—"

"Yeah, that was me," I interrupted. "You're Detective Mark Hamilton, aren't you?"

"Yes, that's me."

"Thanks. Can someone move this police car?" I said, trying to smile. I didn't want to talk about tracking down my malware-hacking neighbors who were now either in prison or out of the country. Somehow discussing the cases I worked on revived all the trauma that went with each one. Not fun for me, since I tend to run hot when it comes to apprehension and worry.

"Ever think of becoming a cop?" he asked as he opened the police car door.

"That would be a resounding no," I said. "I don't have the temperament. Besides, I'm too old."

He backed his police car out of my way. As he slowly moved past me, he stuck his head out of the driver's side window. "No, you're not. You've got good instincts," he said.

"I'll think about it," I called out to the cop as I backed up and headed for home. "That will never happen," I mumbled to myself as I pressed down the accelerator.

Chapter 33

Although I planned to go home and try to sort out what actually happened tonight, and the man who tried to run me off the road, I turned left onto the freeway and headed to Lena's house. I spoke into my phone.

"Text Lena."

"What do you want to say?" answered the friendly voice. As weird as it seems, I like to think that that friendly voice is not floating around in space but is secure inside my cellphone.

"*I'm coming over. Period. Need to talk. Period. Send.*"

Within sixty seconds, Lena sent me an *OK*.

Although it was almost eight and moving from a quiet dusk to the deep blue of a late summer night, Dr. T was outside entertaining the local kids with stories about his work as a physician in the San Francisco Emergency Room. The hood was up on his beloved black Charger, and the boys and girls stood next to him, peering at the engine as he talked. They were waiting for him to say, "Can someone start the car for me?" at which time there would be a fight and numerous "Me" "Me" "Pick me" from the kids.

"Hey Trisha," he said as I parked out in front of the small house. "Love the stitches. Let me take a look." I stood quietly as he prodded the ten stitches under the bandage on my forehead. "Nice job," he said.

Lena was sitting on the steps to the front porch, holding the chubby hands of Little T as he attempted to walk up steps that were half his size.

"You won't believe what just happened," I said.

"If you're involved, I probably won't," said Dr. T. "Kids, okay, that's it for this evening. Tomorrow we'll continue with more tales from the ER. Maybe I'll tell you about the kid who lost his first tooth. He was lying on the couch at the time, and it fell into his ear and his parents couldn't get it out, so they brought him to the ER."

"Gross," said the kids in unison.

"Now get on home," he said, shooing them away. "So? What happened to you?" he asked. He reached over and picked up his son, who immediately grabbed his father's nerdy black-framed glasses. He took Lena's hand and pulled her to her feet.

"Your story about the tooth fairy's strange extraction sounds interesting, too," I said, following Lena into their home. "So here it is. Las Vegas mobsters have come to Marin,"

They both turned around and stared at me.

"Say what?" asked Dr. T.

"I got a bunch of emergency texts from Justine Barlow, Harrison Barlow, Daria, and her twin basically saying, 'We need your help, now!'"

"And of course, you responded." said Lena.

"I called 911 first."

"Trisha to the rescue. Did you wear your cape?" asked Dr. T.

I glared at him. "Not funny. They reached out to me. What was I supposed to do?"

I described the scene I walked in on when I arrived. Zip tied mother and son. Frantic Daria about to attack me with a plunger.

"And why did this happen?" asked Dr. T.

"Evidently Andy Barlow had racked up more than two million dollars in debt from some Vegas gangster. The guy sent these thugs to threaten the family if they didn't pay his bills. And I think these were the guys who tried to run into Dad and me."

"Wow," was all Lena could say as she listened to the story.

"I'd say the police hadn't heard a story like this before from all the reactions and facial expressions. They questioned me as well, but since I didn't know anything about anything …"

"Not true," said Lena.

"Well, they didn't need to know that," I said. "Anyway, I left. And here I am."

Terrel shook his head. "Understanding you the way I do …we do …" he said, pointing at Lena, "what are you going to do? Let it drop is what I recommend."

I started pacing around the living room, thinking out loud. "What if these gangsters tried to get their money back earlier, like one or two months ago. They quickly found out that Andy didn't have anything worth of value left, so they threatened him and then killed him. They could be the murderers."

Lena walked down the hall to Little T's room and called out to me, "That doesn't make sense. If they knew Andy was dead—and they would, especially if they killed him—how could they get their money back? Were they trying to shake down the family? He must have owned things they could sell to clear the debt. His house, that boat. I bet more than that."

"Well, his secretary told me the house and boat were owned by some offshore company. I wouldn't be surprised if everything else he owned was in that offshore company."

"What happened to the family?" Lena asked as she walked back to the living room.

"I honestly don't know. I left. I probably should check in with them," I said, reaching for my phone.

I called Harrison and he picked up immediately.

"Are the police still there?" I asked. I heard the sound of a car engine and some chit chat in the background.

"No, they left not long after you did."

"What did they tell you to do?" I asked.

Justine responded. "They said go somewhere else for a few days."

"Am I on speaker phone?" I asked.

"Yes," responded four voices.

"Are you going to Marty's house?" I asked.

"No," said Justine, "The police think these thugs know about that, too."

"Well, what then? Are you going to a hotel?"

"We're going to your house, right now," said Harrison.

My house buzzed with frantic activity and loud voices when I walked in the front door. The twins stood in the kitchen making peanut butter and jelly sandwiches with the help of Earl. Justine and Harrison sat in the living room. Fortunately, Dad turned the LED wall off, so all that surrounded them was plain old calming paint. Dad listened as they rambled on about gangsters, Las Vegas, the police, and debts, big debts. Instead of offering compassion and maybe some sympathy, he bit his lower lip. He was trying not to laugh.

"I'm sorry I didn't get a chance to explain what was up," I said.

"Well, there was that foggy text you sent that said company was on its way over."

I made a face. "Not clear, was it?"

"No Trisha, it wasn't. Can you follow me for a moment?" He took Justine's hand as he stood up. "Now you wait right here. I need to have a little chat with my daughter." As he walked by me, he grabbed my arm. "This way."

He pulled me down the hall into his bedroom and quietly closed the door.

"Why are these people here?"

"I don't know. I didn't invite them. They came up with the idea themselves when the police told them to find another place to stay for a while."

"A while? Don't you think you should have at least asked Earl?

Maybe mentioned it to me before they showed up."

"I was over at Lena's telling them about what happened at Justine's house. The police let me go and I needed to talk this big mess through, so I drove to…"

"What did the police want with you?"

"Nothing. That's why they let me go. I showed them the texts everyone, meaning all four of them, sent me. But I had nothing else to tell them."

"Why did they text you?"

"I don't know. Ask them. I wasn't trying to blindside you and Earl. When I called to check up on them, that's when they told me they were headed this way."

"Oh Trisha, how did you get yourself in the middle of this mess?"

"I didn't mean to." I walked over and hugged him. "I'm sorry. I didn't know this would happen."

By the time Dad and I rejoined the group in the rest of the house, Earl had found a place for everyone to sleep. Dawson and Harrison were installed in a room that normally would be called the basement, but a very elegant basement.

Justine and her niece/stepdaughter Daria were in a room next to Dad. Earl put out fresh towels in all five of the bathrooms, dug up comfy robes, and made sure there was a pot of herbal tea at the ready in the kitchen. Earl, the consummate host, glowed as he organized his new guests. Handling four unexpected people who had just been traumatized was a piece of cake for the retired entrepreneur.

The house settled into a peaceful calm. I sat in the living room by myself, wondering if the puzzle of Andy Barlow's death had solved itself. I understood that the man who loaned Andy money wanted it back, so he sent some guys to terrorize the family. Did they hire someone to kill Andy out on the bay? Was that someone on board when the Nereus left the dock? But how did I fit in the picture? Had I become an opponent looking for Andy's lost money?

I tucked my feet underneath me. My phone jiggled. Brad wanted to see me again. I deleted it. Another text from Brad pleading me to meet him. Another delete. What a mistake I made spending the night with him. Although I had to admit, our little interlude satisfied me more than I wanted to say. Somewhere down deep I knew I needed to have a conversation with Jon about my indiscretion. That might mean the end of my relationship with him. I couldn't let this stand the way it was. He deserved better than that. I texted him.

Talk soon?

Lost in thought, I never heard Justine pad down the hall, wrapped in one of Earl's comfortable robes.

"Oh!" She started when she saw me. "I thought everyone was in bed."

"Not yet," I said.

"I'm going to get some tea. Want a cup?" she asked with a tired smile.

"Sure."

In a few minutes, she anchored herself on the other end of the couch, gave me the tea, and stared off into space.

"Can I ask you a question?" I said to the deflated woman.

"Do you have to? I'm not in a mood to talk about anything."

I ignored her. "Why did you ever marry your dead husband's brother? Were you in love with him?"

Justine sampled her tea like she was pondering the meaning of life.

"I'm not sure," was all she said. She took another sip of the amber liquid. "Life with Andy had its ups and downs. Recently more down than up. I knew there was a problem with the company, but he wouldn't say what. Yes, he was a gambler. I knew that before I married him. And I'm not one of those women who never looked at the bank account. I did and I saw money flying out the door. Our house had a second mortgage on it. Credit cards were maxed out. And you know what Andy did about it? He swam. He took himself out on that expensive boat we didn't need and spent hours in the Bay. That was his escape.

"Then there was his eye for the ladies. Girls, actually. He used his niece Daria to meet her friends and then, well, one thing led to another, so to speak."

"But these girls were underage."

"He didn't care. He always led a privileged life getting whatever he wanted. Now the money was gone. He knew the business was about to go under. He owed money to everyone. And he was running after teenagers."

I sat in shock listening to Justine. "Did you ever—"

She cut me off. "What? Talk to him? Of course. Threaten to leave? More times than I can say. In fact, I'd made up my mind to divorce him and move to London to be closer to Harrison. The only person I could talk to was Marty. He'd listen. He was kind and said he could offer me a better future. That I should think about it. Then Andy died and Marty's proposal seemed a way out of an empty life. He promised that Harrison could continue on with his studies in London. That was the clincher for me. So, I married him."

Justine lifted herself off the couch with a heavy sigh. "Need to try and sleep. I never expected that today I'd be bound and gagged by someone from the Las Vegas mafia."

"That's who they were?" I was hoping for more information.

"Who else would do something like that to get their money back?"

She had a point. I didn't know much about gambling with someone else's money or the mafia or loan sharks in Las Vegas, but Justine's reasoning made sense to me.

With the house now in complete silence, my mind drifted to everything I knew about Andy Barlow. My ecards circled my brain with all of Andy's facts and traits: brother, husband, father, swimmer, financial advisor, excessive gambler, risk taker, pedophile, destroyer of companies, not connected to reality when it came to money. Would that make him delusionary? Or someone with an addictive personality?

Was that enough on the negative side to get him killed? I thought so.

"Time will tell," I mumbled to the room around me. As I moved toward the stairs anxious to fall into bed, my phone pinged twice: another text from ex-husband Brad. "Please, just go away," I said to black cell phone

Want to see you

Not good for me, I replied.

I hit delete. Again. I did not want to see him again … but deep down I was having doubts.

The other text was from Jon.

Did you fall off the face of the earth? Call me.

I deleted that too. How could I tell him about my tete-a-tete with Brad? Was I prepared for his reaction, whatever it might be? I knew the answer to that question. No, I wasn't. I wanted nothing to do with his reaction. Could I forget Brad ever showed up? If I ignored the whole thing, maybe I could convince myself it never happened.

Chapter 34

The Coast Guard station where the Barlows' boat had been towed originally took up one corner of the harbor. Anchored below the north tower of the Golden Gate Bridge, the small station lodged on the San Franisco Bay side of the bridge.

I parked my car and watched as one of their forty-seven foot motor lifeboats powered out under the bridge into the Pacific Ocean. White caps whipped spray over the bow in building surf. The boat bounced its way through the waves that had streamed across the Pacific toward San Francisco.

Strolling toward the station, I hesitated at the gate, wondering if it was proper to walk in and knock on the door. A quiet "Can I help you?" came from behind me. Wearing a dark blue shirt, bright red jacket tied around his waist, and a Coast Guard ball cap, the stocky young man smiled.

"Yeah, you can. Do you have a few minutes?"

"Sure. What do you need?"

"Answers. Answers to some questions about a body found off a boat. Maybe a month ago."

"Well, we're not supposed to talk about the recovery of bodies."

Maybe I could soften him up. "This station does a lot of that, right?"

"Yeah, we're one of the busiest search and rescue stations on the

Pacific coast. We cover north to Point Reyes and south to Año Nuevo."

"The place with all the elephant seals sunbathing on the sand?"

"That's the one."

"So, you rescue people and boats in the Bay and up and down the coast?"

He nodded. "Wanna guess how many people we rescue in a year?" he asked with a smile.

"A hundred or so," I said, thinking my number was too large.

He laughed out loud. "You're not even close," he said. "Try six hundred a year, give or take a few."

"Seriously, six hundred people need help in the bay and off the coast?"

He nodded. "You got it. But I have a feeling that's not what you wanted to talk about."

"No, but it's interesting information. About a month ago, an open water swimmer had a terrible accident. Got chewed up by the propeller of his boat."

"Yes, I remember that. Pretty grisly."

"The boat was towed back here. I think there was someone, maybe more than one person on board. Is that normal? To tow boats back to the closest Coast Guard station?"

"It depends. Usually we take them to the nearest marina and call the EMTs if that's what's needed."

"And that's what you did in this case?"

"Well, if I remember correctly. The swimmer wasn't too far away from this harbor, so we radioed ahead for EMTs to meet us at our dock," he said, pointing to the Coast Guard dock stretching out into Horseshoe Bay in front of us.

"Do you remember anything about the person on board the boat?"

"He seemed pretty shaken up."

"You're sure it was a male?"

"Yep."

"I'd been told it was the swimmer's brother."

"Think it was a relative, but I couldn't be certain."

Well, that was a twist. "Do you happen to know the name of this person? Was the first name Marty?"

"Don't think so."

"What about Dawson or Harrison?"

"Might be. They sound familiar but I really don't remember."

Another Coastie came walking by. "Hold on there, I'll walk back with you," my new friend said to his buddy. "Hope that helps. Need to get back now," he said with a snappy salute. Then he continued down the path to headquarters.

I sat there watching the fog play hide and seek with the Golden Gate Bridge towers. The occupants of the boat kept changing. Hatch either lied again or didn't really know who went out that day with Andy. I needed to look at this from a different angle.

⁘

Although I had grudgingly agreed to meet Lena at the pool this afternoon, I decided to stop in at Marin Marine only four miles away, close to the waterfront. The boatyard took up a quarter of a block of Sausalito's prime real estate. Not far off the main road, boats of all sizes packed the boatyard entrance. They stood gunnel to gunnel with no more than a few feet between them. Inside the yard itself, men and women wearing heavy duty masks sanded the side of various hulls. I walked into the open yard and bypassed the front office. I wanted to get a feel for the place before I talked to the owner.

"Excuse me," I called up to young, tattooed woman oiling a teak handrail. "Miss?" I tried again. Her ear plugs kept out any sound. She still didn't respond, so I walked around that boat to the next in line. A muscled young man, his hair pulled back in a man bun, looked down at me standing twelve feet below him.

"Hey," he called down. "Looking for something?" he asked.

"The owner. Sorry but I can't remember his name."

"Evan?"

"Yes, that's right. Right. It's Evan."

"He walked through here a minute ago. If you go that way," he said, pointing a dripping paint brush across the yard, "you'll see the back entrance to the office. He's probably there." Then he slipped on his protective face mask and a pair of large goggles, bent down, and disappeared on the floor of the cockpit.

I propelled myself around the boats resting on their trailers, looking like so many turkeys on their oven baking racks. The door to the office straight ahead of me stood open. As I grew closer, Evan came out and stopped, startled.

"Can I help you?" he said. It was the man that helped clean out his mother-in-law's home.

"Sorry to bother you. Do you remember me? My sister, Lena, came by as you were helping your mother-in-law move out of her house. I came back later and picked up some flowerpots."

"Kind of," he said. "I don't have much time to chat. Have to make sure two boats are ready to leave the yard by closing time."

"I get it, but I'd like to talk to you."

"About what? You have a boat that needs repair?"

"No, about the Barlow brothers and their bankrupt business. I know that's why your mother-in-law had to sell her house. She lost all her money because of them."

"You're right about that," he said, walking past me toward the large yard full of non-functioning boats. "She lost everything, poor lady."

"Did you know of anyone else who lost money?"

"I heard that a bunch of business owners here in Sausalito took a hit," he said.

"You, too?" I asked. No answer. He continued putting distance between me and him as he scrambled down a row with boats on trailers high above his head.

"Did you know the Barlow brothers?" I called out in a loud voice as he moved further away. He didn't want to talk to me. I jogged after him.

"Did you ever meet them?" I said, trying to catch up. Again, no answer. This was getting me nowhere. I took my inquiry in another direction.

"What about their boat? The Nereus. Did you work on it?"

He came to a sudden stop and turned around. "We maintain the Nereus, okay? Is that what you want to hear?"

The gruffness of his voice was like a door slammed in my face. I hit a nerve.

"Well … ah … I wasn't trying to bother you. I need some information, that's all."

He walked over to me, slowly, very slowly. "The Barlows are clients of mine, okay? I don't discuss my clients."

"Understand," I said. "Look, I'll be frank. Andy's son thinks his dad was killed by the Nereus. I wondered if someone brought it into your yard for maintenance or repair work after his death?"

"I told you I don't discuss my clients," he said, his voice steely. "Now you can walk through the office to exit the yard." He put his large, strong hands on my shoulders and turned me around so I was facing the office's open door. He gave me a slight push and stood there while I walked away. I turned my head slightly to see if he continued to watch me, but he had turned back toward the yard and moved to a classic sailboat with a large gash dead center of its hull.

When I entered the cramped boatyard office, an older teenager sat at the front desk, a phone glued to her ear. "I'm sorry, Mr. Whitealler, your boat had substantial damage. We're only beginning to come up with an estimate. – Yes, I understand. – No, I'm sorry I don't know. But I'll call you as soon as we have some definite numbers. – Yes, of course. I will. – I'll check with Evan now. Sure. – Okay. Talk to you soon." And she hung up.

"Can I help you?" she asked in an exasperated voice.

"Bad day?"

"Not really, but it's a busy one. What'd you need?"

"Evan just told me that he needs to see you. Right now."

"Okay, I'll track him down." On the desk was one of a pair of walky-talkies. "Oh, he forgot his. Better go find him."

I moved closer to her desk and smiled at her as she squeezed by me. With her out of the office, I looked over at her computer and dove into her files of customers. Within seconds I found the Barlows and their record of repair work. Each time the boat entered the shop, a few words identified the work to be done and who brought the boat in. I quickly scrolled through the maintenance tickets. Only a few. Andy and occasionally Marty brought the boat in. Except for the last two times, when Harrison brought it to the yard. The vague work order said, 'Various Repairs.' I clicked on that one. No mention of what repairs took place. No details. No breakdown for each item and cost. In fact, there wasn't a cost at all.

"Odd," I said out loud. I snapped a picture of the screen so I could look it over later. Before I closed the files, I noticed the dates Harrison brought the boat in. The first time was about two weeks before Andy's death. The second, two weeks later.

Chapter 35

From Sausalito to the pool took less than twenty minutes. How I managed to get there, I couldn't tell you. I don't remember pulling onto the freeway, stopping at stoplights, or driving into the pool parking lot. My mind remained on the conversation with Evan and the computer information from the boatyard. He'd been dramatically elevated in the list of suspects.

The sun drenched the pool's half-empty parking lot as I pulled in. Northern California is fortunate to have outdoor pools that stay open year round, at least in my neighborhood. Lena chatted up the assistant at the pool's front counter as I caught up with her. Midday turned out to be the perfect time to swim since the kids had migrated back to their schools. Long, empty lanes and warm sunshine.

"Hey," said Lena as she held the door open to the women's changing room. "Now. Why don't you want to swim?"

I plopped down on a bench in front of a row of lockers. "You know what I learned?" Lena opened her mouth to answer … something snarky, I'm sure. But I kept going. "Mrs. Gunderson's son-in-law owns Marin Marine, and they take care of the Nereus. And he repaired that boat after Andy's death. And remember Hildie said that they lost money with the Barlows."

"Okay."

"And the person on the boat with Andy Barlow was a man. So says the Coast Guard."

"That's no surprise," said Lena. "Did you think it was Justine or the high school cutie, Daria?"

"No, but then, how would the Vegas thugs fit into this?"

"Maybe they held whoever was driving the boat at gunpoint and were hidden," Lena said.

"I hadn't thought about that."

Lena had put on a swimsuit under her clothes and aimed herself toward the door to the pool in less than five minutes. I followed.

"Why does all this matter?" she asked.

"Because," I said, right on her heels, "I think I've been looking for the wrong person."

"Over here," said my sister, aiming for two lounge chairs by the deep end. She meticulously laid out a towel on one and sat down, surveying the pool as she did. "Look. There's a woman in that lane that I know. She's about my speed. That's where I'll be."

As she stuffed her headful of curls into a cap, she grabbed her tinted goggles and scooted over to the pool, waving at her friend.

"Don't you want to know who may have done it?" I called after her. She didn't turn around. "Guess not," I mumbled to myself.

Three lanes over, my favorite octogenarian stopped at the deep end of the pool and waved at me. "Cookie, look. I've saved a spot for you." He gestured with a skinny arm to the empty lane next to him.

"Okay. Give me a minute." It probably took less than that for me to dash back to the changing room, slip into my swimsuit, and pull on my cap and goggles.

"So, how's by you?" he asked with a kind grin as I sat down at the edge of the pool.

"Perplexed."

"Can I help?" he asked.

I slipped beneath the cool water and popped back up again. "Thanks. But no. I need to figure this out myself."

He nodded, still holding on to the wall. "I'm a good listener."

Having a serious conversation in the pool was not my idea of fun, so I dropped about eighteen inches below the surface and pushed off the wall, surrounded by the muffled sound of voices above me.

The rays of the sun pierced the blue water and turned the pool bottom into an ever-changing kaleidoscope of cool blues and whites. Normally, I delighted in staring at the pool bottom and the efficient arms and legs moving past me. But not today. Over and over, my mind came back to Harrison and Dawson. I had asked the Coastie about them without even realizing it. Deep, somewhere in my mind, I felt they could be more involved than I originally thought. Dawson knew boats. He could easily manipulate his family's powerboat to deliberately run Andy down. Was he his father's accomplice? But why? And Harrison? What reason would he have for killing his father?

I paused at the other end of the pool, stood up, and let the sun engulf me.

"Why?" I must have said out loud.

"Why what?" said my older friend. "Sure you don't want to talk about this?"

"I'm trying to figure out if a death in the Bay was an accident or a murder. I have three suspects. Maybe more. I'm not sure."

"Sounds like you already know this was a murder."

The grandfatherly man with kind eyes patted my damp arm. "Who had the most to gain?" he asked. "On TV, usually the motive is revenge, jealousy, or money. Does that help?"

"It might. It just might. It's possible that Marty, and his son, wanted revenge for Andy destroying the business. The dead guy also had a thing for teenage girls. Maybe the son was worried about his twin sister. And then there's … Why didn't I think of it before? Thank you. Thank you," I said, giving the slim old man a hug.

"Now you stop that," he said, surprised by the embrace. "I'm not that kind of man. I'm married, you know."

I barely heard his last words.

"Race you to the other end," I called out as I pushed off the wall, and sprinted away.

⚜ • ——————— • ⚜

I stayed in the pool for thirty minutes more. Every now and then, I'd catch a glimpse of my sister charging up and down the next lane. Instead of enjoying the sense of weightlessness and cool beauty, I concentrated on the Marty, Dawson, Harrison conundrum.

With my mind still running on its hamster wheel, I left the pool, changed, and tried to relax on a lounge chair while waiting for Lena. I checked my phone. A text from Jon popped up. Jon's texts had become more insistent over the last week.

Wanna get together?

Hello?

????

??

Did your phone die?

Come on Trisha. Wake up!

When one of his texts popped up, I turned off my phone and threw it under the bed or a chair, put it in my backpack, or managed to lose it in one of the many rooms of Earl's house.

Finally, with people splashing and swimming fifty feet away, I rehearsed a speech about how I needed to talk to him about a very serious matter and that it needed to be done as soon as possible. And in person. I prepared myself to come clean and live with the consequences of my cozy rendezvous with my soon-to-be ex-husband. Frankly, I shouldn't distinguish it by calling it a rendezvous. It was basically a booty call.

As I asked my phone to call Jon, my heart rate spiked and I saw blue spots in front of my eyes. His phone rang. I held my breath, hoping I wouldn't pass out. My eyes closed and I sucked in a long deep breath. The pickup. Voicemail. Stupid voicemail. So much for all my good intentions.

"Hey Jon. I really am alive. Just busy. The whole Barlow family is now living at my house. Major confusion. Give me a ring. I'll tell you all about it." And I hung up. I'm such a coward.

I waved to Lena as I headed for the parking lot. One tanned arm lifted high out of the water as she waved back. Shuffling over to my car, I concentrated on kicking a marble-sized stone. What an imbecile I was when it came to men. The gloomy emotional cloud escorted me to my car. Slipping in the driver's seat, I absentmindedly reached up to straighten the rearview mirror.

"What the …?" My mirror angled away from the back window. Instead, it faced the passenger door. As I reached up to fix it, I saw movement in the back seat and a flash of green. Before I had a chance to scream, a man's hand reached around and clapped over my mouth. His other hand wrapped around my throat.

"Stay still and shut up and you won't get hurt," said a gravelly voice. I clutched at his hands, desperate to pull them off. He yanked my head back against the headrest.

"What do you want with the Barlows?" he muttered into my ear.

"Mmmm," was all I could say. I reached around and scratched at his face. Then I bit down as hard as I could on his fleshy fingers.

"You bitch." He tightened his grip on my neck and over my mouth. My arms flailed in front of me, looking for something, anything to grab so I could hammer him.

"You want the money? You're not getting the money. That comes to us. Leave the Barlows alone. Got it?"

As I struggled to grab his hair, I remembered my smart watch. All I had to do was hit a button to call 911.

"You've been following us. But you stop now. Do you hear? Now."

I sucked in short shallow breaths through my nose and crashed my wrist into the side window. The watch face texted me, *It looks like you took a hard fall. Should I call for help?*

I managed to press the 'yes' button the same time I bit down on the man's hand again, moving my head from side to side. His skin ripped and I tasted blood.

"Fuck," he yelled, shaking his hand. He let go of me and jumped out the door. Waiting for him was the other man in the white sedan.

⁕ ⸺ • ⸺⸺ • ⸺ ⁕

When the police showed up, Detective Mark Hamilton walked over to me and I repeated the story I told the other officers.

"These were the same men who broke into Justine Barlow's home. They want me to leave the Barlows alone. They think I'm after some money. But I don't know what they're talking about."

"What money?" asked Det. Hamilton.

"I don't know. Insurance money, maybe. Andy Barlow was a gambler and he owed someone in Las Vegas for millions."

The questions continued until I pleaded to go home. Det. Hamilton gave me yet another of his cards.

"Before I let you go, can you remember anything, anything at all … even the littlest details about the man in the car with you?"

I closed my eyes. "He was white, big fat fingers. About five-seven to five-eight. A burly guy wearing a green shirt. He had a smoker's voice, kind of rumbly, and he smelled of vinegar and rotten onions."

Chapter 36

I dreaded going into the house when I got home. All those people. So much noise. I didn't want to tell anyone what happened. But, to my surprise, no one answered when I called out, "Hello." No cars filled up the parking spaces outside. I shot up the stairs, bolted into my room, slammed the door, and threw myself on the bed. The Barlows were involved with some bad people, whether they knew it or not.

I turned my wallpaper into a view of the Scottish Highlands and started to warm the bathroom floor. Eventually, I slipped into a warm bath and my heart rate finally mellowed. Thirty minutes later, I wrapped myself in a warm towel and climbed into bed … more tired than I had ever been in my life.

⚯ ⚯

"Trisha? Trisha," said Dad hesitantly. "I have breakfast for you." He walked in with a tray. "Are you sick?"

My head exploded as I sat up, pounding like waves crashing on the shore.

"Didn't feel well. Went to sleep when I came home yesterday." I squinted out at the deck. Fog lifted off the redwoods and blue sky peaked through.

"What time is it?"

"About eight."

"Got to get up."

"You stay in bed. Come down when you're ready. Picked up your favorite donuts and that great coffee you like." He quietly shut the door behind him.

Had yesterday even happened? Did someone really try to choke me? I shivered. Instead of dipping down into the bed, I threw back the covers and picked up the tray with Dad's goodies. I planned on eating my way to good mental health.

Something else happened yesterday and I couldn't quite remember. The pool, swimming, my eighty-year-old lane mate. Yes, that was it. My octogenarian swim friend casually asked who had the most to gain by Andy Barlow's death. I hadn't approached the question like that. But honestly, I didn't know. Marty? Harrison? Dawson? Justine? Maybe the boys could tell me, if I could get them together to talk.

I texted both, but each one had reasons why they couldn't meet later today. I pushed, telling them I was rounding up the case and needed to run something by them as soon as possible. Reluctantly, they agreed to meet at the boat after Dawson got out of school.

I planned to arrive early. Maybe stop in and talk with Hatch again. I found him to be sketchy at best. Or maybe he just didn't like telling the truth.

With time to spare, I pulled out the tablet with my ecards and copied information, including the papers that Marty Barlow sent to Lena's neighbor, the flowerpot lady. Did he really think that the firm had a chance to survive? Or was it a ploy to scam more clients out of money?

⚜ • —— • ⚜

Surprisingly, both boys reached the boat before I did. And they were doing things guys their age did: playing games on their phones.

"Bang! Eh! Grr! Pow!" I could hear Dawson say as I walked down the side pier.

"Sup," nodded Harrison when I climbed on board. He never looked up, but I watched his thumbs fly over the small keyboard on his mobile. I stood there for a moment trying to remember what I did when I was their age and cellphones weren't even on my radar.

"Guys, can you put the phones down for a minute or two? I need to have an honest talk with you." Both glanced up at the same time, then glanced down for a second longer, sighed, and turned off their phones almost in unison.

"Let's go below," said Dawson, and he led the way to the quiet cabin.

They took seats on the settee and looked at me expectantly without saying anything.

I propped myself on the table and said, "Tell me everything you know about the Las Vegas creeps who broke into Harrison's house."

They looked at each other and shrugged.

"Never saw them before," said Harrison.

"Ditto," said Dawson.

An awkward silence hung in the air.

I stood up. "Okay. Well, why were they there?"

Both boys shrugged again.

"Come on. Help me out here. Please. I'm doing this because you asked me to, Harrison. The reason your dad died may not be what you first thought."

"What did you think happened to him?" asked Dawson, glancing at Harrison now fixated on the floor of the boat.

"Dunno," he said. "I had weird thoughts then."

Dawson turned and stared directly at him. "Like what?"

The air in the cabin stilled. I could hear both boys breathing. A seagull squawked outside and I flinched.

"Well," said Harrison reluctantly. "I thought your dad killed mine when they were out on the boat."

Dawson jumped off the settee. "I knew it. That is so fucked up. So fucked up. Why would you think that?"

Harrison ran his hands through his hair. "I don't know. I thought your dad was mad at mine."

"Mad enough to kill him? Why would he be mad anyway? That is fucked up, bro."

"Did you guys know there was a money problem with their business?" I asked. Again, a long silence. I stared at both of them. "Did you?"

They mumbled over each other, not making eye contact.

"Your dad was a pedo," said Dawson.

"Bullshit. Take that back," said Harrison. He grabbed Dawson by the collar and stuck his face close to him.

"Yeah, he was. He liked my sister's friends."

"I'm going to kill you," said Harrison, swinging at his cousin and connecting with his nose, which immediately started to bleed. The two boys lurched at each other and ended up on the cabin floor.

"Stop it. Stop it. Now," I yelled and tried to pull them apart.

Dawson crawled away and stuffed the paper towels I gave him around his nose. Blood leaked through and dripped onto the floor. His voice sounded hollow behind the paper towels. "All you have to do is ask Daria, Harrison. Everyone knew."

Harrison pulled himself up and took a step toward the boat's galley. He leaned over the sink, his head hanging in defeat.

"I knew," he said. "Daria tried to tell me once, but I ignored her. Told her she was a lying bitch. But I knew. I'd seen him with some of her water polo friends." He turned around. His eyes filled with tears. "I even tried to tell my mom." He looked out the porthole of the boat, as if carried back to that conversation.

Again, the air froze.

"And?" I asked. "What did she say?"

"She didn't believe me. Said I was imagining things."

"That was it?" I asked.

"Yeah. I never said anything about it again."

I sighed.

"Why are we here?" said Dawson, whose nose had finally stopped bleeding.

"I wanted to find out what you guys knew about the Las Vegas stuff. They're bad people and could hurt you. Please tell me if you think they killed your dad, Harrison."

Neither boy looked at each other.

"My dad never talked too much about business at home," said Dawson.

"Did he ever say anything about cutting back? Limiting expense?"

Dawson shook his head no.

"Harrison?"

"He once said things were getting tight, that I might have to leave England and finish school in California."

"And?" I asked.

"I didn't like that. I wanted to stay where I was."

"If I offend you, I'm sorry. But Harrison, your dad had a gambling problem. Did you know that?"

Harrison shrugged. "He liked to have fun. He went to Vegas all the time. My mom was more of a stay-at-home mom. Know what I mean? She used to go with him but then stopped, saying she needed to be home for me."

"Dawson, did your father ever talk about cutting back or problems with the business?"

"No." The answer was curt, dry and, to my way of thinking, probably a lie.

"Do you know where your dad played in Vegas?"

"Nah," said Harrison. "I went with him once. I think we stayed at Twenty-One. It was on the Strip. But I was little then. Around nine or ten."

"Did you ever hear him say anything about your uncle's gambling?" I asked Dawson.

"Check that drawer," he said, pointing to a side drawer by the galley. I pulled it open and along with utensils, knives, and some candles, there was a plastic bag full of matchbooks, coasters, and menus from a variety of Las Vegas spots. "Uncle Andy was always bringing in shit like that and storing it here on the boat.”

I plucked a few of them out of the bag. “Okay if I borrow these for a bit?” Both boys shrugged in unison.

“I gotta go. Anything else?” asked Dawson.

I shook my head. “Thanks guys.”

Harrison scrambled off the boat at breakneck speed, not saying goodbye or managing a look backward.

Dawson stayed. He clearly had something to say.

“His dad *was* a pedo. I’m not lying,” he said to me.

“I’ve heard the rumors before. Do you think he ever moved on your sister?”

“I know he did. That sicko. In fact, I found them together. He had his arms around her and was kissing her. So gross.”

“What happened?”

“I pulled him off her. Daria was crying. She didn’t know what to do. I think he’d been grooming her for this or whatever. As much as she would tell me, they never ever did it. But he wanted to.”

“Did you talk to your dad?”

“I tried. But he didn’t want to listen. I even went to my aunt. But you heard Harrison. She didn’t want to hear about it.”

“You let it drop?”

“I told Daria not to be alone with him anymore. Ever. I think she fancied herself in love with him.” I couldn’t believe what he was saying. Andy Barlow was deeply troubled. “You know, I even thought about going to my counselor at school.”

“Really?”

“I changed my mind at the last minute. If I talked about it, I’d have blown up the whole family. I didn’t want to do that.”

“Do you think Daria would talk to me?” I asked the pensive teenager.

“Not likely. She doesn’t like to talk about it. Water under the bridge is what she says now.”

“Fair enough,” I said.

"I gotta go," said Dawson. He stood up and started to clean up the boat's cabin, putting blue cushions back on the settee, scrubbing up the remaining dark red thick blood from the cabin floor, and giving the interior a quick look over before we climbed the few short steps to the deck. He fitted the hatch boards into place and secured the lock. Gracefully, he stepped off the boat, offering me a hand onto the dock. We walked silently past the other boats. At the metal gate, he turned and said, "When I was little, I loved being around my uncle, but he turned into a scumbag. And everyone knew it."

He walked away quickly toward the parking lot. I moved much more slowly, wondering why life couldn't be easier for everyone.

Chapter 37

Jon wanted to see me. I'd avoided him long enough but I knew it was time. He offered dinner and an evening of movies. He suggested *Jaws*, which I'd seen. I said I'd make dessert, my irresistible fudge. Jon loved my thick chocolatey fudge with peppermint sprinkles on top. Maybe I could send him into a sugar coma before I told him about Brad.

Brad continued texting me daily. I refused to answer. Truth be told, I now felt wishy-washy about him. But I signed the divorce papers and mailed them back to his lawyer. I didn't tell anyone, least of all Brad. Why was I on the down low about the divorce papers? I didn't have a logical answer. I refused to see him because I didn't want to end up in bed with him. Which was a possibility. What was wrong with me? I responded to him like an addictive drug. I had to finalize my contact with Brad now. I pulled out my phone and started to text.

Divorce papers are signed. Sent to your lawyer. I don't want to see you again. You're bad medicine for me.

The response was immediate.

?

??

Let's have a drink and say goodbye.

I still didn't answer.

Please. Irish coffee?

I don't drink. No. I wish you well. Now leave me alone.

He sent back a crying emoji:

With that, I blocked his number, picked up the fudge, and went out the front door.

Patches of bright pink drifted out over the Pacific Ocean as I approached the Golden Gate Bridge. The Bay area glowed in early fall. Winds dropped to a whisper as the sun fell into the sea. If the air remained calm and the water still, I'd see the Farallon Islands, twenty miles due west, or at least their silhouette. These lonely islands were a wildlife refuge and known as hunting grounds for great white sharks.

It was a slow day on the bridge. A few fishing boats came back in from the Pacific on the first of the flood tide. Off to the left, the San Francisco city front basked in the sun, washing the buildings stark white. The Transamerica Pyramid stuck out like a needle into the sky. On the eastern side, the newer Salesforce obelisk, a glass and steel tower, sucked in the light and reflected it back over the city.

Normally the beauty of San Francisco enchanted me as I drove across the Golden Gate Bridge. But now I wondered if the view, and Jon, would change. I pulled into a parking lot not far from the Hyde Street Pier, and instead of walking toward his apartment, I headed for Aquatic Park. The last time I was here, Brad found me. I scanned the concrete bleachers down to the sidewalk and the beach. Out in the protected waters of the cove, swimmers moved along the Balclutha, one of the tall ships, and headed west against the flood tide. I was stalling and I knew it. I took one long last look at the swimmers in the water.

⁂

Jon opened the door before I knocked and grabbed the plate of fudge from my hands. I smiled but couldn't speak. His apartment smelled like smooth, rich red tomato sauce.

"Spaghetti?" I said quietly, walking into his small kitchen, lifting a lid, and inhaling the thick, spicy sauce with whiffs of oregano. "Smells wonderful." But then I walked over toward the big plate glass window and looked out at the masts of the tall ships below. The place I had just been.

"You're quiet today," said Jon, coming up behind me. I took a step away. He cocked his head and glanced at me. "What's going on?"

I shrugged.

"Tell me," he said. "Too involved with the Barlow case?"

I couldn't face him. I found my way to his couch and finally looked up. "I have to tell you something."

I patted the couch seat next to me. The quirky smile turned to concern as he moved toward me and sat down.

"Trisha, you're scaring me. What happened?"

My mouth dried up like I was eating sand. I tried to speak but nothing came out.

"I need water," I gagged. He brought me a glass and watched me drink. I stared at the bottom of the glass, closed my eyes, and began.

"You know I was married."

"Sure, the guy's name was Brad Carson and he walked out on you."

I nodded. "Well, last week, he walked back in."

"What?"

"He's here. He came to San Francisco so that I could sign the divorce papers."

A big smile spread across Jon's face. "That's making you so grim?" he said, taking my hand. I pulled it back and slipped it under my leg.

"No."

"Oh." He pulled back. "Did you decide not to sign them?"

"No! Nothing like that. They're signed and I sent them off to his lawyer."

"Trisha, I don't understand. What are you trying to tell me?"

The words tumbled out like a waterfall dropping into a crevice. "He found me and Lena at Aquatic Park."

"Okay."

"And I slept with him."

"You had sex outside? At Aquatic Park?"

"I went back to his Airbnb and stayed. I stayed the whole night. I don't know why. Well, I do know why. But that's over. I'm never going to see him again. Ever. I promise."

Jon let out a long sigh and rested his head on the back of the couch. "You know. You're a lot of trouble for me."

"I'm sorry." I managed to glance over at him. He stared at the ceiling. "Do you want me to leave?" I asked, not sure what to do.

"I don't know," he said. He moved a few inches away from me on the couch. The apartment was quiet except for the bubbling of the tomato sauce on the stove. "Why would you do that?"

"I'm not sure."

"You said you knew why. Tell me."

I stood up and started to pace back and forth in front of him, not wanting to tell him why I had sex with my soon-to-be ex-husband. But if anything positive was to come out of this conversation, it had to start with the truth, which I had managed to tell so far. But the hard part was coming up.

"I think I wanted to prove something to him. Maybe to me. He left me so long ago. Walked out and never came back. Do you know what that feels like? A loser. I felt like a loser until I came crawling back to Marin to a bedroom in my sister's house."

He leaned over, propped his elbows on his knees, and rested his head in the hands. He talked to the floor.

"What in god's name did you need to prove?" He looked up, wounded and hurt.

"Jon, can't you guess? When he left, I felt like an empty garbage bag. I spent the next six months eating and drinking. I wanted him to see how I had changed, grown and became … ah … desirable."

"He's a guy, Trisha. Of course, he'd think you're desirable. Did he force you?"

"No."

"Did he promise you a future?"

"I didn't want one."

"What did you want?"

"Sex," I blurted out. "All I wanted was sex from him. He had to see what he lost when he left me."

The word 'sex' was like a slap in the face for Jon. His head jolted back and bumped into the wall behind him.

"That was fucking blunt," he said.

"That's all it was. I wanted him to see me as hot."

In a bitter voice, Jon said, "Did he?"

I walked closer to the window and peered out at the flags flying off the tall ships in the distance. "I don't know. And I don't care. You may not believe this, but I think it made me clearer about you."

"Don't go there," he said. "Don't give me the 'I had to know if I really loved you or my ex, so I fucked him' routine."

"I think it's true."

"You're so shallow. Can't you see what you're doing? Manipulating me. Manipulating him, even. You better leave."

"Jon, please. I didn't have to tell you, but I wanted you to know."

"To make yourself feel less guilty, right?"

"I don't know."

"Yeah, you do." He walked over to the front door and opened it without saying a word.

"Jon, can we talk? Maybe tomorrow or later."

He said nothing. I grabbed my backpack hanging on the back of one of his chairs and shuffled over to the door. I slowly looked up and watched the face I'd learn to love and trust turn blank as he looked at me.

"I'm sorry. I truly am," I said. As I walked into the hall, the fragrance of rich spicy tomato sauce disappeared as Jon shut the door.

Chapter 38

The next few days dragged on. No Jon. My fault. I texted him a few times but he never responded. Not that I blame him. But was what I did really so awful? A mistake. Yes. But … but … but. Who was I kidding? That internal flush of emotion took over. In a way, I knew exactly what I was doing. Although the only one I'd admit it to was me. I refused to discuss my indiscretion with my family members or the teens still living in the house.

To get my mind off the consequences of my stupidity, I thought about the death of Andy Barlow. I wanted to learn about the investigation involving the Las Vegas loan shark who sent his thugs to harass the Barlows. So, I called Detective Hamilton.

He agreed to see me, and we met at a café on their outside patio. For a change, the fall fog blocked the sun out, leaving the sky a dirty gray. The empty patio stretched in front of other shops and restaurants. Cool air kept the diners inside and the kids out of a small fountain of whales playing in a wave. A colony of soggy polka-dotted red umbrellas chained to cement metal tables surrounding the fountain waited for customers.

"So, are you taking me up on joining the force?" Detective Hamilton said, inhaling the rich cup of coffee in his hands.

"No. I'm past my mid-forties. That's not the age of a police rookie. Need to change the subject. I'd like to know whatever you know about those guys from Las Vegas that broke into the Barlow house and tied the mom and son up."

The detective clicked his teeth and sucked in his cheeks.

"I can't talk about an ongoing investigation," he said, staring down at the table.

"Nothing? Nothing at all?"

He glanced up. The look on his face said he was dying to talk about it.

"This might help." I pulled out the stash of coasters and matchbook covers I picked up from the boat. "These are places Andy frequented in Vegas." Then I grabbed a small, folded piece of paper from my wallet. "Andy had a burner phone. It seems like he used it to call a casino in Reno and a tough-sounding guy who lent him money."

He scrutinized each piece of paper meticulously. "Thanks. We'll check it out."

"Look, I'm helping, or at least I'm trying to help, Harrison Barlow. He still feels his dad was murdered. That his death wasn't an accident."

"Oh yeah. We talked to him more than once. But I got to tell ya, we found nothing." He spread out his thick hands on the white table. "The Coast Guard found nothing suspicious either. The kid's upset, of course, looking for someone to blame. But there's nothing there."

"Do you think the death connects with the Vegas people?"

"Officially, the death was an accident. But me? Personally? It's possible. The guy was a compulsive gambler. Was in way over his head with some loan sharks, and they wanted their money." He leaned back in his chair placing both hands behind his head. "Terrorizing the family is not smart but it may make them cough up with some money."

A little dog barked in agreement with the detective and pulled on his leash that was tied to the table next to me.

"Look, there's no reason for these thugs to kill him if they wanted him to pay up. How can he do that if he's dead?"

"That's what my sister said," I agreed. "But something isn't right.

It doesn't make sense. The Barlows' business had gone belly up, thanks to Andy. Is it possible that the Las Vegas creeps rented a boat? They found out when Andy Barlow was going out and they followed him and somehow pushed him overboard and into the propeller?"

"You won't let that Vegas connection go, will you? What do they gain? If it's all about money, killing him doesn't help."

"Did you ever follow up on his family, his extended family? All of them lost big time." I spread my arms out.

"You have an overactive imagination. Trisha, this was a tragic accident. Nothing more."

Detective Hamilton's radio started to chatter. "Look, I have to go. But play this out, step by step, and you'll see it doesn't make sense. Who told them Andy Barlow was going out? Who took Andy Barlow out? How did they get connected and why?"

"Money. Somebody wanted money. Or revenge," I said, not knowing where to go next with my far-flung idea.

"That part is probably true. But the rest doesn't work. Not the way I'm looking at it." He stood up and stretched. His dark blue shirt stretched tight against the bullet-proof vest underneath. "Keep thinking about it. There could be an idea somewhere in that cockamamie story you came up with."

As I watched him walk back to his squad car, my mobile phone exploded. It rang, vibrated, and danced all over the metal table. Urgent, it said with each vibration.

It was Justine Barlow. "Hey, Justine, I was just thinking about you. Are you still at Earl's?"

"All the kids are. But no, I'm back home and I need to see you. It's urgent."

"What do you mean?"

"I can't talk about it right now. When can you get here?"

"About twenty minutes."

"Make it faster," she said. "Hurry." And then she hung up. I glared at the phone. The Barlows treated me like a yo-yo. Come here. Do that. Do this. Help me. What did they want from me now? It didn't take profound intuition to unmask their true clingy personalities. Entitled. Arrogant. Pretentious. Demanding. They want what they want. I'd become someone to order around. Like a servant. And I didn't like it.

"This is the last time I do this for them," I mumbled to myself as I struggled to find my dirty Honda in the parking lot. You'd think the dirt would make it stand out, but no such luck.

It was time to put this case to bed. Whoever did it or didn't do it was no longer a concern of mine. I had other things to obsess about, like how to win back a boyfriend that I loved … yeah, I said it out loud … loved and continued to hurt. While I sat in the front seat, I texted Jon a one-word message again.

Sorry

But it didn't go through. Jon had blocked me. "Good for him," I said to myself with a sigh, although my eyes started to water. He's a good guy, a great guy, and he doesn't need someone that whores around as a serious girlfriend. I sounded tough, even to myself. But that wasn't the case. With a self-serving careless action, I pushed away the one steady, one good thing in my life. No tears this time. No reaching out to my sister or father. It wasn't their fault. It was mine.

"I'm getting what I deserve," I continued, talking to myself. "Forget about him. Go stand up to Justine and her son and tell them to find someone else to figure out if their dear departed husband and father was killed."

Maybe he was so unhappy with how his life turned out, he killed himself. I pressed on the accelerator a little too hard, and the tires spun out and almost launched me into the car across from me.

Suicide never crossed my mind before. But that might be the answer that no one wants to bring up. Maybe it was all too much for the gambler that took down his own financial security company and, in the process, destroyed his family. I never thought I had something in common with the dead swimmer. But both he and I knew how to kill a family vibe.

Justine paced around the pool. I watched her walk back and forth, sipping on a clear drink in a plastic glass decorated with gray dolphins swimming in an endless circle. She never looked at me or said a word.

I leaned on the back of a lounge chair. "Justine, we need to talk."

That didn't stop her. So, I joined her, walking laps around her pool.

"I can't do this anymore unless I'm paid."

She never looked my way, although I was right next to her elbow. We made the turn at the deep end of the pool.

"This … you … you're useless. I don't know anything more about what happened to my husband—"

I cut her off. "Your previous husband."

That stopped her. "Well, aren't you sarcastic." She glowered at me.

"I'm only telling the truth. You married your first husband's brother before … ah, before."

"You're going to say, 'Before he was cold in the ground.' Well, that's not where he is, is he? His ashes are out in the bay," she snapped at me. "And it's none of your business who I marry and when. Okay. Here it is. Dawson killed Andy."

"What? Are you sure?"

"He hated him. He thought—and he was wrong—that he seduced his sister Daria. But that never happened. She's his niece, for god's sake," Justine said.

Talk about a dysfunctional family. I spun around and almost tripped over a lounge chair. "What proof do you have that number one: Dawson killed Andy, and number two: that Andy seduced or tried to seduce Daria?"

"I overheard Harrison talking to someone on his phone."

"What was he saying?" I asked.

"I didn't hear all of it. But he said something about Daria and Andy. Then I heard the word pedo."

"Did you talk to Dawson, or at very least talk to Harrison?" I continued.

"Are you crazy? I can't talk to either of them about this."

"Justine, could you sit down for a second?"

She slinked away and tossed me a nasty look.

"Please." I rested my hand lightly on her arm and guided her to the chaise in front of me. I stayed standing, shuffling from foot to foot.

"Well?" she asked.

"Do you think Andy was aware of the problems he caused his firm because of his gambling?"

Instead of sounding off at me, she looked down at the pool deck and her empty dolphin glass on the small white metal table next to her. After a long pause, she spoke again in a voice caked with ice.

"He was a gambler. Reality wasn't his strong point. He always felt he could recover the money he lost and put everything right. We fought about it all the time. He never wanted to talk about business at home. Normally, he'd cut me off and leave. Or maybe go jump in our pool and swim some laps. Anything to get away from the truth."

"Was he unhappy, maybe depressed enough to consider … ah … taking his own life?"

"What? No, never." Justine stood up and took a step toward me. I inched back. "That's horrible you'd ever think of such a thing. Do you think he swam into that propeller? Who would do such a thing?"

She moved closer. I glanced back at the pool, now just inches from me.

"It was only a question. It had to be asked," I said, now breathing harder. I put my hands on her shoulders, pushing her back. Her reactions were surprisingly quick. She grabbed both my arms and pushed.

I fought to regain my balance, but I slipped off the deck. For a few seconds, I floated in mid-air. Not going up. Not going down. Only hanging above the blue water and gazing at Justine's face twisted into a mask of agony. Then gravity took over and pressed me, flat on my back, arms flailing, into the pool. I sank until my feet touched the bottom, hair floating around my face. The hushed stillness surrounded me. I didn't want to see Justine again. I wanted to stay here where it was calm and soundless. But my chest tightened and I needed a breath of air. I pushed off the bottom and broke the surface. A hand reached out to me. Instead of taking it, I dog-paddled to the shallow end of the pool and climbed up the steps, holding on to the metal rail. Justine moved quickly toward me with a towel.

"I'm so sorry," she said.

"Don't come near me," I said, wrapping my arms around my torso. I grabbed the towel and draped it over my head. From underneath the towel, a torrent of pent-up emotions came spurting out.

"Your son asked me to help." I pulled the towel off and dropped it on the wet deck. "He thought your husband … your new husband … killed Andy and wanted me to prove it. Now you think Dawson killed him." I took a step closer and she moved back in the direction of the house, not the pool. "Which one is it? The uncle, the kid, the thugs from Las Vegas? Do you have any proof? Not guesses, but real, hard proof. I hoped I could help your son. But I think your whole family is crazy."

I started walking toward my car, water leaking out of my shoes.

"I'm so sorry," said Justine, following me and reaching out a hand. "I'm upset. But Andy would never kill himself."

"What about you? Would you kill him? You had the most to gain with him dead."

"What? Me? Never. I wouldn't do anything like that." Justine's hand sliced through the air as if she was cutting me off.

"But I bet you'd plan it, wouldn't you? With one of your family members. Who was it? Marty? Dawson? Maybe Marty and Dawson together? How about your dear son Harrison? Was he involved?"

"How dare you! Leave. Leave now."

"I'm going, but get the kids … all the kids … out of Earl's house."

I opened the car door and fell into the driver's seat, spraying water on both front seats and the dusty console. I pulled down the driver's mirror and looked at myself. Drenched hair remained plastered to my head. Rivulets of pool water dripped down my face. I looked awful.

Justine stood a distance from the car and called out, "Stay away from my house."

Chapter 39

The warmth of my heated bathroom floor reduced a fraction of the anger I felt toward Justine Barlow. What a bitch! After all I'd done to help her and her son. If I hadn't already cashed her retainer and spent it, I'd walk away from the Barlows. But Justine paid for a service and I had to deliver. The heated towel holders were a plus at times like these. They melted my stress. I threw a warm blue towel around my head, turban style, and wrapped a small toasty throw rug of a towel around my body. Once out of the steamy bathroom, I examined the large whiteboard next to the desk with the laptop.

I'd seen this on TV detective shows and thought it made sense. Map out who's connected to who with thick black lines. In the center was Andy Barlow, and potential suspects extended out like spokes on a wheel. Under Marty's name, a small line listed his potential locations, the Philippines/Thailand, and the word 'bank' with a question mark after it. Next to Marty were his kids, a line for Dawson and one for Daria. Under Andy, another line for Harrison and one for Justine. Off to the right was a circle for the Las Vegas creeps and a circle for Marin Marine with a line extending from both to Andy. The line for the secretary Vivian extended to both the brothers.

Witnesses or people who had something to say about the case were documented, one under the other. The kid at the café who told me about Andy and the teenage girls, the flowerpot woman down the street from Lena who lost everything, the baseball fan honored at the ballpark, and finally Hatch Grey, the old salt berthed on the same dock as the Barlows' boat.

I threw on a stretched-out Giants shirt and a faded pair of jeans while my eyes skimmed over the chart. Back and forth I looked. I didn't think Daria had anything to do with the death, but she could have been a motive for Dawson. Dawson was unhappy with his uncle's pursuit of his sister and her friends, but was he angry enough to kill him? Of the whole group, except for Hatch, he seemed to have the most boat knowledge. Harrison asked me to conduct an investigation, so he didn't seem likely. All he seemed to care about was his college in England and returning as soon as possible.

Harrison suspected Marty, still in another country and already married to Justine. If Andy was permanently out of the picture, maybe he could resurrect his business. Justine took up the last spot in the family. She didn't strike me as being the brightest person in the group, but my gut told me she was conniving and out for herself and maybe her son. I stared at her name on the chart. The more I thought about it, the clearer her connection to her husband's death became. She had the most to gain: insurance, a new husband, and a way to keep her son in England so she could continue on with an unblemished life. Did she know enough about boats to do the actual killing? Not likely. But Marty did.

Of the extras, there were investors who lost money and weren't happy, or family members of those who lost money. But it seemed a long shot that they would band together and kill one of the brothers. The accountant seemed all wrong. She worried about her dog and herself. Although she knew she had committed a crime, she never said a cruel word about her bosses. Finally, Hatch. He seemed like Madame Defarge from *A Tale of Two Cities*. During the French Revolution, she sat silently and knitted and watched the world go by in the Dickens classic. True, she was almost invisible, but her actions helped the revolutionaries. Could Hatch play that role? He knew much more than he let on.

While glued to my whiteboard, a loud cheer went up from downstairs. I could hear parts of the conversations. "Home." "Dad." I walked over to the staircase and peered one flight down.

"What's going on?" I tried to shout over the commotion.

Daria managed to hear me and said, "We're leaving."

"To where?" I asked.

"Home."

The kids were on the move.

I smiled at the commotion below. "When is she coming to get you?"

"Who?" asked Daria and Dawson in unison.

"Your aunt, Justine."

They burst into laughter. "No. Not her. It's Pops. He's back."

"What was that all about?" asked Earl, coming out of his office down the hall from my bedroom.

"Your guests are checking out of Chez Cunningham."

"You don't say."

"That I do, and they are going home. To which home I couldn't tell you. But according to them, their father is back in the country after visiting his money ... wherever he keeps it ... and is on his way over to pick them up."

Earl nodded. "I think I hear a car driving up the road."

Earl padded down the stairs with me following. I detoured into the kitchen while he walked to the open front door and looked out, then winced. "Is it a parent" I asked, digging around the cupboard for a cookie, a cracker, even a stale piece of bread.

"No," is all Earl said. He headed back to the staircase. "Come on Babe. I have work to do."

"Well, who is it?" I asked, stretching my head to one side, hoping to see the car.

"Yep," is all Earl said. He walked up the stairs with his back to me.

"Why are you acting so ..." I stopped and looked out the front door at the car and driver in front of the house. It was Brad. One ex-husband too many had come to visit.

254

Chapter 40

The large redwood trees shaded the path Brad and I took leading into La Cruz Canyon. I didn't want to talk to him in the house. Earl's not an eavesdropper, but my father would be home soon. Let's just say Brad is not one of his favorites.

The soft scrape of our feet moving across the dirt trail down to the reservoir blanketed my galloping breathing. He was quiet. So was I. As the sun dipped behind Mt. Tam, the air grew cooler and the light faded. In a duskier corner of the canyon, an owl hoot-hooted.

"You're living out here in nature," said Brad, gazing into the trees.

"That's the first sentence you uttered since we left the house." I turned to stare at him. "Why are you here? I filled out and signed the divorce papers like you asked. There's nothing more for me to do."

Brad wouldn't look at me. "It's not about that. Well, maybe it is," he said, still looking into the trees. I planted myself in front of him so he was forced to stop and see me.

"Why are you here?" I asked again. He circled around me like a stream flowing by a rock and kept going.

I chased after him. "Brad. Talk to me. Stop." I grabbed his arm and pulled him back.

He sighed, took a deep breath, and finally said, looking me straight in the eye, "I don't want a divorce. I want you and me to get back together."

"No way." The words were out of my mouth before I could stop myself. "What could you possibly be thinking?" I dropped his arm and took a few steps back.

"Listen," he said. "I know this comes out of the blue."

I crossed my arms and kept moving back, baby step after baby step.

"After the other day, when we … you know …"

"Had sex, yes, I know."

"I realized that I still had feelings for you. Even after all these years, I need to be around you."

"No, Brad. No. I lost someone because of that. Someone that honestly loves me."

"But we had fun together, Trish. Remember? All those hikes in the mountains? Just the two of us."

"What I remember were all those trips to the local bars. You disappearing and me … well, me disappearing in my own way. I've finally found my own life, who I am."

"Once I got my shit together, I left my brother's house and I moved back to Colorado. That was last year," said Brad. "Please think about moving there. We could start over. This time it would work."

Since Jon disappeared from my life, I had to admit to myself that Brad popped into my mind too often. I even checked out one of my favorite Colorado parks on the internet, admiring the mountains and remembering a favorite camping spot Brad and I enjoyed.

A little further down the trail, a bench carved out of a fallen redwood pressed against a redwood. I aimed toward it, skirting Brad without touching any part of him. Once I sat down, I could see the end of the reservoir. He wanted me back. Those are words I waited years to hear. Is there a possibility that it's true?

"You know, I've been swimming in that reservoir," I said to no one in particular.

"You can't swim," said Brad, sitting down next to me. "Lena's the swimmer. You're the driver."

"Those days are long gone," I said. "I'm a pretty good swimmer now, thanks to Lena's encouragement. I've even competed in a few open water races."

A huge smile crossed Brad's face. "You don't have to lie, Trisha. I like … love you … the way you are."

"You don't believe I could do that, do you?" I asked.

"Well, it was never your thing. You told me that you hated the water."

"That was then. This is now."

"You don't have to try and impress me," Brad said, putting an arm around my shoulder. I jerked back at his touch.

"I'm not trying to impress anyone. I've been swimming in pools and some lakes, rivers, and a reservoir."

"Of course," he said with a smile on his face.

"Don't be so condescending. I'm not as fast as Lena, but I have a good stroke, or so I've been told."

"Sure," he said.

"Why don't you believe me?" I stood up and walked across the path, toward the reservoir. Then I turned back and smiled sadly. "This is who you are, isn't it? I tried so hard to be someone I wasn't. To be the person you wanted me to be: the mountain hiker, beer drinker wife. I bet you got bored with that person. Looking back on it, I was so puzzled when you left. I did everything you asked of me. I probably bored you to tears. I later learned that didn't add up to a strong relationship. It took years of rethinking and starting from the bottom. I learned that I was good at some things that came as a real surprise, like solving crimes."

Brad started to speak.

"No. Wait until I'm through. I've turned into a pretty good amateur detective as well as a swimmer. Bet you never thought you'd hear that from me."

Brad nodded. "I don't know what to say."

"Come on, let's go," I said and I started up the trail back to Earl's house.

"You're a detective?" he asked.

"No, I just act like one sometimes. And I solve crimes. Real crimes, like people getting killed."

Brad shook his head. "I don't believe it."

"That's what I do on the side. My other job is working for the San Francisco Giants in Guest Services. Basically, I work the games."

Brad was tongue-tied. "You're … you're an office assistant. That's all you ever wanted to be. That and married."

I slowed down so Brad could catch up with me. If I tilted my head and looked up, I could see Earl's house between the trees. That's where I wanted to be, and I wanted Brad to leave.

"That's not all I wanted to be. I had Lena to take care of. You really didn't know me, did you? Well, it's not your fault. I didn't know me either. Then. I do now."

We were standing at the top of the trail. "I'm not going back to Colorado. I signed the divorce papers because that's what I wanted to do. I've moved on with my life. Maybe you should too."

Brad shrugged and shook his head. "You've changed. That's all I can say. If you're interested, I liked the old Trisha better."

What a jerk, I thought to myself. But I smiled, leaned over, and gave him a kiss on the cheek. "Enjoy the rest of your life." Then I walked over to the big house, my shoes sending up puffs of dirt, and trekked up the front stairs, never looking back.

⚮

Dad and Earl sat like statues in the living room off the deck when I walked in. They stared straight ahead at the baseball playoffs on the TV. They didn't say anything. They never looked my way. They tried so hard to ignore me.

"Dad? Earl?" I said quietly.

"Hi, Trish. Where you been?" asked Dad. His head swiveled in my direction, then snapped back to the television.

"Were you eavesdropping on my conversation with Brad? I bet you both heard every word I said. Right?"

"Me? Never. Been watching the game." Their responses jumbled together as I walked over and blocked their view of the TV.

"If you heard everything, then I don't have to repeat it, right?"

"Well, not everything," said Earl. "Wanna give us a wrap-up?"

"I want to make sure you sent that man away. For good," said Dad.

"She did. Remember?" said Earl. "She told him to have a good life or something like that."

"I didn't hear that part," said Dad. "What'd she say again?"

They looked past me like I had evaporated into thin air.

"Hello? I'm standing right here."

"I know, and you're in the way," said Earl. "I'm going to miss the next batter. Could you move over?"

I took a quick sidestep and stared at the two men, who continued to ignore my existence. "You don't want to know what I said to Brad?"

"Is he coming back?" asked Dad, eyes still on the batter who was now trotting to first base, taking off his gloves and batting helmet with each step.

"He shouldn't have walked him," said Earl. "Now they've got a guy on first and one in scoring position."

"No," I responded.

"I'm fine then," he said.

I aimed myself at the staircase.

"Wait," said Dad. This time he looked at me. "What about Jon?"

"I screwed that up," I said.

"But, I thought …" started Dad again.

"I don't want to talk about it." And I didn't. I moved quickly up the stairs toward my bedroom.

Earl and Dad began mumbling. "Don't talk about me," I yelled over the banister.

"We're not. It's this guy on the mound. Time to make a change. Both Earl and I agree. Oh, and here comes the manager. He must have heard us."

Earl snickered. "Must have heard us. That's a good one."

I sighed, walked into my suite of rooms and closed the door.

I checked my phone. Jon hadn't unblocked me. Not a good sign.

I gave my sister a call and filled her in on my conversations with both Justine and Brad. I looked out at La Cruz Canyon from my deck, fixated on a brown squirrel with a bushy tail leaping from branch to branch.

"Trish. Trisha? Are you still there?" asked Lena.

"I'm here."

"Something bothering you?"

"Well," I started.

"It's how you treated Jon, right?"

"I signed and mailed in the divorce papers. I have no husband and no boyfriend. This has not been my best moment."

"Stop whining. Do something. Forget these guys, both of them, and do something. You have a crime to solve and I bet you're more than halfway there. So, solve it," she said.

She hung up.

"So solve it," I repeated in a high-pitched whining voice.

A new text popped up on my phone.

Big misunderstanding. Want to see you. Meet me on the boat. Sent from the newly returned Marty Barlow.

"Well, that's something to do," I said to the almost-dark La Cruz Canyon.

Chapter 41

Marty pushed off the invitation when I asked for specifics. It took a week, but eventually, I nailed him down to a day and time. I arrived at the marina early evening as long shadows crept across the boats at the dock.

"What's the misunderstanding?" I asked Marty after I climbed aboard the Nereus and settled on the deep blue cushioned settee.

"Want a drink?" he asked, pulling out a bottle of bourbon—good bourbon—and two plastic glasses from a cabinet in the galley. I shook my head no. "Do you mind if I do?"

He didn't wait for my reply. He poured until the glass inched above the halfway full mark. Whatever he had to say to me needed some liquid encouragement. Silence quivered in the air, broken only by the occasional screech of a seagull.

"Congratulations on your marriage," I started, hoping I could get him talking. He nodded and took another gulp. "Have you decided where you'll live? Your house? Or Justine's?"

He shrugged and looked out into the stern of the boat.

"Did you enjoy the Philippines?" I asked.

"I'm waiting for the kids," he said, ignoring my questions.

"You never said they were coming. Why did you invite them?" I asked.

"Had enough of them when they were at your house?"

"No. Not at all. They're good kids. All three of them. But I thought you had something to tell me. You said there was a misunderstanding."

"You don't like me, do you?" Marty frowned at me as each word left his mouth.

"That's pushing it," I said. "I really don't know you. I have no reason to dislike you. But I do have a lot of questions for you, about your business, your brother … that kind of thing."

"Hey Dad," yelled Dawson as he and Daria walked down the finger pier.

"You two, get the boat ready to leave the dock," Marty commanded like the skipper he was.

"Wait a minute." I hopped up and tried to climb the steps to the stern of the boat, but Marty blocked my way.

"You're staying here," he said as he sat on the steps and watched Daria pull up the bumpers cushioning the side of the boat from the dock. Dawson silently switched on the motor and began to back the large boat out of its slip.

"No. I'm not," I said, pushing him aside and taking the steps two at a time. I had planned to jump off the boat and land hopefully on the dock, but we were further away than I had hoped. I could jump but I'd land in the water not on the pier.

My heartbeat jolted into overdrive.

"Let me off," I said, my voice raising.

"Come on back. I'm not going to hurt you," said Marty.

"I want to get off," I yelled, now beginning to panic. Land moved further away. Where were they taking me and why?

"Head toward the back of Angel Island," Marty told Dawson. "We can anchor while we talk. And then move on." He looked over at me. "Come back down below. Get out of the wind."

"No. I'm fine right here," I said, and I sat on one of the white boat cushions out of arm's reach from Marty. The setting sun turned the bay a deep shade of blue. Seagulls flew overhead, monitoring the water below. When they saw something tasty, they folded their wings tight against their solid bodies and dove beak first into the bay with barely a splash. I'd watched this scene before, when Jon took me from Marin to Berkeley. Then it was beautiful. Now it was treacherous. And no Jon to the rescue.

I reached for my phone. But Marty grabbed it out of my hand.

"Where are we going?" I asked, starting to shiver, not from the slight breeze but from fear. I hugged myself and stuck my hands close to my armpits for warmth. Marty ducked into the cabin and came back with a jacket. When I didn't move, he draped it around my shoulders.

"This will warm you up," he said, looking at me. I glanced down at the deck, not meeting his eyes. "Take me back. Now," I ordered. But he walked forward to chat with Dawson, who piloted the boat.

We passed a small sailboat in the light breeze, and a kayak taking advantage of the calm waters. I watched the Tiburon peninsula as we motored past, with its hidden waterfront homes and stretched out docks. We crossed Raccoon Strait, the mile and a half water corridor of water between Tiburon and Angel Island, and powered through a small tidal rip that bounced the boat around. I grabbed on to a stanchion, not wanting to slip off my seat. But no one else took any precautions.

The quiet air and subdued waters continued as we snuck behind Angel Island. "Look for a spot and let's anchor," Marty said to his kids. Dawson powered a little further on and then put the engine in neutral while he dropped an anchor off the bow of the boat. The current secured it as it pushed the boat backward and the anchor dug into the bottom. The boat began to swing gently.

"Okay," said Marty. "Kids, come here. I want you to help me tell this story."

I started first. "Bringing me out here is a big mistake." No reaction from the three of them.

Marty sat down directly opposite me, his kids on either side. "First," he said, "thank you for keeping my family safe when Andy's

Las Vegas contacts showed up at Justine's place. You protected them. For that I'm grateful. And so are they." He looked first to his right at Dawson and then at Daria, who frowned. "Kids?"

In unison, the words "thank you" slid from their mouths.

"You know I had to leave the country for a while. Dawson told me Harrison, and evidently you, think that I killed my brother. I would never do anything like that."

"Right," I said under my breath.

"You don't believe me? Okay. What's the best way for me to prove it to you? Why would I do that? He was my brother."

"Oh, I don't know. Maybe because his gambling had ruined your business? Maybe because both of you were running a Ponzi scheme and duping your clients? Maybe because you were in love with his wife?"

"What's a Ponzi scheme?" asked Dawson.

"I'll tell you later," said Daria, leaning behind her dad to talk to her brother.

"Not true," said Marty. "And you know something else that's not true? The police's decision to call his death an accident. I don't think it was. In fact, I'm sure it wasn't."

"And who do you think killed him? The thugs from Las Vegas? Justine? Harrison? Your kids? Disgruntled clients?"

"I have my ideas, but I can't say."

"Why not? Please take me back to the dock," I said, attempting to sound firm. Angel Island was not that far away. If I jumped off the boat, could I swim to shore? Would the current push me away from land? Or would Marty back over me and trash my body to bits like he did his brother?

"Where's the proof?" I asked Marty as I continued to eye the tree-lined shore of Angel Island. I could make out a small sandy beach. If I reached that, I would have to climb up through the dense trees, walk to the ferry dock about three miles away, but then what? Would anyone be there?

"I can't tell you," he said. "You have to trust me."

I stood up and threw one leg over the side. "Take me back now or I'm jumping off this boat," I said.

Marty reached and pulled me back into the cockpit. "Not yet. Daw, hit it. Turn around and drive up Raccoon Strait to the place we talked about."

Dawson clambered back up to the boat's controls, maneuvered the anchor back on to the boat, and pushed the throttle forward. The boat jerked and moved rapidly toward Raccoon Strait.

"Daria, go get your swimsuit." She moved quickly down the steps to the cabin. Marty stared at me. "My daughter's going to give you her suit. Put in on."

"I will not," I said in the firmest voice I could muster. My breath rushed through my body. My head began to spin. Not now, I said to myself. Don't faint. They'll throw you overboard. I sat down, leaned over, and dropped my head between my knees. The fuzziness cleared and I used the few seconds to look around the deck from this upside-down angle. Some tools rested just out of reach, but if I stretched, maybe I could grab them.

"Go below," he ordered, pulling me to a standing position and pushing me toward the steps into the cabin.

"No," I said, grabbing onto the deck opening.

"Yes," he said, pushing my arms down and almost throwing me into the cabin. "You wanted to get in the water before. Now you'll have your chance."

At the bottom of the steps, Daria stood with a swimsuit in her hand. "You have to put this on. Go change in the head," she said, pointing to the small bathroom.

I shook my head no.

"Please," she said. "If you don't come do it, Pops will come down and probably strip you. You don't want that, do you?"

Resigned, I pulled the swimsuit from her hand and squeezed into the tiny head. Smaller than an airplane's bathroom, it took some weird moving around before I could take my clothes off and pull on her suit. I glanced into the mirror. The suit was at least two sizes too small, and the material barely covered my necessities. I opened the door.

"Okay, I have it on. Now I'm putting my clothes back on over it."

"Don't bother," said Daria. We're almost there. Put the jacket on and go back on the deck."

This time I did as I was told. The wind had picked up when we headed west up Raccoon Strait. The boat bounced over the chop. I knew I would soon be in that water. Everything that Lena had said about swimming in the Bay flew out of my mind. The only words I could remember were cold and current. The Golden Gate Bridge looked like a trinket in the distance as we passed the western edge of the island.

"Now," Marty said. Daria had climbed up on deck behind me. She took one arm. Marty took the other. They dragged me over to the side.

"Jump," said Marty.

"No," I said. "I can't move." The water looked deep blue, but cold, very cold.

"Jump. Or I'll push you."

"I'm not moving," I said. Both of my hands clung to the person on either side.

"Dad, I don't want to do this," said Daria.

"Push her off," said Marty. Daria shook her head. Marty reached behind me and shoved his daughter to the side. "Jump," he said again. When I didn't move, his hands slipped to the small of my back and propelled me off the boat toward into the bay. All sound disappeared. Nothing registered during the two freakishly long seconds in the air. I inhaled, held my breath, and fused my arms to my sides.

The plunge didn't register at first. Then my senses exploded. Cold. Bone chilling cold. I opened my eyes beneath brownish water. The silt-filled Bay obstructed views of my arms and legs. Where they still there? I couldn't tell. I clawed for the surface. Off to the side was the hull of the boat, a large dirty white blob. I gasped and spat out what seemed like gallons of Bay water, half salt, half not. The three people on the boat looked over the side at me. Dawson was in shock. Daria was crying. And Marty? Well, Marty was expressionless.

"What the fuck?" I yelled, treading water, taking in as much water as I spit out. "What's wrong with all of you? Get me out of here."

No one said a word. Then it hit me. They were going to kill me like they killed Andy. Goosebumps spread across my arms and down my legs. Was it from the chilly water or fear? While my feet pumped below me, I turned around while choppy little waves slapped my neck and face. Angel Island was behind me. Tiburon was across Raccoon Strait. The distance from one to the other was about a mile. I was closer to the boats anchored in Ayala Cove, the little anchorage off the island. Maybe a quarter to a half mile. I could swim that if the Nereus didn't run me down first. Without a look back, I sighted on the nearest sailboat and started to swim. Without goggles, water blurred my vision, but I kept going. About eight strokes in, I heard the voices on the boat behind me.

"Come back," Daria yelled.

"We're coming to pick you up," said Dawson. "Swim toward us."

Maybe it was the adrenaline, but as I moved my arms and kicked, and with my head above the water so I could see where I was going, the chill faded. The goosebumps disappeared. But I had to keep moving. I knew from what Lena had told me about swimming in cold open water that as soon as I stopped, I would get cold, and it would be harder to warm up. I inched toward the anchored sailboat in front of me. I could see a man standing on the bow near the anchor line looking in my direction.

"Help," I yelled, waving one arm. He waved back but didn't move. Maybe he couldn't hear me. I saw him point to a spot behind me. A quick look told me what I thought. The bow of the Nereus was approaching. It followed me but stayed off to the side. It glided closer and closer.

"Here. Grab this," called out Daria as she hurled the life ring in my direction. "We'll pull you around to the ladder."

"No thanks," I said, swallowing water and coughing. The ladder was right next to the outboard engines and certain death. If I was going to die here in the Bay between Angel Island and the Tiburon peninsula, they would have to chase me down. I kept swimming toward the sailboat, kicking as hard as I could. From the side, the large powerboat passed me and pulled between me and the sailboat.

Marty had hauled in the life ring and was getting ready to throw it again.

"I'm not trying to kill you," he said, flinging the ring in my direction. "Grab it," he bellowed.

The brief but frenetic swim in the chilly waters and the fear of drowning or being attacked by an outdoor engine sapped my strength. Panic made my movements in the water choppy and fruitless. I did what Lena said not to do. I stopped swimming. The tide pulled me closer to the boat and the life ring. I could hear the outboards purring like a waiting wild animal. I drifted toward the stern of the boat and the engines.

"Kill the engine," Marty shouted to Dawson. Silence penetrated the cool air. "Swim toward the rear of the boat."

Daria came to one side carrying a boat hook. "Grab on. I'll pull you in," she called.

I had no more strength, so I did.

Chapter 42

Daria held two warm washcloths up to my face. I couldn't feel anything. She had draped a big beach towel around me and helped pull off my swimsuit.

"I'm really sorry," Daria said, almost in tears.

"I can't remember the last time someone undressed me so enthusiastically," I was about to say. But I stopped. The image of me and Brad popped into my mind.

"Thanks, Daria," I said instead.

"We're all sorry. We wanted to show you something," she said again. "Get your clothes on as fast as you can." She handed me a cup of tea. "You ready for Dad to come down?"

"No, I don't want to talk to him. What was he trying to do, kill me?"

"He wasn't doing that at all. Just listen to him, okay?" She stuck her head out of the cabin. "You can come down now," she called out.

My clothes felt damp and sticky. I grabbed a blanket that Daria laid out beside me. I cocooned in its warmth and took the two warm washcloths and strung them around my neck. I sat close enough to the galley that I grabbed another mug and covered it up with the blanket. If Marty came close to me, I intended to whack him in the head with it. I watched his boat shoes pause at the top step. Then slowly, he climbed down into the cabin. I tightened my grip on the mug.

When he was fully in the cabin, he stood back against the steps, not moving.

"Is it okay if I walk over and sit across from you?" he asked, still not moving.

I nodded.

He crept across the teak floor, never turning away from me, and sat down on the settee in slow motion.

We stared at each other in complete stillness.

"Are you getting warmer?" he asked.

"You and your family are crazy, you know that?"

"Look, I'm sorry—we're all sorry—that we pushed you in the water. Maybe it wasn't the best idea. But I needed to show you that I didn't kill my brother. No matter what Harrison or maybe even Justine says."

That's odd. Why would his blushing bride think that her new husband killed her old one?

"By getting you in the Bay, moving closer to the propellers, there are ways that you, the swimmer, can keep yourself safe. You saw that, right?"

"That wasn't on my mind. Frankly, I didn't remember much except attempting to sprint to the anchored boat ahead of me. If you were a skilled boat handler, I think you could have run me right over. I don't believe a swimmer, no matter how fast they can swim, would be able to keep themselves safe."

Marty stood up and sighed. "This idea, taking you out and ... ah ... helping you in the water so you could see what was possible, or not possible, was my kids' idea."

"Right. Blame them," I said.

"Dad's telling the truth," Daria said. "He didn't kill Uncle Andy and I thought this might convince you. When it came time to push you in the water, I got scared and couldn't do it. But I wanted you to see that it's not that easy to run someone over."

"The one thing I learned from this, this stunt, was that someone could be killed, but it wouldn't be easy. The boat would have to be driven by someone who knew what they were doing. Someone with boat handling skills. That still could be you, Marty. Or maybe Dawson."

"Don't bring me into this," Dawson yelled from the cockpit. "It wasn't my idea. At least not the pushing you into the water part."

"I don't care whose idea it was. I want to go back to the dock. I'm shivering and soggy." I tucked the blanket tighter around me, but my teeth still chattered. "I do have one thing I need to clear up. Were any of you on the boat when Andy went out for a swim? Did you take him?"

"Not me," said Dawson as he increased the speed and the boat headed back down Raccoon Strait.

"You?" I asked, staring at Marty.

"No. I told you that earlier."

I glanced at Daria. Her eyes didn't meet mine, but she shook her head no.

"Well, somebody took him out. There was a person on board when the Coast Guard brought his body back."

Marty shook his head. "It wasn't me," he said firmly.

The three of us were silent, leaving only the sounds of the muffled engine and the greenish-brown water slapping against the hull.

"Daria," Marty said to his daughter, "go up to the cockpit and help your brother. I need to talk to Trisha."

Daria took off.

"I can't believe that pushing me off the boat was her idea," I said as I watched her scramble up the ladder to the cockpit.

"I have to tell you something that is very sensitive to Daria. Sensitive to the whole family," Marty said. "I've tried to make it clear that I didn't kill my brother. But to be honest, I wanted to. Since my wife died, I've tried to parent my kids. They were just starting middle school when she passed away. That's a tough time for any kid, without a mom … Well, some days were better than others."

Marty began pacing around the small cabin. Every now and then he would shoot a glance in my direction. "Justine offered to help me with them and so did Andy, and I gladly took them up. At first the kids loved being at their aunt and uncle's home, even though Harrison could be strange. But when they reached thirteen years old, something changed. Daria would cry if I dropped her off there. Dawson would rather spend time here on the boat. I finally sat them down and said, 'You're not leaving this room until you tell me what's going on.'"

"Your brother was making moves on the lovely young developing Daria. Right?"

"How did you know?"

"I've had more than one person tell me about Andy's predilection for young girls."

Marty stared at me. "Really?"

"Really. And how Daria was used as bait to attract her friends and introduce them to her uncle."

"Well, you're right. Evidently, Dawson walked in on Marty and Daria in the laundry room. He was holding Daria in a clench and had one hand on her breast, the other trying to reach down her jeans. Daria was frozen. She didn't know what to do. This, after all, was her beloved uncle. According to Dawson, she kept saying, 'Leave me alone, stop.' Dawson pulled him off her and they both stayed far away from him until I came to pick them up. I vaguely remember that I thought the twins had had one of their many disagreements. They weren't talking to each other or me. I pressed them and pressed them until Daria burst into tears. When they told me, I didn't believe it. I really couldn't. My brother wouldn't do something like that. It took a while, but I realized that not only was Andy destroying our business, he was destroying our family. Did I want revenge for that? You bet. But killing him? Then who would take care of my kids? They both would be more vulnerable. My plan was to keep them away from Andy, no matter how wonderful Justine had been to them."

I watched Marty carefully as he told me his story. His face

grimaced with each sentence. What he said rang true, especially after thinking about what the boy from the diner said to me weeks back. And the conversation with Dawson.

"Well, if you didn't do it, or your kids weren't involved, what about Justine? Or Harrison?" I asked.

"Not likely. They have more to lose with him dead. I'm thinking it was probably one of our clients who lost their savings," Marty said.

"Like who?"

Marty shrugged. "I've looked over our clients list more than once to narrow it down. There's a few you might be interested in checking out. We have … well, had … a number of investors in the yachting world. Some worked in the industry and were local; others kept their boats in different corners of the world."

"Dad," called Dawson from the cockpit. "Could you come up here?"

"Wait," I said as Marty took the stairs two at a time. I heard him walking toward the front of the boat. Following him, I called out, "Marty, who are these customers?" The grumble of the engine smothered any sound more than two feet away. Approaching Marty and Dawson from behind, I noticed a red light blinking on the dashboard of the boat.

"Turn everything off. We have enough power to glide into the slip," said Marty.

"Marty," I tried again.

"Can't talk now. Having engine problems. Daria, get the bumpers out. Trisha, as soon as we're in the slip, get off the boat, grab the lines on the dock, and throw them to Daria." Marty glanced at me. "Sorry. We'll talk later," he said and turned back to Dawson.

Chapter 43

"What is it with this Barlow family?" I asked Lena. "Two of them have pushed me in the water. I'm not supposed to get my stitches wet for another ten days. They're still there, aren't they? The stitches?"

Lena didn't bother to look. "That's what he said? The boat was having engine problems?" asked Lena.

I nodded. "Seemed true to me. A red light blinked on the dashboard. Anyway, that was a few days ago, and he still hasn't given me the name of his suspects. I've texted him daily but no response."

We strolled outside the empty flowerpot lady's home, Lena beside me, pushing Little T in his stroller.

"I don't know why we're here," she said. "The house looks deserted."

She was right. Drawn blinds, dried overgrown grass, and newspapers piling up at the front door confirmed our suspicions.

"What do you know about Hildie, her daughter?" I asked Lena as we continued down the street.

"Not much. She seemed devoted to her mother before all this happened. I often saw her husband's truck parked on the street."

"Do you know anything about them?"

"Not really. I think she's a dental hygienist and her husband owns Marin Marine in Sausalito. We talked about this, remember?"

Another neighbor walked past us and stopped to play with Little T.

"You are getting so big," she said, reaching over to pat his chubby little hand. "I saw you looking at the Gunderson house. Thinking of buying it?"

"Is it on the market already?" asked Lena. "They're not wasting any time."

"Mrs. Gunderson needs the money to move on. She's living at her daughter and son-in-law's. They don't seem to mind, but the mother is fiercely independent and wants out."

"Do you know anything about the son-in-law?"

"Oh yeah. He's a big shot on the Sausalito waterfront. And I think he sits on the Sausalito City Council. Does boat repair and maintenance. Been around for years."

The big golden retriever was clearly annoyed that his walk had come to a stop and started pulling on the leash. "Gotta go. Tramp is unhappy with me."

She and Tramp took off, crossing the street in the other direction.

"Are you thinking what I'm thinking?" I asked Lena.

"What?"

"The son-in-law has the means, the boat smarts, and the political clout to take out Andy Barlow."

Chapter 44

I knew that connecting Marin Marine to the killer was key. Harrison's input became crucial. If he could move away from his original theory. there might be something … anything … that would lead me to the murderer. I arranged to meet him down at the Nereus on Friday, saying I needed to see the approximate spot where his dad died. More people hustled around the harbor, more than usual since it was late afternoon at the start of the weekend. I parked away from the main lot and watched sailors go down to their boats, carrying satchels of groceries or pulling wagons piled to the brim with supplies. From this vantage, I should be able to see him when he drove up.

"There he is now," I said to my dirty Honda as I watched him walk across the main parking lot. Before I jumped out of the car, I reached for my phone and quick dialed Detective Hamilton and left a message.

"Come down to Gaspar de Portola Yacht Harbor. I'm going out on the Nereus with Harrison. I learned something you need to know. Can you find where Evan Gunderson from Marin Marine was on the day Andy Barlow died?"

"Harrison. Wait up," I called. His head snapped around. A fake smile was plastered on his face. In the weeks he'd been in California, his British affect had begun to fade. Strands of dirty blond hair grew from his scalp, creating a sharp line next to the existing black. His dark cape that he wore one of the first times I saw him had been replaced with a "Take a Hike" hoodie with Yosemite National Park printed on the back. His eyes met mine and he stopped. I caught up with him, but he didn't say anything, so we walked in silence. His pure white sneakers (no more black ankle boots) padded toward the pier. He opened the metal gate for me and I went down the gangway first.

"I appreciate you taking me out. All this time I've been working on your dad's case, I never saw the spot where he died. I think it's time, don't you?" I said with a smile. He nodded.

"So, you're leaving tomorrow?" I asked awkwardly, trying to make small talk. We continued walking in silence until we reached the Nereus. He climbed over the lifelines first, unlocked the combination lock and pulled out the wooden slats leading to the cabin. I stood there on the finger pier, waiting for him to tell me to board. It didn't look like that was going to happen, and I climbed on.

"A quick question. Hope you don't mind. It's a little personal. Your mom said that because of Andy's gambling, all the credit cards were maxed out. How are you paying for a plane flight back to England?"

"What's this all about?" he asked as he walked up the narrow stairway and sat down next to me.

"Just curious. Money seems to be a problem. And I wanted to see the distance between where your father was found and the Coast Guard station near the north tower of the Golden Gate Bridge," I lied. "I told you that."

He fidgeted with a line wrapped around one of the boat's winches.

"I bought a round-trip ticket with an open return date before I left," he mumbled.

"I don't know too much about boats. Do they need regular work done on them like cars?"

"They do. We take the Nereus to Marin Marine. They're the best yard in the north bay."

"You bring the boat in?"

"Me? No. That used to be Dad, Uncle Marty, or even Dawson's

job."

"Did it go into the shop after your father's accident?"

"Don't remember. Is that what you wanted to talk about? You could have texted me," he said.

"How well do you know Evan Gunderson?"

"Who?"

"The owner of Marin Marine."

"Only seen him a few times.," he said.

"Do you think he was on board when your father died?

"You think he killed him? Why would he do that?"

"He lost a lot of money when Barlow & Barlow went belly up."

"You don't know that," he said, standing up abruptly and moving toward the helm. "Still want to go out?"

I nodded and the engines started.

"Pull in those fenders," he said, pointing to the cylindrical white bumpers hanging off the cleats. I hoisted in three of them that had been protecting the hull of the boat from bumping the finger pier.

"Stow them under the seats," he said, still not looking at me. With one motion, I flipped up the seats to see a long white storage bin.

"Here?" I asked.

"Yeah. There," he called back.

The rumble of the outboards behind me muffled all spoken sound. I held on to the railing and inched myself up toward Harrison. I was outside the cabin by the controls but standing right next to him.

"Hey, you're blocking my view," he said. I shuffled back until I could sit down. I shuddered, remembering how Marty and Daria had pushed me off this very same boat a few days ago. I hoped Harrison didn't have that in mind.

Still looking out into the bay as we traveled around Tiburon point into the Raccoon Strait, he asked, "What's this all about??"

"Help me with the timeline of what happened."

"Ok." I only heard the 'k' over the grumbling engines.

"Your dad goes out for a training swim with someone."

"Uncle Marty."

"We don't know that for sure. He jumps in the water to swim. The Nereus backs over him."

Harrison nodded.

"The Coast Guard brings the boat in, and the sheriff calls you and your mom to discuss the accident."

Harrison nodded again.

"So, you were already here in Marin and heard about your dad's death when your mother did?"

Harrison's automatic reaction stopped in mid-nod.

"You were here before the accident?" I asked.

"Why does it matter?" he asked, keeping his eyes ahead.

"I'm just asking," I said.

He slowed the engines as we passed Ayala Cove, the anchorage for Angel Island. A few anchored boats swayed back and forth with the current, bows pointed east. The tide was going out, flowing toward the Pacific Ocean.

"You're right," he said, turning to look at me. "I came home before he died." Even with the reduced power of the engine, the current pushed us along toward the Pacific Ocean.

I stood up and took a step toward him. He kept one hand on the wheel as he stared at me.

"Harrison, I really don't think that Uncle Marty was on board. Could it be that you were on the boat with him?" The words hung in the air. He shifted his gaze forward. A few minutes passed.

"What are you implying?" he asked as he pushed the throttle forward, increasing the power and heading straight for the Golden Gate Bridge. Sausalito appeared off to our right and Angel Island quickly dropped behind us.

We glided by the Coast Guard station off to the left.

I stood next to him again and said quietly, "Harrison, I think you were the one who killed your father. What I want to know is why?"

He coughed as he gave the throttle another push, almost launching the boat out of the bay. Cold brownish-green water sailed over the bow and flowed back into the cockpit.

"Slow down," I yelled. My hair whipped around my face as I grabbed any available handhold to keep me from flying backward and off the boat, into the bay.

As the Nereus approached the Golden Gate, the suspension bridge grew in size, looking enormous from this angle. Harrison slowed the boat down again.

"I have one day left in the United States. Just one day. Tomorrow by this time, I'll be in the air. I should have made my reservation for today." He chuckled. "You're dim, you know that. It took you all this time to figure it out."

"Tell me why, Harrison. I thought you and your dad were close. That's what you said."

"Why? You want to know why? My father, that tight-ass gambler, told me to come home. That he had run out of money and couldn't afford my 'luxurious Shakespearean education.' His words. Not mine. When I said he had to stop gambling—see, I knew about that. Mom had told me. When I told him that he had … he had to support me … he laughed and said I was an entitled Marin brat who only cared about himself. He stopped paying for my tuition, my room and board. Everything. I had no choice but to fly back here to this place," he said, flinging his arm toward the Marin headlands.

"So I came home and pretended that everything was okay. That I was a good son and would get a job … doing what, I don't know. Then I overheard my parents arguing about his life insurance, and it hit me. He was worth something. If he was dead."

Harrison steered the boat directly underneath the North Tower of the bridge. The choppy cold water slammed against the support. The roadway of the bridge seemed so far overhead, but the muffled roar of traffic seeped down toward us. I knew what Harrison had in mind. A trip into the Pacific maybe close to the Farallon Islands, the hunting grounds of the great white sharks, and a quick shove into the dark cold

Pacific Ocean. That's how these Barlows got rid of their problems.

Harrison continued talking.

"Yes," he admitted. "I killed my dad. I had no other choice."

"Dawson, my cousin, without knowing it, helped me. He taught me how to handle this boat. Uncle Marty was more than happy to have someone else take over Dad's training swims. I practiced my boat skills over and over and then waited for the ideal time."

Harrison pulled back on the throttle again, and we drifted underneath the bridge into the Pacific Ocean covered with white caps. The Nereus pounded against the waves and bounced wildly up and down.

"You want to know how I did it?" he yelled over the wind so I could hear him. "When the tides seemed right, I asked him to pick me up at Travis Marina. The one over there by the Coast Guard station." He pointed back at the small boat basin we'd just passed. "It was a glorious day. Not much wind. Nothing like all these waves today. No fog. Dad sat, head lifted toward the sun. Happy and at peace. I told him I had an energy tablet that helped with endurance during a long swim. I said that he should try it out while he was training and had someone near him if he got in trouble. I'd been talking about this tab for a week or so. I remember him saying, 'Sure. It's worth a try.' He wanted to swim the width of Lake Tahoe in the summer and his training had plateaued. He wasn't that fast of a swimmer to begin with, so he was willing to try anything to pick up some speed. He took the pill. Washed it down with some sort of electrolyte drink. Then I waited. It was a heavy duty sleeping pill. Who knows what else it was laced with. He sat right there where you are and within thirty minutes, he could barely keep his eyes open. I helped him stand up. We walked to the stern of the boat right next to the engines. He tried to back out. 'Harr,' he said, 'I don't feel well. I don't want to do this.'

"'Yeah, you do,' I said and I pushed him in. The cold water revived him for a minute or two and he started to swim, but then he had trouble moving his arms. His eyes closed. I maneuvered the boat right in front of him and then I hit reverse. I backed right over him. Simple. He didn't get out of the way. One scream. That's all. No other noise but a lot of bangs as his body hit the propellers. Over and over again. Blood was everywhere. I thought about sharks as I watched the blood circle the outboards and drift away from the boat. One of his legs and an arm followed it. Then I radioed the Coast Guard sounding all scared."

He sat there lost in the memory, the joy of the memory.

Limbs floating away? Was Harrison a psychopath? But this wasn't the time to analyze his psyche. I needed to save myself. The boat hurtled west in the choppy waters. Waves continued to hit the side of the boat and cold spray washed over me. I didn't want to end up in the Pacific Ocean. The gore he talked about sent him into a trance, giving me a chance to look around the boat. Some tools rested in a canvas bag tucked underneath the driver's seat. I stretched one foot out, and when the boat lurched again, I kicked the bag over and pretended to fall off the seat. In the confusion, I picked up a hammer and tucked it under my hoodie.

As I pushed myself back onto the seat, I asked, "Was your mother involved?"

"No. But I don't think she minded that he was dead. It gave her a chance to move on. Have to say, I didn't think she would move on to Uncle Marty."

With that, he stopped talking and drove the boat farther west into the Pacific Ocean, away from the headlands and the entrance to the San Francisco Bay.

"Where do you want to go in?" he said, matter-of-factly.

"I don't want to go in at all. Please, Harrison. Take me to the dock. Please. Don't do this." I searched the Pacific Ocean for other boats. The empty ocean stared back. It surrounded the two of us out on this lurching boat.

"We're still too close to land," he said almost to himself.

"Harrison, I promise not to tell anyone. You can get the insurance money and go back to England. No one will know."

We powered on for another fifteen minutes, then the engines went quiet. The westerly wind blew spray off the rough seas. Harrison got up and seized my arm. I pulled away and crouched over, touching the wet deck and grabbing hold of the hammer in my pocket. His hands slipped around my waist as he tried to drag me to the side of the boat. This was it. My hand tightened on the tool. In an instant, I slammed my hand up and solidly hit him in the groin.

He immediately doubled over and cried out in pain. I swung at his head and knocked him out. Frantically, I glanced around the boat looking for rope. Every boat had rope, right? But all I located was the rope on the fenders. While he remained unconscious, I pulled his arms behind him and looped it around his wrists. With no one at the helm, the Nereus turned sideways and waves hit us broadside, almost tipping the boat over. More cold spray hit the boat and doused the two of us, but it didn't bring him to. Did I kill him? I prodded the veins on his neck. Still alive, but how much longer would he be out? I grabbed another bumper and looped the rope around his ankles, tying everything off on a cleat. He wasn't going to move, not if I could help it.

I scrambled toward the wheel and picked up the radio. Forget proper radio etiquette. I didn't know it anyway. Pressing the black button on the side, I yelled, "Help," into the speaker. "I'm outside of the Golden Gate floating around on a powerboat in the ocean. Someone tried to kill me."

The next voice I heard was that of the Coast Guard. "Please state the name of your boat and give me your latitude and longitude?"

"The Nereus. I don't know the latitude and longitude, but if you come underneath the Golden Gate Bridge heading west, you'll see the boat. We're the only thing out here. I'm not sure how to make this boat move, but I'll try."

"We're on our way," said the male voice. "Keep the radio close so we can talk to you."

Behind me, Harrison had begun to stir. "I'll kill you for this," he yelled. The wind picked up and swallowed his words. I looked at the instrument cluster in front me. I found the throttle and pushed it forward. The power boat jumped forward, throwing me back into the seat.

"Too much gas, you idiot," Harrison yelled. "Untie me. I'll do it."

"That's not going to happen," I called out over my shoulder. I tried again, this time very slowly, and the boat moved northeast, still taking chilling waves on its side. Cold water dripped down my back, and my hands shook. I gradually turned the wheel so that the boat headed due East toward the Golden Gate Bridge. I pushed the throttle a little further and we moved faster through the waves. The wind, now behind us, pushed us in the right direction. Far ahead, I saw a boat barreling its way underneath the bridge.

"Here comes the calvary," I shouted. An air horn sat in a cloth pocket next to the front seat. I picked it up, held it far away from me, and blasted away. Over and over. The radio barked at me. "We hear you. We see you. You can stop sounding the horn."

But I didn't. Not until the Coast Guard boat pulled up next to me.

"There's a guy back there fastened to the cleat." I tried to point to where I had stowed Harrison, but my arms shook uncontrollably. I more or less pointed to the sky, then the ocean. "He was going to dump me overboard. He killed his dad, Andy Barlow."

"That woman's a liar," called out Harrison from the floor of the boat. "She tried to kill me."

"We'll figure this out when we get back to dry land," said a Coastie, climbing aboard the Nereus.

Chapter 45

The Coast Guard dock erupted in chaos as the rescue boat pulled into the pier. Police cars swarmed the area, blue and red lights swirling. Two fire engines screamed down the winding hill, their sirens wailing and lights flashing. Even an ambulance stood by.

Overhead, the thwop thwop thwop of a news helicopter drowned out the noise on land. "This looks like a movie set for an action film," I said to the Coastie standing next to me. Harrison emerged from below in handcuffs and shuffled onto the dock with security holding his arms. They took him first to an ambulance and then stuffed him into a Marin Sheriff's car.

I went next, minus the handcuffs. Like Harrison, first stop were the EMTs waiting in the ambulance.

"I'm fine … just wet and cold," I told them.

"Her vitals are good. Heart rate and blood pressure higher than normal," said a woman now checking my eyes.

"Well, what do you expect," I said. "This wasn't a Mai Tai cruise. Someone was about to dump me into the Bay." They continued poking and prodding and staring at me. My caregiver draped a silver mylar blanket over my shoulders.

"Stay seated for about ten minutes or so," she said while typing on a tablet.

"Let me through," a familiar voice said, moving toward me. Det.

Hamilton came into view with a concerned look on his face. "You okay?"

"Harrison confessed. I got him to confess. He killed his father for the dumbest reason ever. How did you know I was here?"

"Police radio scan. You know, you sent me to the wrong marina. But when I heard what was going on out in the ocean, I figured it had to be you."

I closed my eyes for a second. "Getting tired."

"I'm taking you home."

"My car is at …"

"Give me your keys. We'll take care of that. Tomorrow. You come in to see me."

I nodded and followed him toward the back of the parking lot.

⁂

The next day, the story of the college student who killed his father had spread across the internet. Lena kept me abreast of each new report. I hadn't been identified in the press yet. For that I was grateful. As requested, I stopped by the Central Marin Police Department and asked to see Detective Hamilton.

"You almost went swimming with the fishes," he chuckled as he escorted me back to a conference room.

"That's not funny. But I finally found out who killed Andy Barlow."

"That you did. Now I have some questions for you."

With that, I talked, replied to his inquiries, and talked some more, telling him everything that happened from the moment I arrived at the marina. He taped my epic and nodded as I spoke.

"Okay. My office may want to see you again. One more thing. I checked out Evan Gunderson. He was working an exhibit table at a marine conference in San Diego the day Barlow died. We know now he didn't do it. But it was a lead we never followed up. Good work."

"What happened to Harrison?"

"He's in jail and charged with premeditated murder."

"And Marty? He defrauded hundreds of people."

"He lawyered up. He and his brother committed a serious white-collar crime. Although he went to jail, he was out on bail almost immediately."

"What's going to happen to him?

"It depends how much he cooperates. The SEC. the Commodity Futures Trading Commission, the FBI, and the Department of Justice could all get involved. It's not a pretty picture."

As he talked, I thought about his twins and what would happen to them. "Not a pretty picture at all," I said. "Were you able to track down the Vegas loan sharks from the info I gave you?"

Detective Hamilton smiled and formally said, "The information that you gave us was very helpful. Thank you. Both men that you met are now behind bars, due to you."

"How so?"

"We gave Vegas police the description you gave us. It seems that the smell of vinegar that you detected often indicates diabetes. They ran that through their database and lo and behold, there he was. It was only a matter of hours before they picked him up, and his partner."

For the first time in about two months, my adrenaline level sunk below high gear. I felt incredibly tired, again.

"You've been really helpful, Trisha," the detective said as he walked me to the door. "But we would have figured it out."

"You don't know that," I said, laughing as I walked out the front door to my car.

Chapter 46

During the weeks that followed, Daria developed a warm friendship with Dad and Earl. She stopped by the house one afternoon to drop off some homemade muffins.

"What a kind gesture, Ms. Daria," said Dad. As they sat around the kitchen table, I heard Daria say that the marriage between Justine and Marty had collapsed.

"It had something to do with insurance money," Daria said. "Dad filed for it, whatever that means, and Aunt Justine said the money belonged to her." My father shot a knowing look at Earl.

"Don't expect to see that money soon. The insurance payout is probably on hold until everything about your father's business is settled," said Earl.

"What happened to Vivian, the longtime secretary and bookkeeper?" I asked.

"I heard Dad talking about a plea deal for her. He's getting one of those too. I think. He wants to stay out of jail. And that's what I want," Daria said.

I felt sorry for the befuddled teen. What a steep drop from the rich bitch.

<hr>

The late fall day felt crisp in the shade and toasty when Lena and I walked into the warm patches. We hiked down the trail next to Earl's house into the canyon.

"The Barlows are getting what they deserve," I told Lena. As the sun filtered through the trees, it created puzzle pieces on the packed dirt trail.

"What about the kids?" Lena asked.

"This has got to be hard for them," I said, looking down the path ahead trying to see the reservoir at the bottom of the canyon. "Everyone has lost somebody. Justine lost her husband, and her son's in jail. The twins could lose their dad."

"Will they come back and live with you?" Lena asked with a grin.

"Oh no. I don't plan on being a mother to twins," I said.

"And Harrison?"

"He won't be going back to England anytime soon. Since he's over eighteen, he could end up in prison for a long time. How did he think he would get away with this?"

"There are a lot of entitled Marin kids, but they don't go around hacking up their parents with an outboard motor just because they don't get what they want."

"True," I nodded.

The green-brown waters of the reservoir now stretched out in front of us. We couldn't reach it from this trail, but I could see a few swimmers in the water and beachgoers sitting on the sand.

"Wanna go for a swim?" asked Lena.

I shook my head.

"What's up with you?" my sister asked. "Normally, when you close a case and everyone says how great you are, you're glowing. But not this time. You wanna tell me why?"

"I'm not sure I can explain it. These were good people, except maybe for Harrison the psychopath."

"And the pedophile," added Lena. "Or Marty, the guy who knew that his brother was milking their brokerage for every penny in the bank. They were running a Ponzi scheme, for god's sake. And then there's a widow who marries her dead husband's brother before the dust settles. Trisha, these are not good people."

"You have a point," I said. "But I feel bad about the whole thing, especially the twins."

We walked on for a few minutes in silence until we reached the tall wooden fence that separated us from the reservoir.

"I hate to ask …" started Lena.

"Then don't," I said.

"But—"

"I know what you're going to say. Don't. Just don't." I turned around and stared at her. "Okay, look, you're going to ask about Jon and maybe Bradley. I have tried to reach Jon and he doesn't reply. Bradley's on his way back to where he came from. I signed the divorce papers, mailed them, and said goodbye."

"And?" asked Lena.

"I screwed up."

"You got that right."

"I was such an idiot."

Lena reached over and took my hand. She smiled in my direction. "You still have me," she said with a little laugh.

"How did I get so lucky?" I said with the last bit of snark I had left.

"Let's run back up to the house," she challenged, beginning to jog away. She stopped for a minute, turned toward me. "Come on. When you can't breathe, you stop worrying about your problems."

But I remained standing for a second.

"Move!" she yelled. Lena walked back down the hill, grabbed my arm, and pulled me into a slow jog. "You can worry about whatever is bothering you whenever you want. But how about for a few minutes, just think of putting one foot in front of the other."

For once, my sister had a good idea.

About the Author

If you want to find Glenda, she'll be in, on, or under water—and writing about it. She understands water sports on a very personal level since she swims, surfs and sails.

Glenda wrote a weekly sailing column for the *Marin Independent Journal* for 19 years. She also wrote for local, national and international sailing publications. She branched into travel writing and her features have appeared in the *San Francisco Chronicle, Travel & Leisure, Ford Times, Chevron USA, Defenders of Wildlife*, and *Bay & Delta Yachtsman*.

The Trisha Carson series is set in the San Francisco Bay area. Her books have a swimming undercurrent, based on her own experience in open water swimming. She has raced in more than 150 open water events in Northern California, as well as Hawaii and Perth, Australia. She is listed in Openwaterpedia.com

Glenda tutors first-generation high school and college students in English and History. She has an M.A. from Miami University, Oxford, Ohio and a B.A. from Indiana University, Bloomington, Indiana. She is the president of the Northern California Chapter of Sisters in Crime and is a member of Mystery Writers of America.

She lives in San Rafael, Ca with her dog McCovey.